The Gringos
Bower, B.M.

Published: 1913
Categorie(s): Fiction, Action & Adventure, Romance, Westerns

Bertha Muzzy Sinclair or Sinclair-Cowan, née Muzzy (November 15, 1871 – July 23, 1940), best known by her pseudonym B. M. Bower, was an American author who wrote novels and fictional short stories about the American Old West.

Chapter 1

The Beginning of it

If you would glimpse the savage which normally lies asleep, thank God, in most of us, you have only to do this thing of which I shall tell you, and from some safe sanctuary where leaden couriers may not bear prematurely the tidings of man's debasement, watch the world below. You may see civilization swing back with a snap to savagery and worse—because savagery enlightened by the civilization of centuries is a deadly thing to let loose among men. Our savage forebears were but superior animals groping laboriously after economic security and a social condition that would yield most prolifically the fruit of all the world's desire, happiness; to-day, when we swing back to something akin to savagery, we do it for lust of gain, like our forebears, but we do it wittingly. So, if you would look upon the unlovely spectacle of civilized men turned savage, and see them toil painfully back to lawful living, you have but to do this:

Seek a spot remote from the great centers of our vaunted civilization, where Nature, in a wanton gold-revel of her own, has sprinkled her river beds with the shining dust, hidden it away under ledges, buried it in deep canyons in playful miserliness and salved with its potent glow the time-scars upon the cheeks of her gaunt mountains. You have but to find a tiny bit of Nature's gold, fling it in the face of civilization and raise the hunting cry. Then, from that safe sanctuary which you have chosen, you may look your fill upon the awakening of the primitive in man; see him throw off civilization as a sleeper flings aside the cloak that has covered him; watch the savages fight, whom your gold has conjured.

They will come, those savages; straight as the arrow flies they will come, though mountains and deserts and hurrying rivers bar their way. And the plodding, law-abiding citizens who kiss their wives and hold close their babies and fling hasty, comforting words over their shoulders to tottering old mothers when they go to answer the hunting call—they will be your savages when the gold lust grips them. And the towns they build of their greed will be but the nucleus of all the crime let loose upon the land. There will be men among your savages; men in whom the finer stuff outweighs the grossness and the greed. But to save their lives and that thing they prize more than life or gold, and call by the name of honor or friendship or justice—that thing which is the essence of all the fineness in their natures—to save that and their lives they also must fight, like savages who would destroy them.

There was a little, straggling hamlet born of the Mission which the padres founded among the sand hills beside a great, uneasy stretch of water which a dreamer might liken to a naughty child that had run away from its mother, the ocean, through a little gateway which the land left open by chance and was hiding there among the hills, listening to the calling of the surf voice by night, out there beyond the gate, and lying sullen and still when mother ocean sent the fog and the tides aseeking; a truant child that played by itself and danced little wave dances which it had learned of its mother ages agone, and laughed up at the hills that smiled down upon it.

The padres thought mostly of the savages who lived upon the land, and strove earnestly to teach them the lessons which, sandal-shod, with crucifix to point the way, they had marched up from the south to set before these children of the wild. Also came ships, searching for that truant ocean-child, the bay, of which men had heard; and so the hamlet was born of civilization.

Came afterwards noblemen from Spain, with parchments upon which the king himself had set his seal. Mile upon mile, they chose the land that pleased them best; and by virtue of the king's word called it their own. They drove cattle up from the south to feed upon the hills and in the valleys. They brought beautiful wives and set them a-queening it over spacious homes which they built of clay and native wood and furnished with the luxuries they brought with them in the ships.

They reared lovely daughters and strong, hot-blooded sons; and they grew rich in cattle and in contentment, in this paradise which Nature had set apart for her own playground and which the zeal of the padres had found and claimed in the name of God and their king.

The hamlet beside the bay was small, but it received the ships and the goods they brought and bartered for tallow and hides; and although the place numbered less than a thousand souls, it was large enough to please the dons who dwelt like the patriarchs of old in the valleys.

Then Chance, that sardonic jester who loves best to thwart the dearest desires of men and warp the destiny of nations, became piqued at the peace and the plenty in the land which lay around the bay. Chance, knowing well how best and quickest to let savagery loose upon the land, plucked a handful of gold from the breast of Nature, held it aloft that all the world might be made mad by the gleam of it, and raised the hunting call.

Chance also it was that took the trails of two adventurous young fellows whose ears had caught her cry of "Good hunting" and set their faces westward from the plains of Texas; but here her jest was kindly. The young fellows took the trail together and were content. Together they heard the hunting call and went seeking the gold that was luring thousands across the deserts; together they dug for it, found it, shared it when all was done. Together they heeded the warning of falling leaf and chilling night winds, and with buckskin bags comfortably heavy went down the mountain trail to San Francisco, that ugly, moiling center of the savagery, to idle through the winter.

Here, because of certain traits which led each man to seek the thing that pleased him best, the trail forked for a time. One was caught in the turgid whirlpool which was the sporting element of the town, and would not leave it. Him the games and the women and the fighting drew irresistibly. The other sickened of the place, and one day when all the grassy hillsides shone with the golden glow of poppies to prove that spring was near, almost emptied a bag of gold because he had seen and fancied a white horse which a drunken Spaniard from the San Joaquin was riding up and down the narrow strip of sand which was a street, showing off alike his horsemanship and his drunkenness. The horse he bought, and the outfit, from the silvertrimmed saddle and bridle to the rawhide riata hanging coiled upon one side of the narrow fork and the ivory-handled Colt's revolver tucked snugly in its holster upon the other side. Pleased as a child over a Christmas stocking, he straightway mounted the beautiful beast and galloped away to the south, still led by Chance, the jester.

He returned in a week, enamored alike of his horse and of the ranch he had discovered. He was going back, he said. There were cattle by the thousands—and he was a cattleman, from the top of his white sombrero to the tips of his calfskin boots, for all he had bent his back laboriously all summer over a hole in the ground, and had idled in town since Thanksgiving. He was a cowboy (vaquero was the name they used in those pleasant valleys) and so was his friend. And he had found a cowboy's paradise, and a welcome which a king could not cavil at. Would Jack stake himself to a horse and outfit, and come to Palo Alto till the snow was well out of the mountains and they could go back to their mine?

Jack blew three small smoke-rings with nice precision, watched them float and fade while he thought of a certain girl who had lately smiled upon him—and in return had got smile for smile—and said he guessed he'd stick to town life for a while.

"Old Don Andres Picardo's a prince," argued Dade, "and he's got a rancho that's a paradise on earth. Likes us gringos—which is more than most of 'em do—and said his house and all he's got is half mine, and nothing but the honor's all his. You know the Spaniards; seems like Texas, down there. I told him I had a partner, and he said he'd be doubly honored if it pleased my partner to sleep under his poor roof—red tiles, by the way, and not so poor!—and sit at his table. One of the 'fine old families,' they are, Jack. I came back after you and my traps."

"That fellow you bought the white caballo from got shot that same night," Jack observed irrelevantly. "He was weeping all over me part of the evening, because he'd sold the horse and you had pulled out so he couldn't buy him back. Then he came into Billy Wilson's place and sat into a game at the table next to mine; and some kind of a quarrel started. He'd overlooked that gun on the saddle, it seems, and so he only had a knife. He whipped it out, first pass, but a bullet got him in the heart. The fellow that did it—" Jack blew two more rings and watched them absently—"the Committee rounded him up and took him out to the oak, next morning. Trial took about fifteen minutes, all told. They had him hung, in their own minds, before the greaser quit kicking. I *know* the man shot in self-defense; I saw the Spaniard pull his knife and start for him with blood in his eye. But some of the Committee had it in for Sandy, and so—it was adios for him, poor devil. They murdered him in cold
blood. I told them so, too. I told them—"

"Yes, I haven't the slightest doubt of that!" Dade flung away a half-smoked cigarette and agitatedly began to roll another one. "That's one reason why I want you to come down to Palo Alto, Jack. You know how things are going here, lately; and Perkins hates you since you took the part of that peon he was beating up,—and, by the way, I saw that same Injun at Don Andres' rancho. Now that Perkins is Captain, you'll get into trouble if you hang around this burg without some one to hold you down. This ain't any place for a man that's got your temper and tongue. Say, I heard of a horse—"

"No, you don't! You can't lead me out like that, old boy. I'm all right; Bill Wilson and I are pretty good friends; and Bill's almost as high a card as the Committee, if it ever came to a show-down. But it won't. I'm not a fool; I didn't quarrel with them, honest. They had me up for a witness and I told the truth—which didn't happen to jibe with the verdict they meant to give. The Captain as good as said so, and I just pleasantly and kindly told him that in my opinion Sandy was a better man than any one of 'em. That's all there was to it. The Captain excused me from the witness chair, and I walked out of the tent. And we're friendly enough when we meet; so you needn't worry about me."

"Better come, anyway," urged Dade, though he was not hopeful of winning his way.

Jack shook his head. "No, I don't want anything of country life just yet. I had all the splendid solitude my system needs, this last summer. You like it; you're a kind of a lone rider anyway. You never did mix well. You go back and honor Don Andres with your presence—and he is honored. If the old devil only knew it! Maybe, later on—So you like your new horse, huh? What you going to call him?"

Dade grinned a little. "Remember that picture in Shakespeare of 'White Surry'? Or it was in Shakespeare till you tore it out to start a fire, that wet night; remember? The arch in his neck, and all? I hadn't gone a mile on him till I was calling him Surry; and say, Jack, he's a wonder! Come out and take a look at him. Can't be more than four years old, and gentle as a kitten. That poor devil knew how to train a horse, even if he didn't have any sense about whisky. I'll bet money couldn't have touched him if the man had been sober."

He stopped in the doorway and looked up and down the street with open disgust. "Come on down to Picardo's, Jack; what the deuce is there here to hold you? How a man that knows horses and the range, can stand for this—" he waved a gloved hand at the squalid street—"is something I can't understand. To me, it's like hell with the lid off. What's holding you anyway? Another señorita?"

"I'm making more money here lately than I did in the mine." Jack evaded smoothly. "I won a lot last night. Whee-ee! Say, you played in some luck yourself, old man, when you bought that outfit. That saddle and bridle's worth all you paid for the whole thing. White Surry, eh? He has got a neck—and, Lord, look at those legs!"

"Climb on and try him out once!" invited Dade guilefully. If he could stir the horseman's blood in Jack's veins, he thought he might get him away from town.

"Haven't time right now, Dade. I promised to meet a friend—"

Dade shrugged his shoulders and painstakingly smoothed the hair tassel which dangled from the browband. The Spaniard had owned a fine eye for effect when he chose jet black trappings for Surry, who was white to his shining hoofs.

"All right; I'll put him in somewhere till after dinner. Then I'm going to pull out again. I can't stand this hell-pot of a town—not after the Picardo hacienda."

"I wonder," grinned Jack slyly, "if there isn't a señorita at Palo Alto?"

He got no answer of any sort. Dade was combing with his fingers the crinkled mane which fell to the very chest of his new horse, and if he heard he made no betraying sign.

Chapter 2

The Vigilantes

Bill Wilson came to the door of his saloon and stood with his hands on his hips, looking out upon the heterogeneous assembly of virile manhood that formed the bulk of San Francisco's population a year or two after the first gold cry had been raised. Above his head flapped the great cloth sign tacked quite across the rough building, heralding to all who could read the words that this was BILL WILSON'S PLACE. A flaunting bit of information it was, and quite superfluous; since practically every man in San Francisco drifted towards it, soon or late, as the place where the most whisky was drunk and the most gold lost and won, with the most beautiful women to smile or frown upon the lucky, in all the town.

The trade wind knew that Bill Wilson's place needed no sign save its presence there, and was loosening a corner in the hope of carrying it quite away as a trophy. Bill glanced up, promised the resisting cloth an extra nail or two, and let his thoughts and his eyes wander again to the sweeping tide of humanity that flowed up and down the straggling street of sand and threatened to engulf the store which men spoke of simply as "Smith's."

A shipload of supplies had lately been carted there, and miners were feverishly buying bacon, beans, "self-rising" flour, matches, tea—everything within the limits of their gold dust and their carrying capacity—which they needed for hurried trips to the hills where was hidden the gold they dreamed of night and day.

To Bill that tide meant so much business; and he was not the man to grudge his friend Smith a share of it. When the fog crept in through the Golden Gate—a gate which might never be closed against it—the tide of business would set towards his place, just as surely as the ocean tide would clamor at the rocky wall out there to the west. In the meantime, he was not loath to spend a quiet hour or two with an empty gaming hall at his back.

His eyes went incuriously over the familiar crowd to the little forest of flag-foliaged masts that told where lay the ships in the bay below the town. Bill could not name the nationality of them all; for the hunting call had reached to the far corners of the earth, and strange flags came fluttering across strange seas, with pirate-faced adventurers on the decks below, chattering in strange tongues of California gold. Bill could not name all the flags, but he could name two of the bonds that bind all nations into one common humanity. He could produce one of them, and he was each night gaining more of the other; for, be they white men or brown, spoke they his language or one he had never heard until they passed through the Golden Gate, they would give good gold for very bad whisky.

Even the Digger Indians, squatting in the sun beside his door and gazing stolidly at the town and the bay beyond, would sell their souls—for which the gray-gowned padres prayed ineffectively in the chapel at Dolores—their wives or their other, dearer possessions for a very little bottle of the stuff that was fast undoing the civilizing work of the Mission. The padres had come long before the hunting cry was raised, and they had labored earnestly; but their prayers and their preaching were like reeds beneath the tread of elephants, when gold came down from the mountains, and whisky came in through the
Golden Gate.

Jack Allen, coming lazily down through the long, deserted room, edged past Bill in the doorway.

"Hello," Bill greeted with a carefully casual manner, as if he had been waiting for the meeting, but did not want Jack to suspect the fact. "Up for all day? Where you headed for?"

"Breakfast—or dinner, whichever you want to call it. Then I'm going to take a walk and get the kinks out of my legs. Say, old man, I'm going to knock a board off the foot of that bunk, to-night, or else sleep on the floor. Was wood scarce, Bill, when you built that bed?"

"Carpenter was a little feller," chuckled Bill, "and I guess he measured it by himself. Charged a full length price, though, I remember! I meant to tell you when you hired that room, Jack, that you better take the axe to bed with you. Sure, knock a board off; two boards, if you like. Take *all* the boards off!" urged Bill, in a burst of generosity. "You might better be making that bunk over, m'son, than trying to take the whole blamed town apart and put it together again, like you was doing last night." In this way Bill tactfully swung to the subject that lay heavy on his mind.

Jack borrowed a match, cupped his fingers around his lips that wanted to part in a smile, and lighted his before-breakfast cigarette—though the sun hung almost straight overhead.

"So that's it," he observed, when the smoke took on the sweet aroma of a very mild tobacco. "I saw by the back of your neck that you had something on your mind. What's the matter,
Bill? Don't you think the old town needs taking apart?"

"Oh, it needs it, all right. But it's too big a job for one man to tackle. You leave that to Daddy Time; he's the only reformer—"

"Say, Bill, I never attempted to reform anybody or anything in my life; I'd hate to begin with a job the size of this." He waved his cigarette toward the shifting crowd. "But I do think—"

"And right there's where you make a big mistake. You don't want to think! Or if you do, don't think out loud; not where such men as Swift and Rawhide and the Captain can hear you.
That's what I mean, Jack."

Jack eyed him with a smile in his eyes. "Some men might think you were afraid of that bunch," he observed with characteristic bluntness. "I know you aren't, and so I don't see why you want me to be. You know, and I know, that the Vigilance Committee has turned rotten to the core; every decent man in San Francisco knows it. You know that Sandy killed that Spaniard in self-defense—or if you didn't see the fracas, I tell you now that he did; I saw the whole thing. You know, at any rate, that the Vigilantes took him out and hung him because they wanted to get rid of him, and that came the nearest to an excuse they could find. You know—"

"Oh, I know!" Bill's voice was sardonic. "I know they'll be going around with a spy-glass looking for an excuse to hang you,
too, if you don't quit talking about 'em."

Jack smiled and so let a thin ribbon of smoke float up and away from his lips.

Bill saw the smile and flushed a little; but he was not to be laughed down, once he was fairly started. He laid two well-kept fingers upon the other's arm and spoke soberly, refusing to treat the thing as lightly as the other was minded to do.

"Oh, you'll laugh, but it's a fact, and you know it. Why, ain't Sandy's case proof enough that I'm right? I heard you telling a crowd in there last night—" Bill tilted his head backward towards the room behind them—"that this law-and-order talk is all a farce. What if it is? It don't do any good for you to bawl it out in public and get the worst men in the Committee down on you, does it?

"What you'd better do, Jack, is go on down to Palo Alto where your pardner is. He's got some sense. I wouldn't stay in the darned town overnight, the way they're running things now, if it wasn't for my business. Ever since they made Tom Perkins captain there's been hell to pay all round. I can hold my own; I'm up where they don't dare tackle me; but you take a fool's advice and pull out before the Captain gets his eagle eye on you. Talk like you was slinging around last night is about as good a trouble-raiser as if you emptied both them guns of yours into that crowd out there."

"You're asking me to run before there's anything to run away from." Jack's lips began to show the line of stubbornness. "I haven't quarreled with the Captain, except that little fuss a month ago, when he was hammering that peon because he couldn't talk English; I'm not going to. And if they did try any funny work with me, old-timer, why—as you say, these guns—"

"Oh, all right, m'son! Have it your own way," Bill retorted grimly. "I know you've got a brace of guns; and I know you can plant a bullet where you want it to land, about as quick as the next one. I haven't a doubt but what you're equal to the Vigilantes, with both hands tied! Of course," he went on with heavy irony, "I have known of some mighty able men swinging from the oak, lately. There'll likely be more, before the town wakes up and weeds out some of the cutthroat element that's running things now to suit themselves."

Jack looked at him quickly, struck by something in Bill's voice that betrayed his real concern. "Don't take it to heart, Bill," he said, dropping his bantering and his stubbornness together. "I won't air my views quite so publicly, after this. I know I was a fool to talk quite as straight as I did last night; but some one else brought up the subject of Sandy; and Swift called him a name Sandy'd have smashed him in the face for, if he'd been alive and heard it. I always liked the fellow, and it made me hot to see them hustle him out of town and hang him like they'd shoot a dog that had bitten some one, when I *knew* he didn't deserve it. You or I would have shot, just as quick as he did, if a drunken Spaniard made for us with a knife. So would the Captain, or Swift, or any of the others.

"I know—I've got a nasty tongue when something riles me, and I lash out without stopping to think. Dade has given me the devil for that, more times than I can count. He went after me about this very thing, too, the other day. I'll try and forget about Sandy; it doesn't make pleasant remembering, anyway. And I'll promise to count a hundred before I mention the Committee above a whisper, after this—nine hundred and ninetynine before I take the name of Swift or the Captain in vain!" He smiled full at Bill—a smile to make men love him for the bighearted boy he was.

But Bill did not grin back. "Well, it won't hurt you any; they're bad men to fuss with, both of 'em," he warned somberly.

"Come on out and climb a hill or two with me," Jack urged. "You've got worse kinks in your system, to-day, than I've got in my legs. You won't? Well, better go back and take another sleep, then; it may put you in a more optimistic mood." He went off up the street towards the hills to the south, turning in at the door of a tented eating-place for his belated breakfast.

"Optimistic hell!" grunted Bill. "You can't tell a man anything he don't think he knows better than you do, till he's past thirty.

I was a fool to try, I reckon."

He glowered at the vanishing figure, noting anew how tall and straight Jack was in his close-fitting buckskin jacket, with the crimson sash knotted about his middle in the Spanish style, his trousers tucked into his boots like the miners, and to crown all, a white sombrero such as the vaqueros wore. Handsome and headstrong he was; and Bill shook his head over the combination which made for trouble in that land where the primal instincts lay all on the surface; where men looked askance at the one who drew oftenest the glances of the women and who walked erect and unafraid in the midst of the lawlessness. Jack Allen was fast making enemies, and no one knew it better than Bill.

When the young fellow disappeared, Bill looked again at the shifting crowd upon which his eyes were wont to rest with the speculative gaze of a farmer who leans upon the fence that bounds his land, and regards his wheat-fields ripening for the sickle. He liked Jack, and the soul of him was bitter with the bitterness that is the portion of maturity, when it must stand by and see youth learn by the pangs of experience that fire will burn most agonizingly if you hold your hand in the blaze.

One of his night bartenders came up; and Bill, dismissing Jack from his mind, with a grunt of disgust, went in to talk over certain changes which he meant to make in the bar as soon as he could get material and carpenter together upon the spot.

He was still fussing with certain of the petty details that make or mar the smooth running of an establishment like his, when his ear, trained to detect the first note of discord in the babble which filled his big room by night, caught an ominous note in the hum of the street crowd outside. He lifted his head from examining a rickety table-leg.

"Go see what's happened, Jim," he suggested to the man, who had just come up with a hammer and some nails; and went back to dreaming of the time when his place should be a palace, and he would not have to nail the legs on his tables every few days because of the ebullitions of excitement in his customers. He had strengthened the legs, and was testing them by rocking the table slightly with a broad palm upon it, when Jim came back.

"Some shooting scrape, back on the flat," Jim announced indifferently. "Some say it was a hold-up. Two or three of the Committee have gone out to investigate."

"Yeah—I'll bet the Committee went out!" snorted Bill. "They'll be lynching the Diggers' dogs for fighting, when the supply of humans runs out. They've just about played that buckskin out, packing men out to the oak to hang 'em lately," he went on glumly, sliding the rejuvenated table into its place in the long row that filled that side of the room. "I never saw such an enthusiastic bunch as they're getting to be!"

"That's right," Jim agreed perfunctorily, as a man is wont to agree with his employer. "Somebody'll hang, all right."

"There's plenty that need it—if the Committee only had sense enough to pick 'em out and leave the rest alone," growled Bill, going from table to table, tipping and testing for other legs that wobbled.

Jim sensed the rebuff in his tone and went back to the door, around which a knot of men engaged in desultory conjectures while they waited expectantly. A large tent that Perkins had found convenient as a temporary jail for those unfortunates upon whom his heavy hand fell swiftly, stood next to Bill's place; and it spoke eloquently of the manner in which the Committee then worked, that men gathered there instinctively at the first sign of trouble. For when the Committee went out after culprits, it did not return empty-handed, as the populace knew well. Zealous custodians of the law were they, as Bill had said; and though they might have exchanged much of their zeal for a little of Bill's sense of justice (to the betterment of the town), few of the waiting crowd had the temerity to say so.

Up the street, necks (whose owners had not thought it worth while to wade through the sand to the scene of the shooting) were being craned towards the flat behind the town, where the
Captain and a few of his men had hurried at the first shot.

"They're comin'," Jim announced, thrusting his head into the gambling hall and raising his voice above the sound of the boss's nail-driving.

"Well—what of it?" snapped Bill. "Why don't you yell at me that the sun is going to set in the west to-night?" Bill drove the head of a four-cornered, iron nail clean out of sight in a table top. And Jim prudently withdrew his head and turned his face and his attention towards the little procession that was just coming into sight at the end of the rambling street, with the crowd closing in behind it as the water comes surging together behind an ocean liner.

Jim worshiped his boss, but he knew better than to argue with him when Bill happened to be in that particular mood, which, to tell the truth, was not often. But in five minutes or less he had forgotten the snub. His head popped in again.

"Bill!"

There may be much meaning in a tone, though it utters but one unmeaning word. Bill dropped a handful of nails upon a table and came striding down the long room to the door; pushed Jim unceremoniously aside and stood upon the step. He was just in time to look into the rageful, blue eyes of Jack Allen, walking with a very straight back and a contemptuous smile on his lips, between the Captain and one of his trusted lieutenants.

Bill's fingers clenched suggestively upon the handle of the hammer. His jaw slackened and then pushed itself forward to a fighting angle while he stared, and he named in his amazement that place which the padres had taught the Indians to fear.

The Captain heard him and grinned sourly as he passed on. Jack heard him, and his smile grew twisted at the tone in which the word was uttered; but he still smiled, which was more than many a man would have done in his place.

Bill stood while the rest of that grim procession passed his place. There was another, a young fellow who looked ready to cry, walking unsteadily behind Jack, both his arms gripped by others of the Vigilance Committee. There were two crude stretchers, borne by stolid-faced miners in red flannel shirts and clay-stained boots. On the first a dead man lay grinning up at the sun, his teeth just showing under his bushy mustache, a trickle of red running down from his temple. On the next a man groaned and mumbled blasphemy between his groanings.

Bill took it all in, a single glance for each,—a glance trained by gambling to see a great deal between the flicker of his lashes. He did not seem to look once at the Captain, yet he knew that Jack's ivory-handled pistols hung at the Captain's rocking hips as he went striding past; and he knew that malice lurked under the grizzled hair which hid the Captain's cruel lips; and that satisfaction glowed in the hard, sidelong glance he gave his prisoner.

He stood until he saw Jack duck his head under the tent flaps of the jail and the white-faced youth follow shrinking after. He stood while the armed guards took up their stations on the four sides of the tent and began pacing up and down the paths worn deep in tragic significance. He saw the wounded man carried into Pete's place across the way, and the dead man taken farther down the street. He saw the crowd split into uneasy groups which spoke a common tongue, that they might exchange unasked opinions upon this, the biggest sensation since Sandy left town with his ankles tied under the vicious-eyed buckskin whose riders rode always toward the west and whose saddle was always empty when he came back to his stall at the end of the town. Bill saw it all, to the last detail; but after his one explosive oath, he was apparently the most indifferent of them all.

When the Captain ended his curt instructions to the guard and came towards him, Bill showed a disposition to speak.

"Who's the kid?" he drawled companionably, while his fingers itched upon the hammer, and the soul of him lusted for sight of the hole it could make in the skull of the Captain. "I don't recollect seeing him around town—and there ain't many faces I forget, either."

The Captain shot him a surprised look that was an unconscious tribute to Bill's diplomatic art. But Bill's level glance would have disarmed a keener man than Tom Perkins.

Perkins stopped. "Stranger, from what he said—though I've got my doubts. Some crony of Allen's, I expect. It was him done the shooting; the kid didn't have any gun on him. Allen didn't deny it, either."

"No—he's just bull-headed enough to tough it out," commented Bill. "What was the row about—do yuh know?"

Perkins stiffened. "That," he said with some dignity, "will come out at the trial. He killed Rawhide outright, and Texas Bill will die, I reckon. The trial will show what kinda excuse he thought he had." Having delivered himself, thus impartially and with malice towards none, Perkins started on.

"Oh, say! You don't mind if I talk to 'em?" Bill gritted his teeth at having to put the sentence in that favor-seeking tone, but he did it, nevertheless.

The Captain scowled under his black, slouch hat. "I've give strict orders not to let anybody inside the tent till after the trial," he said shortly.

"Oh, that's all right. I'll talk to 'em through the door," Bill agreed equably. "Jack owes me some money."

The Captain muttered unintelligibly and passed on, and Bill chose to interpret the mutter as consent. He strolled over to the tent, joked condescendingly with the guard who stood before it, and announced that the Captain had said he might talk to the prisoners.

"I did not," said the Captain unexpectedly at his shoulder. "I said you couldn't. After the trial, you can collect what's coming to you, Mr. Wilson. That is," he added hastily, "in case Allen should be convicted. If he ain't, you can do as you please." He looked full at the guard. "Shoot any man that attempts to enter that tent or talk to the prisoners without my permission, Shorty," he directed, and turned his back on Bill.

Bill did not permit one muscle of his face to twitch. "All right," he drawled, "I guess I won't go broke if I don't get it. You mind what your Captain tells you, Shorty! He's running this show, and what he says goes. You've got a good man over yuh, Shorty. A fine man. He'll weed out the town till it'll look like grandpa's onion bed—if the supply of rope don't give out!" Whereupon he strolled carelessly back to his place, and went in as if the incident were squeezed dry of interest for him. He walked to the far end of the big room, sat deliberately down upon a little table, and rewarded himself for his forbearance by cursing methodically the Captain, the Committee of which he was the leader, the men who had witlessly given him the power he used so ruthlessly as pleased him best, and Jack Allen, whose ill-timed criticisms and hot-headed freedom of speech had brought upon himself the weight of the Committee's dread hand.

"Damn him, I tried to tell him!" groaned Bill, his face hidden behind his palms. "They'll hang him—and darn my oldest sister's cat's eyes, somebody'll sweat blood for it, too!" (Bill, you will observe, had reached the end of real blasphemy and was forced to improvise milder expletives as he went along.) "There ought to be enough decent men in this town to—"

'Did you git to see Jack?" ventured Jim, coming anxiously up to his boss.

The tone of him, which was that hushed tone which we employ in the presence of the dead, so incensed Bill that for answer he threw the hammer viciously in his direction. Jim took the hint and retreated hastily.

"No, damn 'em, they won't let me near him," said Bill, ashamed of his violence. "I knew they'd get him; but I didn't think they'd get him so quick. I sent a letter down by an Injun this morning to his pardner to come up and get him outa town before he—But it's too late now. That talk he made last night—"

"Say, he shot Swift in the arm, too," said Jim. "Pity he didn't kill him. They're getting a jury together already. Say! Ain't it hell?"

Chapter 3

The Thing They Called Justice

Jack stared meditatively across at the young fellow sitting hunched upon another of the boxes that were the seats in this tent-jail, which was also the courtroom of the Vigilance Committee, and mechanically counted the slow tears that trickled down between the third and fourth fingers of each hand. A half-hour spent so would have rasped the nerves of the most phlegmatic man in the town, and Jack was not phlegmatic; fifteen minutes of watching that silent weeping sufficed to bring a muffled explosion.

"Ah, for God's sake, brace up!" he gritted. "There's some hope for you—if you don't spoil what chance you have got, by crying around like a baby. Brace up and be a man, anyway. It
won't hurt any worse if you grin about it."

The young fellow felt gropingly for a red-figured bandanna, found it and wiped his face and his eyes dejectedly. "I beg your pardon for seeming a coward," he apologized huskily. "I got to thinking about my—m-mother and sisters, and—"

Jack winced. Mother and sisters he had longed for all his life. "Well, you better be thinking how you'll get out of the scrape you're in," he advised, with a little of Bill Wilson's grimness. "I'm afraid I'm to blame, in a way; and yet, if I hadn't mixed into the fight, you'd be dead by now. Maybe that would have been just as well, seeing how things have turned out," he
grinned. "Still—have a smoke?"

"I never used tobacco in my life," declined the youth somewhat primly.

"No, I don't reckon you ever did!" Jack eyed him with a certain amount of pitying amusement. "A fellow that will come gold-hunting without a gun to his name, would not use tobacco, or swear, or do anything that a perfect lady couldn't do!
However, you put up a good fight with your fists, old man, and that's something."

"I'd have been killed, though, if you hadn't shot when you
did. They were too much for me. I haven't tried to thank you—"

"No, I shouldn't think you would," grinned Jack. "I don't see yet where I've done you any particular favor: from robbers to Vigilance Committee might be called an up-to-date version of
'Out of the frying-pan into the fire.'"

The boy glanced fearfully toward the closed tent-flaps. "Ssh!" he whispered. "The guard can hear—"

"Oh, that's all right," returned Jack, urged perhaps to a conscious bravado by the very weakness of the other. "It's all day with me, anyway. I may as well say what I think.

"And so—" He paused to blow one of his favorite little smoke rings and watch it float to the dingy ridge-pole, where it flickered and faded into a blue haze "—and so, I'm going to say right out in meeting what I think of this town and the Committee they let measure out justice. Justice!" He laughed sardonically. "Poor old lady, she couldn't stop within forty miles of Perkins' Committee if she had forty bandages over her eyes, and both ears plugged with cotton! You wait till their farce of a trial is over. You may get off, by a scratch—I hope so. But unless Bill Wilson—"

"Aw, yuh needn't pin no hopes on Bill Wilson!" came a heavy, malicious voice through the tent wall. "All hell can't save yuh, Jack Allen! You've had a ride out to the oak comin' to yuh for

quite a while, and before sundown you'll get it."

"Oh! Is that so, Shorty? Say, you're breaking the rules, you old pirate; you're talking to the prisoners without permission. As the Captain's most faithful dog Tray, you'd better shoot yourself; it'll save the town the trouble of hanging you later on!" He smoked calmly while Shorty, on guard without, growled a vilifying retort, and the other guards snickered.

"Ah, brace up!" he advised his quaking companion again. "If my company doesn't damn you beyond all hope, you may get out of the scrape. You didn't have a gun, and you're a stranger and haven't said naughty things about your neighbors. Cheer up. Life looks just as good to me as it does to you. I love this old world just as well as any man that ever lived in it, and I'm not a bit pleased over leaving it—any more than you are. But I can't see where I could better matters by letting myself get wobbly in the knees. I'm sorry I didn't make a bigger fight to keep my guns, though. I'd like to have perforated a few more of our most worthy Committee before I quit; our friend Shorty, for instance," he stipulated wickedly and clearly, "and the Captain."

If he were deliberately trying to goad Shorty to further profanity, the result should have satisfied him. The huge shadow of Shorty moving back and forth upon the front wall of the tent, became violently agitated and developed a gigantic arm that waved threateningly over the ridge pole. The other guards laughed and checked their laughter with a suddenness which made Jack's eyes leave the dancing shadow and seek questioningly the closed tent flaps.

"If I'm any good at reading signs, we are now about to be tried by our peers—twelve good men and true," he announced ironically. "Brace up, old man! The chances are you'll soon be out of this mess and headed for home. Don't be afraid to tell the truth—and don't act scared; they'll take that as a sure sign you've got a guilty conscience. Just keep a stiff upper lip; it won't take long; we do things in a hurry, out here!"

"Say, you're a brick, Mr. Allen!" the boy burst out, impulsively gripping the hand of his champion.

Jack jerked his hand away—not unkindly, but rather as if he feared to drop, even for an instant, his flippant defiance of the trick fate had played him. The jerk sent a small, shining thing sliding down to the floor; where it stood upright and quivered in the soft sand.

"Lord!" he ejaculated under his breath, snatching it up as a thief would snatch at his spoils. He looked fearfully at the closed flaps, outside which the trampling of many feet sounded closer and closer; and with a warning shake of his head at the other, slid the dagger into his sleeve again, carefully fastening the point in the stout hem of the buckskin.

"You never can tell," he muttered, smiling queerly as he made sure the weapon was not noticeable.

He was rolling another cigarette when the Captain parted the tent flaps and came stooping in, followed by twelve men of the Committee who were to be the jury, and as many spectators as could crowd after them.

"Gentlemen, be seated," the Captain invited formally, and motioned the jury to the crude bunks that lined one side of the large tent. Jack and the boy he moved farther from the entrance, and took up his own position where his sharp eyes commanded every inch of the interior and where the gun which he drew from its holster and rested upon his knee could speak its deadly rebuke to any man there if, in the upholding of justice, the Captain deemed it necessary.

The jury shuffled to their places, perched in a row upon the edge of the bunks and waited silently, their eyes fixed expectantly upon their Captain. The crowd edged into the corners and along the sides, their hat crowns scraping the canvas roof as they were forced closer to the low wall.

The Captain waited until the silence was a palpable thing made alive by the rhythmic breathing of the men who were to look upon this new travesty of justice.

"Gentlemen," he said at last, his sonorous voice carrying his words distinctly to the crowd without, "we are now ready to proceed with the investigation. I wish to state, for the information of those present, that after the prisoners were placed here under guard, I went to get a statement from the wounded man, Mr.

Texas Bill. I found him dying from a wound inflicted upon his person by a pistol ball which passed through his left lung, above and to the right of his heart. I did not take a written statement, for lack of time and writing materials. But Texas swore—"

"Yeah—I'll bet he swore!" commented Bill Wilson under his breath. Every one looked toward Bill, standing just inside the flaps, and the Captain scowled while he waited for attention.

"Texas swore that he was shot by one of the prisoners, Jack Allen by name, who fired upon him without due provocation, while he was talking to this other prisoner, whose name we have yet to learn. Texas stated that Allen, appearing suddenly from behind some bushes, began shooting with deadly intent and without warning, wantonly murdering Rawhide Jack, who lies dead in Smith's back room, and shooting him, Texas, through the lung. He also stated that Mr. Dick Swift was with him and Rawhide Jack, and was also shot by the prisoner, Jack
Allen, without cause or provocation.

"They had met the stranger and were standing talking to him about his luck in the diggin's. This stranger, who is the other prisoner, was inclined to be sassy, and made a pass at Rawhide with his fist, telling him to mind his own business and not ask so many questions. Rawhide struck back; and Allen, coming out from behind some bushes, began shooting."

The Captain stopped and looked calmly and judicially from face to face in the crowd.

"That, gentlemen, is the statement made to me by Texas Bill, who now lies dead in Pete's Place as a result of the wound inflicted by Allen."

"That's a lot of swearing for a man to do that's been shot through the lungs," commented Bill Wilson skeptically.

The Captain gave him a malevolent look and continued. "We will ask Mr. Swift to come forward and tell us what he knows of this deplorable and, if I may be permitted the term, disgraceful affair."

Mr. Swift edged his way carefully through the crowd with his left arm thrust out to protect the right, which was bandaged and rested in a blood-stained sling. He asked permission to sit down; kicked a box into the small, open space between the Captain, the jury, and the prisoners, and seated himself with the air of a man about to perform an extremely painful duty.

"Hold up your right hand," commanded the Captain.

Swift apologetically raised his left hand and gazed steadfastly into the cold, impartial eyes of his Captain.

"You swear that you will tell the truth, the whole truth, and nothing but the truth, so-help-you-God?"

Swift, his purplish eyes wide and clear and honest as the gaze of a baby, calmly affirmed that he did.

Jack grinned and lazily fanned the smoke of his cigarette away, so that he might the better gaze upon this man who was about to tell the whole truth and nothing else. He caught Swift's eye and added a sneering lift to the smile; and Swift's eyes changed from bland innocence to hate triumphant.

"Mr. Swift, you will now relate to us the circumstances of this affair, truthfully, in the order of their happening," directed the deep voice of the Captain.

Mr. Swift carefully eased his wounded arm in its sling, turned his innocent gaze upon the crowd, and began:

"Texas, Rawhide, and myself were crossing the sandy stretch south of town about noon, when we met this chap—the stranger there." He nodded slightly toward the boy. "I was walking behind the other two, but I heard Rawhide say: 'Hello, son, any luck in the diggin's?' The kid said: 'None of your damn business!' That made Rawhide kinda mad, being spoke to that way when he just meant to be friendly, and he told the kid he better keep a civil tongue in his head if he wanted to get along smooth—or words to that effect. I don't," explained Mr. Swift virtuously, "remember the exact words, because I was looking at the fellow and wondering what made him so surly. He sassed Rawhide again, and told him to mind his own business and give advice when it was asked for, and struck at him. Rawhide hit back, and then I heard a shot, and Rawhide fell over. I looked around quick, and started to pull my gun, but a bullet hit me here—" Mr. Swift laid gentle finger-tips upon his arm near the shoulder—"so I couldn't. I saw it was Jack Allen shooting and coming towards us from a clump of bushes off to the right of us. He shot again, and Texas Bill fell. I ducked behind a bush and started for help, when I met the Captain and a few others coming out to see what was the matter. That," finished

Mr. Swift, "is the facts of the case, just as they happened."

The Captain waited a minute or two, that the "facts" might sink deep into the minds of the listeners.

"Were any shots fired by any one except Allen?" he asked coldly, when the silence was sufficiently emphasized.

"There were not. Nobody," Swift flashed with a very human resentment, "had a chance after he commenced!" He flushed at the involuntary tribute to the prowess of his enemy, when he saw that maddening grin appear again on Jack's lips; a grin which called him liar and scoundrel and in the same flicker defied him.

The investigation took on the color of a sensation at that point, when the stranger sprang suddenly to his feet and stood glaring at the witness. There were no signs now of tears or weakness; he was a man fighting for what he believed to be right and just.

"Captain, that man is a dirty liar!" he cried hotly. "He and his precious cronies tried to rob me, out there. I was coming into town from across the bay; I had hired a Spaniard to bring me across in a small sailboat, and the tide carried us down too far, so I told him to land and I'd walk back to town, rather than tack back. And these men met me, and tried to rob me! This man," he accused excitedly, pointing a rageful finger at Swift, "was going to stab me in the throat when he saw I resisted. I was fighting the three, and they were getting the best of me. I never owned a gun, and I just had my fists. The two others had grabbed me, and this man Swift pulled a knife. I remember one of them saying: 'Don't shoot—it'll bring the whole town out!' And just as this one raised his knife to drive it into my throat—they were bending me backwards, the other two—I heard a shot, and this one dropped his knife and gave a yell. There were two other shots, and the two who were holding me dropped. This one ran off. Then—" The boy turned and looked down at Jack, smoking his cigarette and trying to read what lay behind the stolid stare of the twelve men who sat in a solemn row on the bunks opposite him. "This young man—" His lips trembled, and he stopped, to bite them into a more manlike firmness.

"Gentlemen, do what you like with me, but you've got to let this man go! He's the coolest, bravest man I ever saw! He saved my life. You can't hang him for protecting a man from murder and robbery!"

"Young man," interrupted the Captain after a surprised silence, "we admire your generosity in trying to clear your fellow prisoner, but you must let this jury try his case. What's your name?"

"John Belden, of Cambridge, Massachusetts." The young fellow's rage faded to a sullen calm under the cold voice.

The Captain made a startled movement and looked at him sharply. "And what was your hurry to get to town?" he asked, after a minute.

"I wanted to get a ticket on the boat, the *Mary Elizabeth*, that is going to leave for New York to-morrow. I wanted to go—home. I've had enough of gold-hunting!" Youthful bitterness was in his tone and in the look he turned on the jury.

The Captain cleared his throat. When he spoke again, he addressed the twelve before him:

"Gentlemen of the jury, I have reasons for feeling convinced that this young man is in part telling the truth. I am acquainted with his father, unless he has given a name he does not own—and his face is a pretty good witness for him; he looks like his dad. While he has undoubtedly glossed and warped the story of the shooting in a mistaken effort to make things look better for the man who did the killing, I can see no sufficient reason for holding him. This Committee stands for justice and is not backward about tempering it with mercy. Gentlemen of the jury, I recommend that John Belden be released from custody and permitted to go home. He was unarmed when I took him, and there is no evidence of his having dealt anything but hard words to the victims of the shooting. Gentlemen, you will give your verdict; after which we will proceed with the investigation."

The jury looked at one another and nodded to the man on the end of the first bunk; and he, shifting a quid of tobacco to the slack of his right cheek, expectorated gravely into the sand and spoke solemnly:

"The verdict of the jury is all in favor of turnin' the kid loose."

"John Belden, you are released. And we'd advise you to be a little careful how you sass men in this country. Also, you better see about that ticket on the *Mary Elizabeth*. Jack Allen, you may come forward and take the oath."

"This box is just as comfortable as that one," said Jack, "and you needn't worry but what I'll tell the truth!" He took a last pull at his cigarette, pinched out the fire, and ground the stub under his heel. He could feel the silence grow tense with expectancy; and when he lifted his eyes, he knew that every man in that tent was staring into his face.

"I used to believe," he began clearly, "in the Vigilantes. If I had been here when the first Committee was formed, I'd have worked for it myself. I believe it cleared the town of some of the worst scoundrels in the country, and that's saying a good deal. But—"

"The Committee," interrupted the Captain, "would like to hear your story of the shooting. Your private opinions can wait
until the investigation of that affair is ended."

"You're right. I beg your pardon for forgetting that it is not settled yet!" Jack's voice was politely scornful. "Well, then, this kid told the truth in every particular, even when he declared that Dick Swift is a dirty liar. Swift is a liar. He's also a thief, and he's also a murderer—and a few other things not as decent!

"As to the row, I was walking out that way, when I saw this kid coming up from the bay toward the town. The three, Swift, Rawhide Jack, and Texas Bill, met him where the—er—trouble took place. I was too far off to hear what was said; in fact, I didn't pay any attention much, till I saw the kid struggling to get away. I walked towards them then. It was easy enough to see that it was a hold-up, pure and simple. I was about fifty yards from them when I saw Swift, here, raise a knife to jab it into the boy's throat. Texas and Rawhide were both holding the kid's arms and bending him backwards so he couldn't do anything. When I saw the knife, I began to shoot." His eyes sought those of Bill Wilson, standing in the crowd near the door. "That's the truth of the whole matter," he said, speaking directly to Bill. "I didn't try to make trouble; but I couldn't stand by and see a man murdered, no more than any decent man could." He paused; and still looking toward Bill, added: "I didn't even notice particularly who the men were, until I went up to the boy. It all happened so sudden that I—"

The Captain cleared his throat. "You admit, then, that you killed Rawhide Jack and Texas Bill this morning?"

"I surely do," retorted Jack. "And if you want to know, I'm kinda proud of it; it was a long shot—to clean the town of two such blackguards. And right here I want to apologize to the
town for making a bungle of killing Swift!"

"We have two witnesses who also swear that you killed Tex' and Rawhide, though they give a very different version of the trouble with the boy. Would you ask us to believe that Texas
Bill lied with his last breath?"

"If he told the story you say he did, he certainly lied most sinfully with his last breath; but I'd hate to take your word for
anything, so I don't know whether he lied or not."

"Mr. Swift, here, tells the same story that Texas Bill told." The Captain chose to ignore the insults. "I think their testimony should carry more weight with the Committee than yours, or the boy's. You are trying to save your neck; and the boy probably feels that he owes you some gratitude for taking his part. But the Committee's business is to weed out the dangerous element which is altogether too large in this town; and the Committee feels that you are one of the most dangerous. However, we will call another witness. Shorty, you may come forward."

Shorty came scowling up and sat down upon the box Swift had occupied. He took the oath and afterwards declared that he had overheard Jack coaching the boy about what he should tell the Committee. The Captain, having brought out that point, promptly excused him.

"Gentlemen of the jury, you have heard the evidence, and
your duty is plain. We are waiting for the verdict."

The man with the cud looked a question at the Captain; turned and glanced down the row at the eleven, who nodded their heads in unanimous approval of his thoughts. He once more shifted the wad of tobacco, as a preliminary to expectorating gravely into the sand floor, and pronounced his sentence with a promptness that savored of relish:

"The verdict of the jury is that we hang Jack Allen for killin' Texas and Rawhide, and for bein' a mean, ornery cuss, anyway."

The Captain turned coldly to the prisoner. "You hear the verdict. The Committee believes it to be just."

He looked at the group near the door. "Mr. Wilson," he called maliciously, "you will now be given an opportunity to collect from the prisoner what he owes you."

"Jack Allen don't owe me a cent!" cried Bill Wilson hotly, shouldering his way to the open space before the Captain. "But there's a heavy debt hanging over this damned Committee—a debt they'll have to pay themselves one day at the end of a rope, if there's as many honest men in this town as I think there is.

"I helped form the first Vigilance Committee, boys. We did it to protect the town from just such men as are running the Committee right now. When crimes like this can be done right before our eyes, in broad daylight, I say it's time another Committee was formed, to hang this one! Here they've got a man that they know, and we all know, ain't done a thing but what any brave, honest man would do. They've gone through a farce trial that'd make the Digger Injuns ashamed of themselves; and they've condemned Jack Allen, that's got more real manhood in his little finger than there is in the dirty, lying carcasses of the whole damned outfit—they've condemned him to be hung!

"And why! I can tell yuh why—and it ain't for killing Texas and Rawhide—two as measly, ornery cusses as there was in town—it ain't for that. It's for daring to say, last night in my place, that the Committee is rotten to the core, and that they murdered Sandy McTavish in cold blood when they took him out and hung him for killing that greaser in self-defense. It's for speaking his mind, the mind of an honest man, that they're going to hang him. That is, they'll hang him if you'll stand by and let 'em do it. I believe both these boys told a straight story. I believe them three was trying to pull off a daylight robbery, and Jack shot to save the kid.

"Now, men, see here! I for one have stood about all I'm going to stand from this bunch of cutthroats that've taken the place of the Committee we organized to protect the town. To-night I want every man that calls himself honest to come to my place and hold a mass meeting, to elect a Committee like we had in the first place. I want every man—"

"Bill, you're crazy!" It was Jack, white to the lips in sheer terror for Wilson, Jack who refused to blench at his own dire strait, who sprang up and clapped a hand over the mouth that was sealing the doom of the owner. "Take him out, Jim, for God's sake! Take him—Bill, listen to me, you fool! What was it you were telling me, there in your own doorway, to-day? About not thinking out loud? You can't save me by talking like that! These men—those that don't hate me—are so

scared of their own necks that they wouldn't lift a finger to save a twin brother. Take him out, boys! Bill doesn't mean any harm." He tried
to smile and failed utterly. "He likes me, and he's—he's—"

Shorty it was who jerked him away from Bill. The Captain, on his feet, was dominating the uneasy crowd with his cold stare more than with the gun he held in his hand.

"This Committee," he stated in his calm, judicial tone, which chilled the growing fire of excitement and held the men silent that they might listen, "this Committee regrets that in the course of its unpleasant duties it must now and then rouse the antagonism of a bad man's friends. But this Committee must perform the duties for which it was elected. This Committee is sorry to see Mr. Wilson take the stand he takes, but it realizes that friendship for the condemned man leads him to make statements and threats for which he should not be held responsible. Gentlemen, this court of inquiry is dismissed, and it may not be amiss to point out the necessity for order being maintained among you. The Committee would deeply regret
any trouble arising at this time."

"Oh, damn you and your Committee!" gritted Bill Wilson, out of the bitterness that filled him. He gave Jack one glance; one, and with his jaws set hard together, turned his back.

The crowd pushed and parted to make way for him. Jim, his face the color of a pork rind, followed dog-like at the heels of his boss. And when they had passed, the tent began to belch forth men who walked with heads and shoulders a little bent, talking together under their breaths of this man who dared defy the Committee to its face, and whose daring was as impotent as the breeze that still pulled at the flapping corner of the cloth sign over the door of his place.

Bill glanced dully up at the sign before he opened his door. "Better get the hammer and nail that corner down, Jim," he said morosely, and went in. He poured a whisky glass twothirds full of liquor and emptied it with one long swallow—and Bill was not a drinking man.

"God! This thing they call justice!" he groaned, as he set down the glass; and went out to make an attempt at organizing a rescue party, though he had little hope of succeeding. Jack was a stranger to the better class of business men, and those who did know him were either friends of the Committee or in deadly fear of it. Still, Bill was a gambler. He was probably putting the mark of the next victim on himself; but he did not stop for that.

Chapter 4

What Happened at the Oak

Jack sat looking after the crowd that shuffled through the doorway into the sunlight. He thought he had believed that he would receive the sentence which the juryman had spoken so baldly; yet, after the words had been actually spoken, he stared blankly after Bill and the others, and incredulously at the Captain, who seated himself upon a bunk opposite to watch his prisoner, his pistol resting suggestively upon his knee. The boy lingered to shake Jack's unresponsive hand and mutter a broken sentence or two of gratitude and sympathy. But Jack scarcely grasped his meaning, and his answer sounded chillingly calm; so that the boy, wincing under the cold stare of the Captain and the seeming indifference of the prisoner, turned away with downy chin a-tremble and in his eyes the look of horrified awe which sometimes comes to a youth who has seen death hesitate just over his head, pass him by, and choose another. In the doorway he stopped and looked back bewildered. Jack had said that he loved life and would hate to leave it; and yet he sat there calmly, scraping idly with his boot-toe a little furrow in the loose sand, his elbows resting on his knees, his face unlined by frown or bitterness, his eyes bent abstractedly upon the shallow trench he was desultorily digging. He did not look as the boy believed a man should look who has just been condemned to die the ignominious death of hanging. The boy shuddered and went out into the sunlight, dazed with this glimpse he had got of the inexorable hardness of life.

Jack did not even know when the boy left. He, also, was looking upon the hardness of life, but he was looking with the eyes of the fighter. So long as Jack Allen had breath in his body, he would fight to keep it there. His incredulity against the verdict swung to a tenacious disbelief that it would really come to the worst. So long as he was alive, so long as he could feel the weight of the dagger in his sleeve, it was temperamentally impossible for him to believe that he was going to die that day.

Plans he made and smoothed them in the dirt with his toe. If they did not bind his arms... They had not tied Sandy's arms, he remembered; and he wondered if a dagger concealed in Sandy's sleeve would have made any essential difference in the result of that particular crime of the Committee. He sickened at a vivid memory of how Sandy had ridden away, just a week or so before; and of the

appealing glance which he had sent toward Bill's place when Shorty started to lead the buckskin from before the prison tent with six men walking upon either side and a curious crowd straggling after. Would a dagger in
Sandy's sleeve have made any difference?

Then his thoughts swung to the Mexican who had told him of the trick, only the night before. It had amused Jack to experiment with his own knife; and the very novelty of the thing had impelled him to slip his dagger into the new hiding-place that morning when he dressed. The Captain had not discovered it there—but would it make any difference? It occurred to him that he need not die the death of dangling and strangling at the end of the rope, at any rate; if it came to dying... Jack became acutely conscious of the steady beat in his chest, and immediately afterward felt the same throb in his throat; he could stop that beating whenever he chose, if they did not bind his arms.

"Horse's ready, Captain," announced Shorty succinctly, thrusting his head through the closed flaps; and the Captain rose instantly and made a commanding gesture to his prisoner.

Jack swept the loose dirt back into the furrow with one swing of his foot and stood up. He went out quietly, two steps in advance of the Captain and the Captain's drawn pistol, and advanced unflinchingly towards the horse that stood saddled in the midst of the group of executioners, with the same curious crowd looking on greedily at the spectacle.

"Ever been on a horse?" asked the Captain, his deep voice little more than a growl.

"Once or twice," Jack answered indifferently.

"Climb on, then!"

Jack was young and he was very human. It might be his last hour on earth, but there rose up in him a prideful desire to show them whether he had ever been on a horse; he caught the saddle-horn with one hand and vaulted vaingloriously into the saddle without touching a toe to the stirrup. The buckskin ducked and danced sidewise at the end of the rope in Shorty's hand, and more than one gun flashed into sight at the unexpectedness of the move.

The Captain scowled at the exclamations of admiration from the crowd. "You needn't try any funny work, young man, or I'll tie you hand as well as foot!" he threatened sternly. "Give me that rope, Davis."

Then Jack paid in pain for his vanity, and paid in full. The Captain did not bind his arms—perhaps because of the crowd and a desire to seem merciful. But though he merely tied the prisoner's ankle after the usual manner, he knotted the small rope with a vicious yank, pulled it as tight as he could and passed the rope under the flinching belly of the buckskin to Davis, on the other side. Also he sent a glance of meaning which the other read unerringly and obeyed most willingly. Davis drew the rope taut under the cinch and tied Jack's other ankle as if he were putting the diamond hitch on a pack mule. The two stepped back and eyed him sharply for some sign of pain, when all was done.

"Thanks," drawled Jack. "Sorry I can't do as much for you." Whereupon he set his teeth against the growing agony of strained muscles and congesting arteries, and began to roll a cigarette with fingers which he held rigidly from trembling.

Bill Wilson, returning gloomily to the doorway of his place, grated an oath and turned away his head.

Some day, he promised himself vengefully, those two—yes, and the whole group of murderers moving briskly away from the tent—would pay for that outrage; and he prayed that the day might come soon.

He went heavily into the big room where men were already foregathering to gossip between drinks of the trial and of the man who was to die. Bill bethought him of the young stranger; made some inquiries of certain inoffensive individuals among the crowd, and sent Jim out with instructions to find the kid and bring him back with him.

Bill was standing in the door waiting for Jim to return, when, in a swirl of dust, came Dade galloping around a corner and to the very doorstep before he showed any desire to slow up. At the first tightening of the reins, the white horse stiffened his front legs, dug two foot-long furrows and stopped still. Bill had no enthusiasm for the perfect accomplishment of the trick. He stood with his hands thrust deep into his pockets and regarded the rider glumly.

"Well, you got here," he grunted, with the brevity of utter misery.

"You bet I did! I was away from the hacienda when the peon came, or I'd have got here sooner," Dade explained cheerfully, swinging to the ground with a jingle of his big, Mexican spurs that had little silver bells to swell the tinkly chimes when he moved. "Where's Jack?"

Big Bill Wilson's jaw trembled with an impulse towards tears which the long, harsh years behind him would not let him shed. "They've got him," he said in a choked tone, and waved a hand toward the west.

"Who's got him?" Dade clanked a step closer and peered sharply into Bill's face, with all the easy good humor wiped out of his own.

"The Committee. You're too late; they're taking him out to the oak. Been gone about ten minutes. They had it in for him, and—I couldn't do a thing! The men in this town—" Epithets rushed incoherently from Bill's lips, just as violent weeping marks the reaction from a woman's first silence in the face of tragedy.

Dade did not hear a word he was saying, after those first jerky sentences. He stood looking past Bill at a drunken Irishman who was making erratic progress up the street; and he was no more conscious of the Irishman than he was of Bill's scorching condemnation of the town which could permit such outrages.

"Watch Surry a minute!" he said abruptly, and hurried into the gambling hall. In a minute he was back again and lifting foot to the stirrup.

"How long did you say they've been gone?" he asked, without looking at Bill.

"Ten or fifteen minutes. Say, you can't do anything!"

Dade was already half-way up the block, a swirl of sand-dust marking his flight. Bill stared after him distressfully.

"He'll go and get his light put out—and he won't help Jack a damn bit," he told himself miserably, and went in. Life that day looked very hard to big-hearted Bill Wilson, and scarcely worth the trouble of living it.

It broke the heart of Dade Hunter to see how near the sinister procession was to the live oak that had come to be looked upon as the gallows of the Vigilance Committee; a gallows whose broad branches sheltered from rain and sun alike the unmarked graves of the men who had come there shuddering and looked upon it, and shuddering had looked no more upon anything in this world.

Until he was near enough to risk betraying his haste by the hoof-beats of his horse, Dade kept Surry at a run. Upon the crest of the slope which the procession was leisurely descending, he slowed to a lope; and so overtook the crowd that straggled always out to the hangings, came they ever so frequent. Reeling in the saddle, he came up with the stragglers, singing and marking time with a half-empty bottle of whisky.

The few who knew him looked at one another askance.

"Say, Hunter, ain't yuh got any feelin's? That there's your pardner on the hoss," one loose-jointed miner expostulated.

"Sure, I got feelin's! Have a d-drink?" Dade leered drunkenly at the speaker. "Jack's—no good anyway. Tol' 'im he'd get hung if he—have a d-drink?"

The loose-jointed one would, and so would his neighbors. The Captain glanced back at them, gave a contemptuous lift to his upper lip and faced again to the front.

Dade uncoiled his riata with aimless, fumbling fingers and swung the noose facetiously toward the bottle, uptilted over the eager mouth of a weazened little Irishman. He caught bottle and hand together, let them go with a quick flip of the rawhide and waggled his head in apology.

"*Excuse* me, Mike," he mumbled, while the Irishman stopped and glared. "Go awn! Have a drink. Mighta spilled it—shame!"

Jack looked back, his heart thumping heavily at sound of the voice, thick though it was and maudlin. Dade drunk and full of coarse foolery was a sight he had never before looked upon; but Dade's presence, drunk or sober, made his own plight seem a shade less hopeless. He did not dare a second glance, with Davis and the Captain walking at either stirrup; but he listened anxiously—listened and caught a drunken mumble from the rear, and a chorus of chuckling laughs coming after.

He looked ahead. The great oak was close, so close that he might have counted the narrow little ridges of red soil beneath; the ridges which he knew were the graves of those who had died before him. The great bough that reached out over the spot where the earth was trampled smooth in horrible significance—the branch from which a noosed rope dangled sinuously in the breeze that came straight off the ocean—swayed with majestic deliberation as if Fate herself were beckoning.

He clasped his hands upon the saddle-horn and, stealthily loosening the dagger-point from the hem of his sleeve, slid the weapon cautiously into his hand. When he felt the handle against his palm, he knew that he had been holding his breath, and that the sigh he gave was an involuntary relief that the others had not glimpsed the blade under his clasped fingers. He would not have to dangle from that swinging rope, at any rate.

"Hello, pard!" Dade's voice called thickly from close behind. "Looking for some rope?"

Jack turned his head just as the looped rawhide slithered past him and settled taut over the head of the startled buckskin. Like a lightning gleam slashing through the dark he saw Dade's plan, and played his own part unhesitatingly.

Two movements he made while the buckskin sat back upon his haunches and gathered his muscles for a forward spring. The first was to lean and send a downward sweep of the dagger across the rope by which Shorty was leading the horse, and the second was a backward lunge that drove the knife deep into the bared throat of the Captain, stunned into momentary inaction by the suddenness of Dade's assault.

The buckskin gave a mighty leap that caught Shorty unawares and sent him into a crumpled heap in the sand. Dade's riata, tight as a fiddle-string at first, slackened as the buckskin, his breath coming in snorts, surged alongside. Jack leaned again—this time to snatch the ivory-handled revolver from the holster on Dade's saddle. As well as he could with his legs held rigid by the rope that tied his ankles, he twisted in the saddle and sent leaden answer to the spiteful barking of the guns that called upon them to halt.

[Illustration: He twisted in the saddle and sent leaden answer to the spiteful barking of the guns.]

Davis he shot, and saw him sway and fall flat, with a smoking gun in his hand. Another crumpled forward; and Shorty, just getting painfully upon his feet, he sent into the sand again to stay; for his skill with small arms was something uncanny to witness, and his temper was up and turning him into a savage like the rest.

But the range was rapidly growing to rifle-length, and death fell short of his enemies after Shorty went down. When he saw his fourth bullet kick up a harmless little geyser of sand two rods in advance of the agitated crowd, he left off and turned to his friend.

"I thought you were drunk," he observed inanely, as is common to men who have just come through situations for which no words have been coined.

"You ain't the only one who made that mistake," Dade retorted grimly, and looked back. "Good thing those hombres are afoot. We'll get on a little farther and then we'll fix a hackamore so you can do your own riding,"

"I can't stand it to ride any farther—"

"Are you shot?" Dade pulled in a little and looked anxiously into his face.

"It's the rope. They tied it so tight it's torture. I'd never have believed it could hurt so—but they gave me an extra twist or

two to show their friendship, I reckon."

Dade rode on beyond a little, wooded knoll before he stopped, lest the crowd, seeing them halt, might think it worth while to follow them afoot.

"They surely didn't intend you to fall off," he said whimsically, when his knife released the strain. But his lips tightened at the outrage; and his eyes, bent upon Jack's left ankle, wore the look of one who could kill without pity.

"They'll never do it to another man," declared Jack, with vindictive relish. "It was Davis and the Captain; I killed 'em both." He rolled stiffly from the saddle, found his feet like dead things and stumbled to a little hillock, where he sat down.

Dade, kneeling awkwardly in his heavy, bearskin chaparejos, picked at the bonds with the point of his knife. "Lucky you had on boots," he remarked. "Even as it is, you're likely to carry creases for a while. How the deuce did you manage to get into

this particular scrape?—if I might ask!"

"I didn't get into it. This particular scrape got me. Say, it's lucky you happened along just when you did."

To this very obvious statement the other made no reply. He cut the last strand of the rope that bound Jack's ankles so mercilessly, and stood up. "You better take off your boots and rub some feeling into your feet while I make a hackamore for that horse. The sooner we get out of this, the better. What's left of the Committee will probably be pretty anxious to see you."

"Oh, damn the Committee!—as Bill remarked after the trial." Jack made an attempt to remove one of his boots, found the pain intolerable and desisted with a groan. "I wish they would show up," he declared. "I'd like to give them a taste of this foottying business!"

Dade went on tying the hackamore with a haste that might be called anxious. With just two bullets left in the pistol and with no powder upon his person for further reloading, he could not share Jack's eagerness to meet the Committee again. When Surry gave over rolling with his tongue the little wheel in his bit, and with lifted head and eyes alert perked his ears forward towards the hill they had just crossed, he slipped the hackamore hurriedly into place and turned to his friend.

"You climb on to Surry, and we'll pull out," he said shortly. "I wouldn't give two pesos for this buckskin, but we're going to add horse-stealing to our other crimes; and while it's all right to damn the Committee, it's just as well to do it at a distance, just now, old man."

The caution fell flat, for Jack was wholly absorbed by the pain in his feet and ankles, as the blood was being forced into the congested veins. Dade led the white horse close, to save him the discomfort of hobbling to it, and waited until Jack was in the saddle before he vaulted upon the tricky-eyed buckskin. He led the way down into a shallow depression which wound aimlessly towards the ocean; and later, when trees and bushes and precipitous bluffs threatened to bar their way, he swung abruptly to the east and south.

"Maybe you won't object so hard to Palo Alto now," he bantered at last, when at dusk he ventured out upon "El Camino Real" (which is pure Spanish for "The King's Highway"), that had linked Mission to Mission all down the fertile length of California when the land was wilderness. "Solitude ought to feel good, after to-day." When he got no answer, Dade looked around at the other.

Jack's face showed vaguely through the night fog creeping in from the clamorous ocean off to the west. His legs were hanging free of the stirrups, and his hands rested upon the high saddle-horn.

"Say, Dade," he asked irrelevantly and with a mystifying earnestness, "which do you think would kill a man quickest—a
slash across the throat, or a stab in the heart?"

"I wouldn't call either one healthy. Why?"

"I was just wondering," Jack returned ambiguously. "If you hadn't happened along—say, how did you happen to come? Was that another sample of my fool's luck?" Since the coincidence had not struck him before, one might guess that he was accustomed to having Dade at his elbow when he was most needed.

"Bill Wilson sent word that you were making seven kinds of a fool of yourself—Bill named a few of them—and advised me to get you out of town. I've more respect for Bill's judgment than ever. I took his advice as it stood—and therefore, you're headed for safer territory than you were awhile ago. It ain't heaven," he added, "but it's next thing to it."

"I'm not hankering after heaven, right now," averred Jack. "Most any other place looks good to me; I'm not feeling a hit critical, Dade. And if I didn't say it before, old man, you're worth a whole regiment to a fellow in a fix."

Chapter 5

Hospitality

If you would enjoy that fine hospitality which gives gladly to strangers and to friends alike of its poverty or plenty, and for the giving asks nothing in return, you should seek the far frontiers; but if you would see hospitality glorified into something more than a simple virtue, then you should find, if you can, one of the old-time haciendas that were the pride of early California.

Time was when the wild-eyed cattle which bore upon their fat-cushioned haunches the seared crescent that proclaimed them the property of old Don Andres Picardo (who owned, by grant of the king, all the upper half of the valley of Santa Clara) were free to any who hungered. Time was when a traveler might shoot a fat yearling and feast his fill, unquestioned by the don or the don's dark-eyed vaqueros.

Don Andres Picardo was a large-hearted gentleman; and to deny any man meat would bring to his cheeks a blush for his niggardliness. That was in the beginning, when he reigned in peace over the peninsula. When the vaqueros, jingling indignantly into the patio of his home, first told of carcasses slaughtered wantonly and left to rot upon the range with only the loin and perhaps a juicy haunch missing, their master smiled deprecatingly and waved them back whence they came. There were cattle in plenty. What mattered one steer, or even a fat cow, slain wastefully? Were not thousands left?

But when tales reached him of cattle butchered by the hundred, and of beef that was being sold for an atrocious price in San Francisco, the old Spaniard was shocked into laying aside the traditions and placing some check upon the unmannerly "gringos" who so abused his generosity.

He established a camp just within the northern boundary of his land; and there he stationed his most efficient watch-dog, Manuel Sepulveda, with two vaqueros whose business it was to stop the depredations.

Meat for all who asked for meat, paid they in gold or in gratitude—that was their "patron's" order. But they must ask. And the vaqueros rode diligently from bay to mountain slopes, and each day their hatred of the Americanos grew deeper, as they watched over the herds of their loved patron, that the gringos might not steal that which they might, if they were not wolves, have for the asking.

The firelight in the tule-thatched hut of Manuel Sepulveda winked facetiously at the black fog that peered in at the open door. A night wind from the north crept up, parted the fog like a black curtain and whispered something which set the flames a-dancing as they listened. The fog swung back jealously to hear what it was, and the wind went away to whisper its wonder-tale to the trees that rustled astonishment and nodded afterward to one another in approval, like the arrant gossips they were. The chill curtain fell straight and heavy again before the door, so that the firelight shone dimly through its folds; but not before Dade, riding at random save for the trust he put in the sure homing instinct of his horse, caught the brief gleam of light and sighed thankfully.

"We'll stop with old Manuel to-night," he announced cheerfully. "Here's his cabin, just ahead."

"And who's old Manuel?" asked Jack petulantly, because of the pain in his feet and his own unpleasant memories of that day.

"Don Andres Picardo's head vaquero. He camps here to keep an eye on the cattle. Some fellows from town have been butchering them right and left and doing a big business in beef, according to all accounts. Manuel hates gringos like centipedes, but I happened to get on the good side of him—partly because my Spanish is as good as his own. An Americano who has black hair and can talk Spanish like the don himself isn't an Americano, in Manuel's eyes."

While they were unsaddling under the oak tree, where the vaqueros kept their riding gear in front of the cabin, Manuel himself came to the door and stood squinting into the fog, while he flapped a tortilla dexterously between his brown palms.

"Is it you, Valencia??" he called out in Spanish, giving the tortilla a deft, whirling motion to even its edges.

Dade led the way into the zone of light, and Manuel stepped back with a series of welcoming nods. His black eyes darted curiously to the stranger, who, in Manuel's opinion, looked unpleasantly like a gringo, with his coppery hair waving crisply under his sombrero, and his eyes that were blue as the bay over there to the east. But when Dade introduced him, Jack greeted his squat host with a smile that was disarming in its boyish good humor, and with language as liquidly Spanish as Manuel's best Castilian, which he reserved for his talks with the patron on the porch when the señora and the young señorita were by.

The distrust left Manuel's eyes as he trotted across the hardtrodden dirt floor and laid the tortilla carefully upon a hot rock, where three others crisped and curled their edges in delectable promise of future toothsomeness.

He stood up and turned to Dade amiably, his knuckles pressing lightly upon his hips that his palms might be saved immaculate for the next little corn cake which he would presently slap into thin symmetry.

"Madre de Dios!" he cried suddenly, quite forgetting the hospitable thing he had meant to say about his supper. "You are
hurt, Señor! The blood is on your sleeve and your hand."

Dade looked down at his hand and laughed. "I did get a
scratch. I'll let you see what it's like."

"You never told me you got shot!" accused Jack sharply, from where he had thrown himself down on a bundle of blankets covered over with a bullock hide dressed soft as chamois.

"Never thought of it," retorted Dade in Spanish, out of regard for his host.

"We had some trouble with the gringos," he explained to Manuel. "There was a little shooting, and a bullet grazed my
arm. It doesn't amount to much, but I'll let you look at it."

"Ah, the gringos!" Manuel spat after the hated name. "The patron is too good, too generous! They steal the cattle of the patron, though they might have all they need for the asking. Like the green worms upon the live oaks, they would strip the patron's herds to the last, lean old bull that is too tough even for their wolf teeth! Me, I should like to lasso and drag to the death every gringo who comes sneaking in the night for the meat which tastes sweeter when it is stolen. To-day Valencia rode down to the bayou—"

While he told indignantly the tale of the latest pillage, he bared the wounded arm. Jack got stiffly upon his swollen feet to look. It was not a serious wound, as wounds go; a deep gash in the bicep, where a bullet meant for Dade's heart had plowed under his upraised arm four inches wide of its mark. It must have been painful, though he had not once mentioned it; and a shamed flush stung Jack's cheeks when he remembered his own complaints because of his feet.

"You never told me!" he accused again, this time in the language of his host.

"The Señor Hunter has the brave heart of a Spaniard, though his blood is light," said Manuel rebukingly. "The Señor Hunter would not cry over a bigger hurt than this!"

Jack sat down again upon the bull-hide seat and dropped his face between his palms. Old Manuel spoke truer than he knew. Dade Hunter was made of the stuff that will suffer much for a friend and say nothing about it, and to-day was not the first time when Jack had all unwittingly given that friendship the test supreme.

Manuel carefully inspected the wound and murmured his sympathy. He pulled a bouquet of dry herbs from where it hung in a corner, under the low ceiling, and set a handful brewing in water, where the coals were golden-yellow with heat. He tore a strip of linen off Valencia's best shirt which he was saving for fiestas, and prepared a bandage, interrupting himself now and then to dart over and inspect the tortillas baking on the hot rock. For a fat man he moved with extraordinary briskness, and so managed to do three things at one time and do them all thoroughly; he washed and dressed the wound with the herbs squeezed into a poultice, rescued the tortillas from scorching, and spake his mind concerning the gringos who, he declared, were despoiling this his native land. Then he lifted certain pots and platters to the center of the hut and cheerfully announced supper; and squatted on the floor, facing his guests over the food.

"There's another thing that bothers me, Manuel," Dade announced humorously, when they three were seated around the pot of frijoles, the earthen pan of smoking carne-seco (which is meat flavored hotly after the Spanish style) and a stack of the tortillas Manuel's fat hands had created while he talked.

Manuel, bending a tortilla into a scoop wherewith to help himself to the brown beans, raised his black eyes anxiously. "But is there further hurt?" he asked, and glanced wistfully at the tortilla before laying it down that he might minister further to the señor.

"No—go on with your supper. There's a buckskin horse out there that the gringos may say I stole. I don't want the beast; he's about fourteen years old and he's got a Roman nose to

beat Caesar himself, and a bad eye and a wicked heart."

"Dios!" murmured Manuel over the list of equine shortcomings and took a large, relieved bite of tortilla and beans. The señor was pleased to jest with a poor vaquero, but the señor would doubtless explain. He chewed luxuriously and waited, his black eyes darting from this face which he knew and liked, to that strange one of the blue eyes and the hair that was like the dullest of dull California gold.

"I don't like that caballo," went on Dade, helping himself to meat, "and so I'd hate like the deuce to be hung for stealing him; sabe?"

Manuel licked a finger before he spread his hands to show how completely he failed to understand. "But if the caballo does not please the señor, why then did the señor steal—"

"You see, I wanted to bring my partner—Señor Jack Allen—down here with me. And he was riding the caballo, and he couldn't get off—"

Manuel swore a Spanish oath politely, to please his guest who wished to amaze him.

"Because he was tied on." Dade failed just there to keep a betraying hardness out of his voice. "The Viligantes were—going to—hang him." The last two words were cut short off with the click of his jaws coming together.

Manuel thereupon swore more sincerely and spilled beans from his tortilla scoop. He knew the ways of the Committee. Four months ago—when the Committee was newer and more just—they had hanged the third cousin of his half-sister's husband. It is true, the man had killed a woman with a knife; yet Manuel's black beard bristled when he thought of the affront to his hypothetical kinship.

"I had to take the two together," Dade explained, trying with better success to speak lightly. "And now, if I turn the buckskin loose, he may go back—and he may not. I was wondering—"

Manuel cut him short. "To-morrow I ride to town," he said. "I will take the caballo back with me, if that pleases the señors. I will turn him loose near the Mission, and he will go to his stable.

"The señor," he added, "was very brave. *Madre de Dios!* To run away with a prisoner of the Vigilantes! But they will surely kill the señor for that; the taking of the horse, that is nothing." His teeth shone briefly under his black mustache. "One can die but once," he pointed out, and emphasized his meaning by a swift glance at Jack, moodily nibbling the edge of a corn cake. "But if the horse does not please the señor—"

Dade caught his meaning and laughed a little over it. "The horse," he said, "belongs to the Committee; my friend does not."

"Sí, Señor—but surely that is true. Only—" he stroked his crisp beard thoughtfully—"the señors would better go to-morrow to the patron. There the gringos dare not come. In this poor hut the señors may not be safe—for we are but three poor vaqueros when all are here. We will do our best—"

"Three vaqueros," declared Dade with fine diplomacy, "as brave as the three who live here, would equal twenty of the
Committee. But we will not let it come to that."

Manuel took the flattery with a glimpse of white teeth and a deprecatory wave of the hand, and himself qualified it modestly afterward.

"With the knife—perhaps. But the gringos have guns which speak fast. Still, we would do our best—"

"Say, if he's going back to town to-morrow," spake Jack suddenly, from where he reclined in the shadow "why can't I write a note to Bill Wilson and have him send down my guns? The Captain took them away, you know; but he won't object to giving them back now!" His voice was bitter.

"The rest of them might. You seem to think that when you killed Perkins you wiped out the whole delegation—which you didn't. What was the row about; if you don't mind telling me?"

"I thought you knew," said Jack quite sincerely, which proved more than anything how absorbed he was in his own part in the affair. He shifted his head upon his clasped hands so that his eyes might rest upon the waning firelight, where the pot of frijoles, set back from supper, was still steaming languidly in the hot ashes.

"You started it yourself, two weeks ago," he announced whimsically, to lighten a little the somber tale. "If you hadn't bought that white horse from that drunken Spaniard, I'd be holding a handful of aces and kings to-night, most likely, in Bill Wilson's place. And my legs wouldn't be aching like the devil," he added, reminded anew of his troubles, when he shifted his position. "It's all your fault, bought the horse."

Dade grinned and bent to hold a twig in the coals, that he might light a cigarette. "All right, I'm the guilty party. Let's have the consequences of my evil deed," he advised, settling back on his heels and lowering an eyelid at Manuel in behalf of this humorous partner of his.

"You bought the horse and broke the Spaniard's heart and ruined his temper. And he and Sandy had a fight, and—So," he went on, after a two-minute break in the argument, "when I heard Swift sneering something about Sandy, last night, I rose up in meeting and told him and some others what I thought of 'em. I was not," he explained, "thinking nice thoughts at the time. You see, Perkins, since he got the lead, has gathered a mighty scaly bunch around him, and they've been running things to suit themselves.

"Then, Swift and two or three others held up a boy from the mines to-day, and I happened to see it. I interfered; fact is, I killed a couple of them. So they arrested both of us, went through a farce trial, and were trying to hurry me into Kingdom Come before Bill Wilson got a rescue party together, when you come along. That's all. They let the kid go—which was a good thing. I don't think they'll be down here after me. In fact, I've been thinking maybe I'd go back, in a day or so, and have it out with them."

"Yes, that's about what you'd be thinking, all right," retorted Dade unemotionally. "Sounds perfectly natural." The tone of him, being unsympathetic, precipitated an argument which flung crisp English sentences back and forth across the cabin. Manuel, when the words grew strange and took on a harsh tang which to his ear meant anger, diplomatically sought his blankets and merged into the shadow of the corner farthest from the fire and nearest the door. The señors were pleased to disagree; if they fought, he had but to dodge out into the night and neutrality. The duties of hospitality weighed hard upon Manuel during that half-hour or so.

Dade's cigarette stub, flung violently into the heart of the fire glow, seemed to Manuel a crucial point in the quarrel; he slipped back the blankets, ready to retreat at the first lunge of open warfare. He breathed relief, however, when Dade got up and stretched his arms to the dried tules overhead, and laughed a lazy surrender of the argument, if not of his opinion upon the subject.

"You're surely the most ambitious trouble-hunter I ever saw," he said, returning to his habitual humorous drawl, with the twinkle in his eyes that went with it. "Just the same, we'll not go back to the mine just yet. Till the dust settles, we're both better off down here with Don Andres Picardo. I don't want to be hung for the company I keep. Besides—"

"I'll bet ten ounces there's a señorita," hazarded. Jack maliciously. "You're like Bill Wilson; but you can preach caution till your jaws ache; you can't fool me into believing you're afraid to go back to the mine. Is there a señorita?"

"You shut up and go to sleep," snapped Dade, and afterward would not speak at all.

Manuel, in the shadow, frowned over the only words he understood—Don Andres Picardo and señorita. The señors were agreeable companions, and they were his guests. But they were gringos, after all. And if they should presume to lift desireful eyes to the little Señorita Teresa—Teresita, they called her fondly who knew her—Manuel's mustache lifted suddenly at one side at the bare possibility.

Chapter 6

The Valley

In the valley of Santa Clara, which lies cradled easily between mountains and smiles up at the sun nearly the whole year through, Spring has a winter home, wherein she dwells contentedly while the northern land is locked in the chill embrace of the Snow King. In February, unless the north wind sweeps down jealously and stays her hand, she flings a golden brocade of poppies over the green hillsides and the lower slopes which the forest has left her. Time was when she spread a deep-piled carpet of mustard over the floor of the valley as well, and watched smiling while it grew thicker and higher and the lemon-yellow blossoms vied with the orange of the poppies, until the two set all the valley aglow.

Now it was March, and the hillsides were ablaze with the poppies, and the valley floor was soft green and yellow to the knees; with the great live oaks standing grouped in stately calm, like a herd of gigantic, green elephants scattered over their feeding-ground and finding the peace of repletion with the coming of the sun.

The cabin of Manuel squatted upon a little rise of ground at the head of the valley. When Jack stood in the doorway and looked down upon the green sweep of grazing ground with the hills behind, and farther away another range facing him, he owned to himself that it was good to be there. The squalidness of the town he had left so tumultuously struck upon his memory nauseatingly.

Spring was here in the valley, even though the mountains shone white beyond. A wind had come out of the south and driven the fog back to the bay, and the sun shone warmly down upon the land. Two robins sang exultantly in the higher branches of the oak, where they had breakfasted satisfyingly upon the first of the little, green worms that gave early promise of being a pest until such time as they stiffened and clung inertly, waiting for the dainty, gray wings to grow and set them aflutter over the tree upon which they had fed. One of them dropped upon Jack's arm while he stood there and crawled aimlessly from the barren buckskin to his wrist. He flung it off mechanically. Spring was here of a truth; in the town he had not noticed her coming.

"You're right, Dade," he declared suddenly, over his shoulder. "This beats getting up at noon and going through the motions of living for twelve or fourteen hours in town. I believe I'll have Manuel get me a riding outfit, if he will. Maybe I'll take you up on that rodeo proposition. Reckon your old don will give me a job?"

"Won't cost a peso to find out," said Dade, coming out and standing beside him in the sun. "I've been talking to Manuel, and he thinks we'd better pull out right away. Valencia's got an extra saddle here, and Manuel says he'll catch a horse for you."

"I believe I'll send a letter to Bill," proposed Jack. "He'll give Manuel enough dust to buy what I need; and I ought to let him know how we made out, anyway."

A blank leaf from the little memorandum book he always carried, and a bullet for pencil—perforce, the note was brief; but it told what he wanted: gold to buy a riding outfit, his pistols which Perkins had taken from him, and news of Bill's well-being. When the paper would hold no more and hold it legibly, he folded it carefully so that it would not smudge, and gave it to his host.

"What if the Committee catches you with that buckskin, Manuel?" he asked abruptly. The risk Manuel would run had not before occurred to him. "Dade he's liable to get into trouble, if they catch him with that horse; let's turn the darned thing loose."

"Me, I shall not ride where the gringos will see me," broke in Manuel briskly. "The señors need not be alarmed. I shall keep away from El Camino Real. At the Mission I will buy what the

señor desires, and I will bring it to him at the hacienda."

"Get the best they've got," Jack adjured him. "An outfit better than Dade's, if you can find one. Bill Wilson has got about twelve hundred dollars of mine; get the best if it cleans the sack." He grinned at Dade. "If you're going to bully me into turning vaquero again, I'm going to have the fun of riding in style, anyway. You've set the pace, you know. I never saw you

so gaudy. Er—what did you say her name is?" "I didn't say."

"Must be serious. Too bad." Jack shook his head dolefully. "Say, Manuel, do you know a good riata, when you see one lying around loose?"

"Sí, Señor. Me, I have braided the riatas and bridles since I was so high." From the height of his measuring hand from the beaten clay beneath the oak, he proclaimed himself an infant prodigy; but Jack did not happen to be looking at him and so remained unamazed.

"Well, you ought to know something about them. Get the best

riata you can find. I leave it to your judgment."

"Sí, Señor. To-morrow I will bring them to you." He hesitated, his eyes dwelling curiously upon the coppery hair of this stranger, whose presence he was not quite sure that he did not resent vaguely. Dade he had come to accept as a man whose innate kindliness, which was as much a part of him as the blood in his veins, wiped out any stain of alien birth; but this blue-eyed one—"The señor himself is perhaps a judge of riatas?" he insinuated, politely veiling the quick jealousy of his nature.

"We-el-l—you bring me one ready to fall all to pieces, and I

reckon I could tell it was poor, after it had stranded."

Dade laughed. "Judge of riatas? You wait till you see him with one in his hand!"

Manuel's teeth shone briefly, but the smile did not come from his heart. "Me, I shall surely bring the señor a riata worthy even of his skill," he declared sententiously, as he walked away with his bridle slung over his arm and his back very straight.

"That sounded sarcastic," commented Jack, looking after him. "What's the matter? Is the old fellow jealous?" Dade flicked his cigarette against the trunk of the oak to remove the white crown of ashes, and shook his head. "What of?" he asked bluntly. "Half your trouble, Jack, comes from looking for it. Manuel's a fine old fellow. I stayed a few days with him here when I first left town, and rode around with him. He's straight as the road to heaven, and I never heard him brag about anything, except the goodness of his 'patron,' and the things some of his friends can do. I'll have to ask you to saddle up for me, Jack; this arm of mine's pretty stiff and sore this morning. Watch how Surry's trained! You wouldn't believe some of the things he'll do."

He turned towards the horse, feeding knee-deep in grass and young mustard in the opening farther down the slope, and whistled a long, high note. The white head went up with a fling of the heavy mane, to perk ears forward at the sound. Then he turned and came towards them at a long, swinging walk that was a joy to behold.

"Do you know, I hate the way nature's trimmed down the life of a horse to a few measly years," said Dade. "A good horse you can love like a human—and fifteen years is about as long as he can expect to live and amount to anything. Surry's four now, by his teeth. In fifteen years I'll still be at my best; I'll want that horse like the very devil; and he'll be dead of old age, if he lasts that long. And a turtle," he added resentfully after a pause, "lives hundreds of years, just because the darned things aren't any good on earth!"

"Trade him for a camel," drawled Jack unsympathetically. "They're more durable."

"Watch him come, now!" Dade gave three short, shrill whistles, and with a toss of head by way of answer, Surry came tearing up the slope, straight for his master. The shadow of the oak was all about him when he planted his front feet stiffly and stopped; flared his nostrils in a snort and, because Dade waved his hand to the right, wheeled that way, circled the oak at a pace which set his body aslant and stopped again quite as suddenly as before. Dade held out his hand, and Surry came up and rubbed the palm playfully with his soft muzzle.

"For a camel, did you say?" Dade grinned triumphantly at the other over the sleek back of his pet.

"What'll you take for him?"

Dade pulled the heavy forelock straight with fingers that caressed with every touch. "José Pacheco asked me that, and I came pretty near hitting him. I don't reckon I'll ever be drunk enough to name a price. But I might—"

Jack glanced at him, and saw that his lips were half parted in a smile born of some fancy of his own, and that his eyes were seeing dreams. Jack stared for a full minute before Dade's thoughts jerked back to his surroundings. Dade was not a dreamer; or if he were, Jack had never had occasion to suspect him of it, and he wondered a little what it was that had sent Dade into dreams at that hour of the morning. But Manuel was returning, riding one pony and leading another; so Jack threw away his cigarette stub and picked up the saddle blanket.

Manuel came up and saddled his mount silently, his deft fingers working mechanically while his black eyes stole sidelong looks at Jack saddling Surry, as if he would measure the man anew. While he was anathematizing the buckskin in language for which he would need to do a penance later on, if he confessed the blasphemy to the padre, Jack threw Valencia's saddle upon the little sorrel pony Manuel had led up for him to ride.

"Truly one would not like to die for having stolen such a beast," stated Manuel earnestly, knotting a macarte around the neck of the buckskin. "He is only fit to carry men to hangings. Come, accursed one! The Vigilantes are weeping for one so like themselves. Adios, Señors!"

He rode away, still heaping opprobrium upon the reluctant buckskin, and speedily he disappeared behind a clump of willows clothed in the pale green of new leaves.

Dade dropped the bullock hide which served for a door, to signify that the master of the house was absent. Though the old don's cattle might be butchered under his very nose, Manuel's few belongings would not be molested, though only the dingy brown hide of a bull long since gone the way of all flesh barred the way; a week, one month or six the hut would stand inviolate from despoliation; for such was the unwritten law of a land where life was held cheaper than the things necessary to preserve life.

On such a morning, when the air was like summer and all the birds were rehearsing most industriously their parts in the opening chorus with which Spring meant to celebrate her return to the northern land, a ride down the valley was pure joy to any man whose soul was tuned in harmony with the great outdoors; and trouble lagged and could not keep pace with the riders.

Half-way down, they met Valencia, a slim young Spaniard with one of those amazing smiles that was like a flash of sunlight, what with his perfect teeth, his eyes that could almost laugh out loud, and a sunny soul behind them. Valencia, having an appetite for acquiring wisdom of various kinds and qualities, knew some English and was not averse to making strangers aware of the accomplishment.

Therefore, when the two greeted him in Spanish, he calmly replied: "Hello, pardner," and pulled up for a smoke.

"How you feel for my dam-close call to-morrow?" he wanted to know of Jack, when he learned his name.

"Pretty well. How did you know—?" began Jack, but the other cut him short.

"José, she heard on town. The patron, she's worry leetle. She's 'fraid for Señor Hunter be keel. Me, I ride to find forsure." Valencia dropped his match, and leaned negligently from the saddle and picked it out of the grass, his eyes stealing a look at the stranger as he came up.

"Good work," commented Jack under his breath to Dade. But Valencia's ears were keen for praise; he heard, and from that moment he was Jack's friend.

"I borrowed your saddle, Valencia," Jack announced, meaning to promise a speedy return of it.

"Not my saddle; yours and mine, amigo," amended Valencia quite simply and sincerely. "Mine, she's yours also. You keep him." While he smoked the little, corn-husk cigarette, he eyed with admiration the copper-red hair upon which Manuel had looked with disfavor.

Before they rode on and left him, his friendliness had stamped an agreeable impression upon Jack's consciousness. He looked back approvingly at the sombreroed head bobbing along behind a clump of young manzanita just making ready to bloom daintily.

"I like that vaquero," he stated emphatically. "He's worth two of Manuel, to my notion."

"Valencia? He's not half the man old Manuel is. He gambles worse than an Injun, and never has anything more than his riding outfit and the clothes on his back, they tell me. And he fights like a catamount when the notion strikes him; and it doesn't seem to make much difference whether he's got an excuse or not. He's a good deal like you, in that respect," he added, with that perfect frankness which true friendship affects as a special privilege earned by its loyalty.

"Manuel's got tricky eyes," countered Jack. "He's the kind of
Spaniard that will 'Sí, Señor,' while he's hitching his knife loose to get you in the back. I know the breed; I lived amongst 'em
before I ever saw you. Valencia's the kind I'd tie to."

"And I was working with 'em when you were saying 'pitty horsey!' My first job was with a Spanish outfit. A Mexican majordomo licked me into shape when I was sweet sixteen. And," he clinched the argument mercilessly, "I was sixteen and drawing a man's pay on rodeo when you wore your pants buttoned on to your waist!"

"And you don't know anything yet!" Jack came back at him. Whereat they laughed and called a truce, which was the way of them.

Chapter 7

The Lord of the Valley

Scattered, grazing herds of wild, long-horned cattle that ran from their approach gave place to feeding mustangs with the mark of the saddle upon them. Later, an adobe wall confronted them; and this they followed through a grove of great live oaks and up a grassy slope beyond, to where the long, low adobe house sat solidly upon a natural terrace, with the valley lying before and the hills at its back; a wide-armed, wide-porched, red-roofed adobe such as the Spanish aristocracy loved to build for themselves. The sun shone warmly upon the great, latticed porch, screened by the passion vines that hid one end completely from view. To the left, a wing stretched out generously, with windows curtained primly with some white stuff that flapped desultorily in the fitful breeze from the south. At the right, so close that they came near being a part of the main structure and helped to give the general effect of a hollow, open-sided square, stood a row of small adobe huts; two of them were tiled like the house, and the last, at the outer end, was thatched with tules.

Into the immaculate patio thus formed before the porch, Dade led the way boldly, as one sure of his welcome. Behind the vines a girl's voice, speaking rapidly and softly with a laugh running all through the tones, hushed as suddenly as does a wild bird's twitter when strange steps approach. And just as suddenly did Dade's nostrils flare with the quick breath he drew; for tones, if one listens understandingly, may tell a great deal. Even Jack knew instinctively that a young man sat with the girl behind the vines.

After the hush they heard the faint swish of feminine movement. She came and stood demurely at the top of the wide steps, a little hoop overflowing soft, white embroidered stuff in her hands.

"Welcome home, Señor Hunter," she said, and made him a courtesy that was one-third politeness and the rest pure mockery. "My father will be relieved in his mind when he sees you. I
think he slept badly last night on your account."

Wistfulness was in Dade's eyes when he looked at her; as though he wanted to ask if she also were relieved at seeing him. But there was the man behind the lattice where the vines were thickest; the man who was young and whom she had found a pleasant companion. Also there was Jack, who was staring with perfect frankness, his eyes a full shade darker as he looked at her. And there was the peon scampering barefooted across from one of the huts to take their horses. Dade therefore confined himself to conventional phrases.

"Señorita, let me present to you my friend, Jack Allen," he
said. "Jack, this is the Señorita Teresa Picardo."

His nostrils widened again when he looked casually at Jack; for Jack's sombrero was swept down to his knees in salute—though it was not that; it was the look in his face that sent Dade's glance seeking Teresita's eyes for answer.

But Teresita only showed him how effectively black lashes contrast with the faint flush of cheeks just hinting at dimples, and he got no answer there.

She made another little courtesy, lifting her lashes unexpectedly for a swift glance at Jack, as he dismounted hastily and went up two steps, his hand outstretched to her.

"We Americanos like to shake hands upon a new friendship," he said boldly.

The señorita laughed a little, changed her embroidery hoop from her right hand to her left, laid her fingers in his palm, blushed when his hand closed upon them eagerly, and laughed again when her gold thimble slipped and rolled tinkling down the steps.

Dade picked the thimble out of a matted corner of a violet bed, and returned it to her unsmilingly; got a flash of her eyes and a little nod for his reward, and stood back, waiting her further pleasure.

"You have had adventures, Señor, since yesterday morning," she said to him lightly. "Truly, you Americanos do very wonderful things! José, here is Señor Hunter and his friend whom he stole away from the Vigilantes yesterday! Did you have the invisible cap, Señor? It was truly a miracle such as the padres tell of, that the blessed saints performed in the books. José told us what he heard—but when I have called my
mother, you yourself must tell us every little bit of it."

While she was talking she was also pulling forward two of the easiest chairs, playing the hostess prettily and stealing a lash-hidden glance now and then at the tall señor with such blue eyes and hair the like of which she had never seen, and the mouth curved like the lips of a woman.

The young man whom she addressed as José rose negligently and greeted them punctiliously; seated himself again, picked up a guitar and strummed a minor chord lazily.

"Don Andres is busy at the corrals," José volunteered, when the girl had gone. "He will return soon. You had a disagreeable experience, Señor? One of my vaqueros heard the story in town. There was a rumor that the Vigilantes were sending out parties to search for you when Carlos started home. Señor Allen is lucky to get off so easily."

Jack held a match unlighted in his fingers while he studied the face of José. The tone of him had jarred, but his features were wiped clean of any expression save faint boredom; and his fingers, plucking a plaintive fragment of a fandango from the strings, belied the sarcasm Jack had suspected. Don Andres himself, at that moment coming eagerly across from the hut at the end of the row, saved the necessity of replying.

"Welcome home, amigo mio!" cried the don, hurrying up the steps, sombrero in hand. "Never has sight of a horse pleased me as when Diego led yours to the stable. Thrice welcome—since you bring your friend to honor my poor household with his presence."

No need to measure guardedly those tones, or that manner. Don Andres Picardo was as clean, as honest, and as kindly as the sunshine that mellowed the dim distances behind him. The two came to their feet unconsciously and received his handclasp with inner humility. Don Andres held Dade's hand a shade longer than the most gracious hospitality demanded, while his eyes dwelt solicitously upon his face, browned near to the shade of a native son of those western slopes.

"I heard of your brave deed, Señor—of how you rode into the midst of the Vigilantes and snatched your friend from under the very shadow of the oak. I did not hear that you escaped their vengeance afterwards, and I feared greatly lest harm had befallen you. Dios! It was gallantly done, like a knight of olden times—"

"Oh, no. I didn't rescue any lady, Don Andres. Just Jack—and he was in a fair way to rescue himself, by the way. It wasn't anything much, but I suppose the story did grow pretty big by the time it got to you."

"And does your friend also call it a little thing?" The don turned quizzically to Jack.

"He does not," Jack returned promptly, although his ears were listening attentively for a nearer approach of the girlvoice he heard within the house. "He calls it one of the big things Dade is always doing for his friends." He dropped a hand on Dade's shoulder and shook him with an affectionate make-believe of disfavor. "He's always risking his valuable neck to save my worthless one, Don Andres. He means well, but he doesn't know any better. He packed me out of a nest of Indians once, just as foolishly; we were coming out from Texas at the time. You'd be amazed at some of the things I could tell you about him—"

"And about himself, if he would," drawled Dade. "If he ever tells you about the Indian scrape, Don Andres, ask him how he happened to get into the nest. As to yesterday, perhaps you heard how it came that Jack got so close to the oak!"

"No—I heard merely of the danger you were in. José's head vaquero was in town when the Vigilantes returned with their Captain and those others, and there were many rumors. This morning I sent Valencia to learn the truth, and if you were in danger—Perhaps I could have done little, but I should have tried to save you," he added simply. "I should not like a clash with the gringos—pardon, Señors; I speak of the class whom you also despise."

José laughed and swept the strings harshly with his thumb. "The clash will come, Don Andres, whether you like it or not," he said. "This morning I saw one more unasked tenant on your meadow, near the grove of alders. What they call a 'prairie schooner.' A big, red-topped hombre, and his woman—gringos of the class I despise; which includes"—again he flung his
thumb across the guitar string—"all gringos!"

Jack's lips opened for hot answer, but Don Andres forestalled him quietly.

"One more tenant does not harm me, José. When the American government puts its seal upon the seal of Spain and restores my land to me, these unasked tenants will go the way they came. There will be no clash." But he sighed even while he made the statement, as if the subject were neither new nor pleasant to dwell upon.

"Why," demanded José bitterly, "should the Americanos presume to question our right to our land? You and my father made the valley what it is; your shiploads of hides and tallow that you sent from Yerba Buena made the town prosper, and called adventurers this way; and now they steal your cattle and lands, and their government is the biggest thief of all, for it tells them to steal more. They will make you poor, Don Andres, while you wait for them to be just. No, I permit no 'prairie schooner' to stop, even that their oxen may drink. My vaqueros ride beside them till they have crossed the boundary. You, Don Andres, if you would permit your vaqueros to do likewise, instead of shaking hands with the gringos and bidding them welcome—"

"But I do not permit it; nor do I seek counsel from the children I have tossed on my foot to the tune of a nursery rhyme." He shook his white-crowned head reprovingly. "He was always screaming at his duenna, one child that I recollect," he smiled.

"Art thou scolding José again, my Andres? He loves to play that thou and Teresita are children still, José; it serves to beguile him into forgetting the years upon his head! Welcome, Señors. Teresita but told me this moment that you had come. She is bringing the wine—"

On their feet they greeted the Señora Picardo. Like the don, her husband, honest friendliness was in her voice, her smile, the warm clasp of her plump hand. The sort of woman who will mother you at sight, was the señora. Purple silk—hastily put on for the guests, one might suspect—clothed her royally. Golden hoops hung from her ears, a diamond brooch held together the lace beneath her cushiony chin; a comfortable woman who smiled much, talked much and worried more lest she leave some little thing undone for those about her.

"And this is the poor señor who was in such dreadful danger!" she went on commiseratingly. "Ah, the wicked times that have come upon us! Presently we shall fear to sleep in our beds—Señor Hunter, you have been hurt! The mark of blood is on your sleeve, the stain is on your side! A-ah, my poor friend! Come instantly and I will—"

"Gracias, Señora; it is nothing. Besides, Manuel put on a poultice of herbs. It's only a scratch, but it bled a little while I rode to the hut of Manuel." If blushes could have shown through the tan, Dade might have looked as uncomfortable as he felt at that moment.

The señorita was already in the doorway, convoying a sloeeyed maid who bore wine and glasses upon a tray of beaten silver; and the smile of the señorita was disturbing to a degree, brief though it was.

Behind the wine came cakes, and the señorita pointed tragically to the silver dish that held them. "Madre mia, those terrible children of Margarita have stolen half the cakes! I ran after them in the orchard—but they swallow fast, those niños! Now the señors must starve!"

Up went the hand of the señora in dismay, and down went the head of the señorita to hide how she was biting the laughter from her lips. "I ran," she murmured pathetically, "and I caught Angelo—but at that moment he popped the cake into his mouth and it was gone! Then I ran after Maria—and she swallowed—"

"Teresita mia! The señors will think—" What they would think she did not stipulate, but her eyes implored them to judge leniently the irrepressibility of her beautiful one. There were cakes sufficient—a hasty glance reassured her upon that point—and Teresita was in one of her mischievous moods. The mother who had reared her sighed resignedly and poured the wine into the small glasses with a quaint design cut into their sides, perfectly unconscious of the good the little diversion had done.

For a half-hour there was peaceful converse; of the adventure which had brought the two gringos to the ranch as to a sanctuary, of the land which lay before them, and of the unsettled conditions that filled the days with violence.

José still strummed softly upon the guitar, a pleasant undertone to the voices. And because he said very little, he saw and thought the more; seeing glances and smiles between a strange man and the maid whom he loved desirefully, bred the thought which culminated in a sudden burst of speech against the gringos who had come into the peaceful land and brought with them strife. Who stole the cattle of the natives, calmly appropriated the choicest bits of valley land without so much as a by-your-leave, and who treated the rightful owners with contempt and as though they had no right to live in the valley where they were born.

"Last week," he went on hotly, "an evil gringo with the clay of his burrowings still upon his garments cursed me and called me greaser because I did not give him all the road for his burro. I, José Pacheco! They had better have a care, or the 'greasers' will drive them back whence they came, like the cattle they are. When I, a don, must give the road to a gringo lower than the peons whom I flog for less impertinence, it is time we ceased taking them by the hand as though they were our equals!" His eyes went accusingly to the face of the girl.

She flung up her head and met the challenge in her own way, which was with the knife-thrust of her light laughter. "Ah, the poor Americanos! Not the prayers of all the padres can save them from the blackness of their fate, since Don José Pacheco frowns and will not take their hand in friendship! How they will gnash the teeth when they hear the terrible tidings—José Pacheco, don and son of a don, will have none of them, nor will he give way to their poor burros on the highway!" She shook her head as she had done over the tragedy of the little cakes. "Pobre gringos! Pobre gringos!" she murmured mockingly.

"Children, have done!" The hand of the señora went chidingly to the shoulder of her incorrigible daughter. "This is foolish and unseemly—though all thy quarreling is that, the saints know well. Our guests are Americanos; our guests, who are our friends," she stated gently, looking at José. "Not all Spaniards are good, José; not all gringos are bad. They are as we are,
good and bad together. Speak not like a child, amigo mio."

The guitar which José flung down upon a broad stool beside him hummed resonant accompaniment to his footsteps as he left the veranda. "Thy house, Señora, has been as my mother's house since I can remember. Until thy gringo guests have
made room for me, I leave it!"

"Señor Allen, would you like to see my birds?" invited Teresita wickedly, her glance flicking scornfully the reproachful face of José, as he turned it towards her, and dwelling with a smile upon Jack.

"Wicked one!" murmured the señora, in her heart more than half approving the discipline.

José had humiliation as well as much bitterness to carry away with him; for he saw the señor with the bright blue eyes follow gladly the laughing Teresita to her rose garden, and as he went jingling across the patio without waiting to summon a peon to bring him his horse, he heard the voice of Don Andres making apology to Dade for the rudeness of him, José.

Chapter 8

Don Andres Wants a Majordomo

"Señor, those things which you desired that I should bring, I have brought. All is of the best. Also have I brought a letter from the Señor Weelson, and what remains of the gold the señor will find laid carefully in the midst of his clothing. So I have done all as it would have been done for the patron himself." In the downward sweep of Manuel's sombrero one might read that peculiar quality of irony which dislike loves to inject into formal courtesy.

Behind Manuel waited a peon burdened with elegant riding gear and a bundle of clothing, and a gesture brought him forward to deposit his load upon the porch before the gringo guest, whose "Gracias" Manuel waved into nothingness; as did the quick shrug disdain the little bag of gold which Jack drew from his pocket and would have tossed to Manuel for reward.

"It was nothing," he smiled remotely; and went his way to find the patron and deliver to him a message from a friend.

Behind Jack came the click of slipper-heels upon the hardwood; and he turned from staring, puzzled, after the stiffnecked Manuel, and gave the girl a smile such as a man reserves for the woman who has entered into his dreams.

"Santa Maria, what elegance! Now will the señor ride in splendor that will dazzle the eyes to look upon!" Teresita bantered, poking a slipper-toe tentatively towards the saddle, and clasping her hands in mock rapture. "On every corner, silver crescents; on the tapideros, silver stars bigger than Venus; riding behind the cantle, a whole milky way; José will surely go mad with rage when he sees. Stars has José, but no moon to bear him company when he rides. Surely the cattle will fall upon their knees when the señor draws near!"

"Shall we ride out and put them to the test?" he asked wishfully, shaking out the bridle to show the beautiful design of silver inlaid upon the leather cheekpiece, and stooping to adjust a big-roweled, silver-incrusted spur upon his bootheel. "Manuel does exactly as he is told. I said he was to get the best he could find—"

"And so no vaquero in the valley will be so gorgeous—" She broke off suddenly to sing in lilting Spanish a fragment of some old song that told of the lilies of the field that "Toil not, neither do they spin."

"That is not kind. I may not spin, but I toil—I leave it to Dade if I don't." This last, because he caught sight of Dade coming across from the row of huts, which was a short cut up from the corrals. "And I can show you the remains of blisters—" He held out a very nice appearing palm towards her, and looked his fill at her pretty face, while she bent her brows and inspected the hand with the gravity that threatened to break at any instant into laughter.

That sickening grip in the chest which is a real, physical pain, though the hurt be given to the soul of a man, slowed Dade's steps to a lagging advance towards the tableau the two made on the steps. So had the señorita sent him dizzy with desire (and with hope to brighten it) in the two weeks and more that he had been the honored guest. So had she laughed and teased him and mocked him; and he had believed that to him alone would she show the sweet whimsies of her nature. But from the moment when he laid her gold thimble in her waiting hand and got no reward save an absent little nod of thanks, the dull ache had been growing in his heart. He knew what it was that had sent José off in that headlong rage against all gringos; though two days before he would have said that José's jealousy was for him, and with good reason. There had been glances between those two who stood now so close together—swift measuring of the weapons which sex uses against sex, with quick smiles when the glances chanced to meet. José also had seen the byplay; and the fire had smoldered in his eyes until at last it kindled into flame and drove him cursing from the place. In his heart Dade could not blame José.

Forgotten while Teresita held back with one hand a black lock which the wind was trying to fling across her eyes, and murmured mocking commiseration over the half obliterated callouses on Jack's hand, Dade loitered across the patio, remembering many things whose very sweetness made the present hurt more bitter. He might have known it would be like this, he told himself sternly; but life during the past two weeks had been too sweet for forebodings or for precaution. He had wanted Jack to see and admire Teresita, with the same impulse that would have made him want to show Jack any other treasure which Chance held out to him while Hope smiled over her shoulder and whispered that it was his.

Well, Jack had seen her, and Jack surely admired her; and the grim humor of Dade's plight struck through the ache and made him laugh, even though his jaws immediately went together with a click of teeth and cut the laugh short. He might have known—but he was not the sort of man who stands guard against friend and foe alike.

And, he owned to himself, Jack was unconscious of any hurt for his friend in this rather transparent wooing. A little thought would have enlightened him, perhaps, or a little observation; but Dade could not blame Jack for not seeking for some obstacle in the path of his desires.

"She says I'm lazy and got these callouses grabbing the soft snaps last summer in the mines," Jack called lightly, when finally it occurred to him that the world held more than two persons. "I'm always getting the worst of it when you and I are compared. But I believe I've got the best of you on riding outfit, old man. Take a look at that saddle, will you! And these spurs! And this bridle! The señorita says the cattle will fall on their knees when I ride past; we're going to take a gallop and find out. Want to come along?"

"Arrogant one! The señorita did not agree to that ride! The señorita has something better to do than bask in the glory of so gorgeous a señor while he indulges his vanity—and frightens the poor cattle so that, if they yield their hides at killing time, there will be little tallow for the ships to carry away!"

The Señorita Teresita would surely never be guilty of a conscious lowering of one eyelid to point her raillery, but the little twist she gave to her lips when she looked at Dade offered a fair substitute; and the flirt of her silken skirts as she turned to run back into the house was sufficient excuse for any imbecility in a man.

Jack looked after her with some chagrin. "The little minx! A man might as well put up his hands when he hears her coming—huh? Unless he's absolutely woman-proof, like you. How do you manage it, anyway?"

"By taking a squint at myself in the looking-glass every morning." Dade's face managed to wrinkle humorously. "H-m. You
are pretty gorgeous, for a fact. Where's the riata?"

Jack had forgotten that he had ever wanted one. He lifted the heavy, high-cantled saddle, flung it down upon the other side and untied the new coil of braided rawhide from its place on the right fork.

"A six-strand, eh? I could tell Manuel a few things about riatas, if he calls that the best! Four strands are stronger than
six, any time. I've seen too many stranded—"

"The señor is not pleased with the riata?"

Manuel, following Don Andres across to the veranda, had caught the gesture and tone; and while his knowledge of English was extremely sketchy, he knew six and four when he heard those numerals mentioned, and the rest was easy guessing.

"The four strands are good, but the six are better—when Joaquin Murieta lays the strands. From the hide of a very old bull was this riata cut; perhaps the señor is aware that the hide is thus of the same thickness throughout and strong as the bull that grew it. Not one strand is laid tighter than the other strand; the wildest

bull in the valley could not break it—if the señor should please to catch him! Me, I could have bought three riatas for the gold I gave for this one; but the señor told me to get the best." His shoulders went up an inch, though Don Andres was frowning at the tone of him. "The señor can return it to the Mission and get the three, or he can exchange it with any vaquero in the valley for one which has four strands. I am
very sorry that the señor is not pleased with my choice."

"You needn't be sorry. It's a very pretty riata, and I have no doubt it will do all I ask of it. The saddle's a beauty, and the bridle and spurs—I'm a thousand times obliged."

"It is nothing and less than nothing," disclaimed Manuel once more; and went in to ask the señora for a most palatable decoction whose chief ingredient was blackberry wine, which the señora recommended to all and sundry for various ailments. Though Manuel, the deceitful one, had no ailment, he did have a keen appreciation of the flavour of the cordial, and his medicine bottle was never long empty—or full—if he could help it.

A moment later Jack, hearing a human, feminine twitter from the direction of the rose garden, left off examining pridefully his belongings, and bolted without apology, after his usual headlong fashion.

Don Andres sat him down in an easy-chair in the sun, and sighed as he did so. "He is hot-tempered, that vaquero," he said regretfully, his mind upon Manuel. "Something has stirred his blood; surely your friend has done nothing to offend him?"

"Nothing except remark that he has always liked a fourstrand riata better than six. At the hut he was friendly enough."

"He is not the only one whose anger is easily stirred against the gringos," remarked the don, reaching mechanically for his tobacco pouch, while he watched Dade absently examining the new riata.

"Señor Hunter," Don Andres began suddenly, "have you decided what you will do? Your mine in the mountains—it will be foolish to return there while the hands of the Vigilantes are reaching out to clutch you; do you not think so? More of the tale I have heard from Valencia, who returned with Manuel. Those men who died at the hand of your friend—and died justly, I am convinced—had friends who would give much for close sight of you both."

"I know; I told Jack we'd have to keep away from town or the mine for a while. He wanted to go right back and finish up the fight!" Dade grinned at the absurdity. "I sat down hard on that proposition." Not that phrase, exactly, did he use. One may be pardoned a free translation, since, though he spoke in excellent Spanish, he did not twist his sentences like a native, and he was not averse to making use of certain idioms quite as striking in their way as our own Americanisms.

Don Andres rolled a cigarette and smoked it thoughtfully. "You were wise. Also, I bear in mind your statement that you could not long be content to remain my guest. Terribly independent and energetic are you Americanos." He smoked through another pause, while Dade's puzzled glance dwelt secretly upon his face and tried to read what lay in his mind. It seemed to him that the don was working his way carefully up to a polite hint that the visit might be agreeably terminated; and his uneasy thoughts went to the girl. Did her father resent—

"My majordomo," the don continued, just in time to hold back Dade's hasty assurance that they would leave immediately, "my majordomo does not please me. Many faults might I name, sufficient to make plain my need for another." A longer wait, as if time were indeed infinite, and he owned it all. "Also I might name reasons for my choice of another, who is yourself, Señor Hunter. Perhaps in you I recognize simply the qualities which I desire my majordomo to possess. Perhaps also I desire that some prejudiced countrymen of mine shall be taught a lesson and made to see that not all Americanos are unworthy. However that may be, I shall be truly glad if you will accept. The salary we will arrange as pleases you, and your friend will, I hope, remain in whatever capacity you may desire. Further, when your government has given some legal assurance that my land is mine," he smiled wryly at the necessity for such assurance, "as much land as you Americanos call a 'section,' choose it where you will—except that it shall not take my house or my

cultivated land—shall be yours for the taking."

"But—"

"Not so much the offer of a position would I have you consider it," interrupted the other with the first hint of haste he had shown, "as a favor that I would ask. Times are changing, and we natives are high-chested and must learn to make room for others who are coming amongst us. To speak praises to the face of a friend is not my habit, yet I will say that I would teach my people to respect good men, whatever the race; and especially Americanos, who will be our neighbors henceforth. I shall be greatly pleased when you tell me that you will be my majordomo; more than ever one needs a man of intelligence and tact—"

"And are none of our own people tactful or intelligent, Don Andres Picardo?" demanded Manuel, having overheard the last sentence or two from the doorway. He came out and stood before his beloved "patron," his whole fat body quivering with amazed indignation, so that the bottle which the señora had filled for him shook in his hand. "Amongst the gringos must you go to find one worthy? Truly it is as Don José tells me; these gringos have come but to make trouble where all was peace. To-day he told me all his thoughts, and me, I hardly believed it was as he said. Would the patron have a majordomo who knows nothing of rodeos, nothing of the cattle—"

"You're mistaken there, Manuel," Dade broke in calmly. "Whether I become majordomo or not, I know cattle. They have a few in Texas, where I came from. I can qualify in cowology any time. And," he added loyally, "so can Jack. You thought he didn't know what he was talking about, when he was looking at that riata; but I'll back him against any man in California when it comes to riding and roping.

"But that needn't make us bad friends, Manuel. I didn't come to make trouble, and I won't stay to make any. We've been friends; let's stay that way. I'm a gringo, all right, but I've lived more with your people than my own, and if you want the truth, I don't know but what I feel more at home with them. And the same with Jack. We've eaten and slept with Spaniards and worked with them and played with them, half our lives."

"Still it is as José says," reiterated Manuel stubbornly. "Till the gringos came all was well; when they came, trouble came also. Till the gringos came, no watch was put over the cattle, for only those who hungered killed and ate. Now they steal the patron's cattle by hundreds, they steal his land, and if José speaks truly, they would steal also—" He hesitated to speak what was on his tongue, and finished lamely: "what is more precious still.

"And the patron will have a gringo for majordomo?" He returned to the issue. "Then I, Manuel, must leave the patron's employ. I and half the vaqueros. The patron," he added with what came close to a sneer, "had best seek gringo vaqueros—with the clay of the mines on their boots, and their red shirts to call the bulls!"

"I shall do what it pleases me to do," declared the don sternly. "Advice from my vaqueros I do not seek. And you," he said haughtily, "have choice of two things; you may crave pardon for your insolence to my guest, who is also my friend, and who will henceforth have charge of my vaqueros and my cattle, or you may go whither you will; to Don José Pacheco, I doubt not."

He leaned his white-crowned head against the high chairback, and while he waited for Manuel's decision he gazed calmly at the border of red tiles which showed at the low eaves of the porch—calmly as to features only, for his eyes held the blaze of anger.

"Señors, I go." The brim of Manuel's sombrero flicked the dust of the patio.

"Come, then, and I will reckon your wage," invited the don, coldly courteous as to a stranger. "You will excuse me, Señor? I shall not be long."

Dade's impulse was to protest, to intercede, to say that he and Jack would go immediately, rather than stir up strife. But he had served a stern apprenticeship in life, and he knew it was too late now to put out the fires of wrath burning hotly in the hearts of those two; however completely he might efface himself, the resentment was too keen, the quarrel too fresh to be so easily forgotten.

He was standing irresolutely on the steps when Jack came back from the rose garden, whistling softly an old love-song and smiling fatuously to himself.

"We're going to take that ride, after all," he announced gleefully. "Want to come along? She's going to ask her father to come, too—says it would be terribly improper for us two to ride alone. What's the matter? Got the toothache?"

Dade straightened himself automatically after the slap on the back that was like a cuff from a she-bear, and grunted an uncivil sentence.

"Come over to the saddle-house," he commanded afterward. "And take that truck off the señora's front steps before she
sees it and has a fit. I want to talk to you."

"Oh, Lord!" wailed Jack, under his breath, but he shouldered the heavy saddle obediently, leaving Dade to bring what remained. "Cut it short, then; she's gone to dress and ask her dad; and I'm supposed to order the horses and get you started. What's the trouble?"

Dade first went over to the steps before their sleeping-room and deposited Jack's personal belongings; and Jack seized the minute of grace to call a peon and order the horses saddled.

He turned from watching proudly the glitter of the trimmings on his new saddle as the peon bore it away on his shoulder, and confronted Dade with a tinge of defiance in his manner.

"Well, what have I done now?" he challenged. "Anything particularly damnable about talking five minutes to a girl in plain sight of her—"

Dade threw out both hands in a gesture of impatience. "That isn't the only important thing in the world," he pointed out sarcastically. If the inner hurt served to sharpen his voice, he did not know it. "Don Andres wants to make me his majordomo."

Jack's eyes bulged a little; and if Dade had not wisely sidestepped he would have received another one of Jack's muscletingling slaps on the shoulder. "Whee-ee! Say, you're getting appreciated, at last, old man. Good for you! Give me a job?"

"I'm not going to take it," said Dade. "I was going to ask you if you want to pull out with me to-morrow."

Jack's jaw went slack. "Not going to take it!" He leaned against the adobe wall behind him and stuck both hands savagely into his pockets. "Why, you darned

chump, how long ago was it that you talked yourself black in the face, trying to make me say I'd stay? Argued like a man trying to sell shaving soap; swore that nobody but a born idiot would think of passing up such a chance; badgered me into giving in; and now when
you've got a chance like this, you—Say, you're loco!"

"Maybe." Dade's eyes went involuntarily toward the veranda, where Teresita appeared for an instant, looking questioningly towards them. "Maybe I am loco. But Manuel's mad because the don offered me the place, and has quit; and he says half the vaqueros will leave, that they won't work under a gringo."

Jack's indignant eyes changed to a queer, curious stare. "Dade Hunter! If I didn't know you, if I hadn't seen you in more tight places than I've got fingers and toes, I'd say—But you aren't scared; you never had sense enough to be afraid of anything in your life. You can't choke that down me, old man.
What's the real reason why you want to leave?"

The real reason came again to the doorway sixty feet away and looked out impatiently to where the señors were talking so earnestly and privately; but Dade would have died several different and unpleasant deaths before he would name that reason. Instead:

"It will be mighty disagreeable for Don Andres, trying to keep things smooth," he said. "And it isn't as if he were stuck for a majordomo. Manuel has turned against me from pure jealousy. He opened his heart, one night when we were alone together, and told me that when Carlos Pacorra went—and Manuel said the patron would not keep him long, for his insolence—he, Manuel, would be majordomo. He's mad as the deuce, and I don't blame him; and he's a good man for the place; the vaqueros like him."

"You say he's quit?"

"Yes. He got pretty nasty, and the don has gone to pay him off."

"Well, what good would it do for you to turn down the offer, then? Manuel wouldn't get it, would he?"

"No-o, he wouldn't."

"Well, then—oh, thunder! Something ought to be done for that ingrowing modesty of yours! Dade, if you pass up that place, I'll—I'll swear you're crazy. I know you like it, here. You worked hard enough to convert me to that belief!"

A sudden thought made him draw a long breath; he reached out and caught Dade by both shoulders.

"Say, you can't fool me a little bit! You're backing up because you're afraid I may be jealous or something. You're afraid you're standing in my light. Darn you, I've had enough of that blamed unselfishness of yours, old man." The endearing smile lighted his face then and his eyes. "You go ahead and take the job, Dade. I don't want it. I'll be more than content to have you boss me around." He hesitated, looking at the other a bit wistfully. "Of course, you know that if you go, old boy, I'll go with you. But—" The look he sent towards Teresita, who appeared definitely upon the porch and stood waiting openly and impatiently, amply finished the sentence.

Dade's eyes followed Jack's understandingly, and the thing he had meant to do seemed all at once contemptible, selfish, and weak. He had meant to leave and take Jack with him, because it hurt him mightily to see those two falling in love with each other. The trouble his staying might bring to Don Andres was nothing more nor less than a subterfuge. If Teresita's smiles had continued to be given to him as they had been before Jack came, he told himself bitterly, he would never have thought of going. And Jack thought he hesitated from pure unselfishness! The fingers that groped mechanically for his tobacco, though he had no intention of smoking just then, trembled noticeably.

"All right," he said quietly. "I'll stay, then." And a moment after: "Go ask her if she wants to ride Surry. I promised her
she could, next time she rode."

Chapter 9

Jerry Simpson, Squatter

The señorita, it would seem, had lost interest in the white horse as well as in his master. That was the construction which Dade pessimistically put upon her smiling assurance that she could never be so selfish as to take Señor Hunter's wonderful Surry and condemn him to some commonplace caballo; though she gave also a better reason than that, which was that her own horse was already saddled—witness the peon leading the animal into the patio at that very moment—and that an exchange would mean delay. Dade took both reasons smilingly, and mentally made a vow with a fearsome penalty attached to the breaking of it. After which he felt a little more of a man, with his pride to bear him company.

Manuel came out from the room which Don Andres used for an office, saluted the señorita with the air of a permanent leave-taking, as well as a greeting, and passed the gringos with face averted. A moment later the don followed him with the look of one who would dismiss a distasteful business from his mind; and entered amiably into the pleasure-seeking spirit of the ride.

With the March sun warm upon them when they rode out from the wide shade of the oaks, they faced the cooling little breeze which blew out of the south.

"Valencia tells me that the prairie schooner which José spoke of has of a truth cast anchor upon my land," observed the don to Dade, reining in beside him where he rode a little in advance of the others. "Since we are riding that way, we may as well see the fellow and make him aware of the fact that he is trespassing upon land which belongs to another; though if he has halted but to rest his cattle and himself, he is welcome. But Valencia tells me that the fellow is cutting down trees for a house, and that I do not like."

"Some emigrants seem to think, because they have traveled over so much wilderness, there is no land west of the Mississippi that they haven't a perfect right to take, if it suits them. They are a little like your countryman Columbus, I suppose. Every man who crosses the desert feels as if he's out on a voyage of discovery to a new world; and when he does strike California, it's hard for him to realize that he can't take what he wants of it."

"I think you are right," admitted Don Andres after a minute. "And your government also seems to believe it has come into possession of a wilderness,

peopled only by savages who must give way to the march of civilization. Whereas we Spaniards were in possession of the land while yet your colonies paid tribute to their king in England, and we ourselves have brought the savages to the ways of Christian people, and have for our reward the homes which we have built with much toil and some hardships, like yourselves when your colonies were young. Twenty-one years have I looked upon this valley and called it mine, with the word of his Majesty for my authority! And surely my right to it is as the right of your people to their haciendas in Virginia or Vermont. Yet men will drive their prairie schooners to a spot which pleases them and say: 'Here,
I will have this place for my home.' That is not lawful, or right."

Ten steps in the rear of them Teresita was laughing her mocking little laugh that still had in it a maddening note of tenderness. Dade tried not to hear it; for so had she laughed at him, a week ago, and set his blood leaping towards his heart. He was not skilled in the ways of women, yet he did not accuse her of deliberate coquetry, as a man is prone to do under the smart of a hurt like his; for he sensed dimly that it was but the seeking sex-instinct of healthy youth that brightened her eyes and sent the laugh to her lips when she faced a man who pleased her; and if she were fickle, it was with the instinctive fickleness of one who has not made final choice of a mate. Hope lifted its head at that, but he crushed it sternly into the dust again; for the man who rode behind was his friend, whom he loved.

It is to be feared that the voice of the girl held more of his attention than the complaint of the don, just then, and that the sting of injustice under which Don Andres squirmed seemed less poignant and vital than the hurt he himself was bearing. He answered him at random; and he might have betrayed his inattention if they had not at that moment caught sight of the interlopers.

Valencia had not borne false witness against them; the emigrants were indeed cutting down trees. More, they were industriously hauling the logs to the immediate vicinity of their camp, which was chosen with an eye to many advantages; shade, water, a broad view of the valley and plenty of open grass land already fit for the plow, if to plow were their intention.

A loose-jointed giant of a man seated upon the load of logs which two yoke of great, meek-eyed oxen had just drawn up beside a waiting pile of their fellows, waited phlegmatically their approach. A woman, all personality hidden beneath flapping calico and slat sunbonnet, climbed hastily down upon the farther side of the wagon and disappeared into the little tent that was simply the wagon-box with its canvas covering, placed upon the ground.

"Valencia told me truly. Señor Hunter, will you speak for me? Tell the big hombre that the land is mine."

To do his bidding, Dade flicked the reins upon Surry's neck and rode ahead, the others closely following. Thirty feet from the wagon a great dog of the color called brindle disputed his advance with bristling hair and throaty grumble.

"Lay down, Tige! Wait till you're asked to take a holt," advised the man on the wagon, regarding the group with an air of perfect neutrality. Tige obeying sullenly, to the extent that he crouched where he was and still growled; his master rested his elbows on his great, bony knees, sucked at a short-stemmed clay pipe and waited developments.

"How d'yuh do?" Dade, holding Surry as close to the belligerent Tige as was wise, tried to make his greeting as neutral as the attitude of the other.

"Tol'ble, thank yuh, how's y'self? Shet your trap, Tige! Tige thought you was all greasers, and he ain't made up his mind yet whether he likes 'em mixed—whites and greasers. I dunno's I blame 'im, either. We ain't either of us had much call to hanker after the dark meat. T'other day a bunch come boilin' up outa the dim distance like they was sent fur and didn't have much time to git here. Tied their tongues into hard knots tryin' to tell me somethin' I didn't have time to listen to, and looked like they wanted to see my hide hangin' on a fence.

"Tige, he didn't take to 'em much. He kept walkin' back and forth between me and them, talking as sensible as they did, I must say, and makin' his meanin' full as clear. I dunno how we'd all 'a' come out, if I hadn't brought Jemimy and the twins out and let 'em into the argument. Them greasers didn't like the looks of old Jemimy, and they backed off. Tige, he follered 'em right up, and soon's they got outa reach of Jemimy, they took down their lariats an' tried to hitch onto him.

"They didn't know Tige. That thar dawg's the quickest dawg on earth. He hopped through their loops like they was playin' jump-the-rope with him. Fact is, he'd learned jump-the-rope when he was a purp. He wouldn't 'a' minded that, only they didn't do it friendly. One feller whipped out his knife and threw it at Tige—and he come mighty nigh makin' dawgmeat outa him, too. Slit his ear, it come that close. Tige ain't got no likin' fer greasers sence then. He thought you was another bunch—and so did I. Mary, she put inside after Jemimy and the twins.

"Know anything about them greasers? I see yuh got a sample along. T' other crowd was headed by a slim feller all tricked up in velvet and silver braid and red sash; called himself Don José Pacheco, and claimed to own all Ameriky from the ocean over there, back to the Allegheny Mountains, near as I could make out. I don't talk that kinda talk much; but I been thinkin' mebby I better get m' tongue split, so I can. Might come handy, some time; only Tige, he hates the sound of it like he hates porkypines—or badgers.

"Mary and me and Tige laid up in Los Angeles fer a spell, resting the cattle. All greasers, down there—and fleas—and take the two t'gether, they jest about wore out the hull kit and b'ilin' of us.

"What's pesterin' the ole feller? Pears like he's gittin' his tongue twisted up ready to talk—if they call it talkin'."

"What is the hombre saying?—" asked the don at that moment, seeing the glance and sensing that at last his presence was noticed.

Dade grinned and winked at Jack, who, by the way, was neither looking nor listening; for Teresita was once more tenderly ridiculing his star-incrusted saddle and so claimed his whole attention.

"He says José Pacheco and some others came and ordered him off. They were pretty ugly, but he called out a lady—the Señora Jemima and dos niños—and—"

"Sa-ay, mister," interrupted the giant Jerry Simpson from the load of logs. "D'you say Senory Jemimy?"

"Why, yes. Señora means madame, or—"

"Ya'as, I know what it means. Jemimy, mister, ain't no senory, nor no madame. Jemimy's my old Kentucky rifle, mister. And the twins ain't no neenos, but a brace uh pistols that can shoot fur as it's respectable fer a pistol to shoot, and hit all it's lawful to hit. You tell him who Jemimy is, mister; and tell 'im she's a derned good talker, and most convincin' in a argyment."

"He says Jemima is not a señora," translated Dade, his eyes twinkling, "but his rifle; and the niños are his pistols."

Don Andres hid a smile under his white mustache. "Very good. Yet I think your language must lack expression, Señor Hunter. It required much speech to say so little." There was a twinkle in his own eyes. "Also, José acts like a fool. You may tell the big señor that the land is mine, but that I do not desire to use harsh methods, nor have ill-feeling between us. It is my wish to live in harmony with all men; my choice of a majordomo should bear witness that I look upon Americanos with a friendly eye. I think the big hombre is honest and intelligent; his face rather pleases me. So you may tell him that José shall not trouble him again, and that I shall not dispute with him about his remaining here, if to remain should be his purpose when he knows the land belongs to me. But I shall look upon him as a guest. As a guest, he will be welcome until such time as he may find some free land upon which to build his casa."

Because the speech was kindly and just, and because he was in the service of the don, Dade translated as nearly verbatim as the two languages would permit. And Jerry Simpson, while he listened, gave several hard pulls with his lips upon the short stem of his pipe, discovered that there was no fire there, straightened his long leg and felt gropingly for a match in the depth of a great pocket in his trousers. His eyes, of that indeterminate color which may be either gray, hazel, or green, as the light and his mood may affect them, measured the don calmly, dispassionately, unawed; measured also Dade and the beautiful white horse he rode; and finally went twinkling over Jack and the girl, standing a little apart, wholly absorbed in trivialities that could interest no one save themselves.

"How much land does he say belongs to him? And whar did he git his title to it?" Jerry Simpson asked, when Dade was waiting for his answer.

Out of his own knowledge Dade told him.

Jerry Simpson brought two matches from his pocket, inspected them gravely and returned one carefully; lighted the other with the same care, applied the flame to his tobacco, made sure that the pipe was going to "draw" well, blew out the match, and tucked the stub down out of sight in a crease in the bark of the log upon which he was sitting. After that he rested his elbows upon his great, bony knees and smoked meditatively.

Chapter 10

The Finest Little Woman in the World

"You tell Mr. Picardy that I ain't visitin' nobody, so he needn't consider that I'm company," announced Jerry, after a wait that was beginning to rasp the nerves of his visitors. "I come here to live! He's called this land hisn, by authority uh the king uh Spain, you say, for over twenty year. Wall, in twenty year he ain't set so much as a fence-post fur as the eye can see. I been five mile from here on every side, and I don't see no signs of his ever usin' the land fer nothin'. Now, mebby the king uh Spain knew what he was talkin' about when he give this land away, and then agin mebby he didn't. 'T any rate, I don't know as I think much of a king that'll give away a hull great gob uh land he never seen, and give it to one feller—more 'n that feller could use in a hull lifetime; more 'n he would ever need fer his young 'uns, even s'posin' he had a couple uh dozen—which ain't skurcely respectable fer one man, nohow. How many's he got, mister?"

"One—his daughter, over there."

"Hum-mh! Wall, she ain't goin' to need so derned much. You tell Mr. Picardy I've come a long ways to find a home fer Mary and me; a long road and a hard road. I can't go no further without I swim fer it, and that I don't calc'late on doin'. I ain't the kind to hog more land 'n what I can use—not mentionin' no names; but I calc'late on havin' what I need, if I can get it honest. My old mother used to read outa the Bible that the earth was the Lord's and the fullness thereof; and I ain't never heard of him handin' over two-thirds of it to any king uh Spain. What he's snoopin' around in Ameriky fur, givin' away great big patches uh country he never seen, I ain't askin'. Californy belongs to the United States of Ameriky, and the United States of Ameriky lets her citizens make homes for themselves and their families on land that ain't already in use. If Mr. Picardy can show me a deed from Gawd Almighty, signed, sealed, and delivered along about the time Moses got hisn fer the Land uh Canyan, or if he can show a paper from Uncle Sam, sayin' this place belongs to him, I'll throw off these logs, h'ist the box back on the wagon and look further; but I ain't goin' to move on the say-so uh no furrin' king, which I don't believe in nohow."

He took the pipe from his mouth, and with it pointed to a spot twenty feet away, so that they all looked towards the place.

"Right thar," he stated slowly, "is whar I'm goin' to build my cabin, fer me and Mary. And right over thar I'm goin' to plow me up a truck patch. I'm a peaceable man, mister. I don't aim to have no fussin' with my neighbors. But you tell Mr. Picardy that thar'll be loopholes cut on all four sides uh that thar cabin, and Jemimy and the twins'll be ready to argy with anybody that comes moochin' around unfriendly. I'm the peaceablest man you ever seen, but when I make up my mind to a thing, I'm firm! Pur-ty tol'able firm!" he added with complacent emphasis.

He waited expectantly while Dade put a revised version of this speech into Spanish, and placidly smoked his little black pipe while the don made answer.

"Already I find that I have done well to choose an Americano for my majordomo," Don Andres observed, a smile in his eyes. "With a few more such as this great hombre, who is firm and peaceful together, I should find my days full of trouble with a hot-blooded Manuel to deal with them. But with you, Señor, I have no fear. Something there is in the face of this Señor Seem'son which pleases me; we shall be friends, and he shall stay and plant his garden and build his house where it pleases him to do. You may tell him that I say so, and that I shall rely upon his honor to pay me for the land a reasonable price when the American government places its seal beside the seal on his Majesty's grant. For that it will be done I am very sure. The land is mine, even though I have no tablet of stone to proclaim from the Creator my right to call it so. But he shall have his home if he is honest, without swimming across the ocean to find it."

"Wall, now, that's fair enough fer anybody. Hey, Mary! Come on out and git acquainted with yer neighbor's girl. Likely-lookin' young woman," he passed judgment, nodding towards Teresita. "Skittish, mebby—young blood most gen'rally is, when there's any ginger in it. What's yer name, mister? I want yuh all to meet the finest little woman in the world—Mrs. Jerry Simpson. We've pulled in the harness together fer twelve year, now, so I guess I know! Come out, Mary."

She came shyly from the makeshift tent, her dingy brown sunbonnet in her hand, and the redoubtable Tige walking close to her shapeless brown skirt. And although her face was tanned nearly as brown as her bonnet, with the desert sun and desert winds of that long, weary journey in search of a home, it was as delicately modeled as that of the girl who rode forward to greet her; and sweet with the sweetness of soul which made that big man worship her. Her hair was a soft gold such as one sees sometimes upon the head of a child or in the pictures of angels, and it was cut short and curled in distracting little rings about her head, and framed softly her smooth forehead. Her eyes were brown and soft and wistful—with a twinkle at the corners, nevertheless, which brightened them wonderfully; and although her mouth drooped slightly with the same wistfulness, a little smile lurked there also, as though her life had been spent largely in longing for the unattainable, and in laughing at herself because she knew the futility of the longing.

"I hope you've taken a good look at Jerry's face," she said, "and seen that he ain't half as bad as he tries to make out. Jerry'll make a fine neighbor for any man if he's let be; and we do want a home of our own, awful bad! We was ten years paying for a little farm back in Illinois, and then we lost it at the last minute because there was something wrong with the deed, and we didn't have any money to go to law about it. Jerry didn't tell you that; but it's that makes him talk kinda bitter, sometimes. He was terrible disappointed about losing the farm. And when we took what we had left and struck out, he said he was going as far as he could get and be away from lawyers and law, and make us a home on land that nobody but the Lord laid any claim to. So he picked out this place; and then along come that Spaniard and a lot of fellows with him and said we hadn't no right here. So I hope you won't blame Jerry for being a little mite uppish. That Spaniard got him kinda wrought up."

Her voice was as soft as her eyes, and winsome as her wistful little smile. She had those four smiling with her in sheer sympathy before she had spoken three sentences; and the two who did not understand her words smiled just as sympathetically as the two who knew what she was talking about.

"Tell the señora I am sorry, and she shall stay; and my mother will give her hens and a bottle of her very good medicine, which Manuel drinks so greedily," Teresita cried, when Dade told her what the woman said, and leaned impulsively and held out her hand. "I would do as the Americanos do, and shake the hands for a new friendship," she explained, blushing a little. "We shall be friends. Señor

Hunter, tell the pretty señora that I say we shall be friends. Amiga mia, I shall call her, and I shall learn the Americano language, that we may talk together."

She meant every word of it, Dade knew; and with a troublesome, squeezed feeling in his throat he interpreted her speech with painstaking exactness.

Mrs. Jerry took the señorita's hand and smiled up at her with the brightness of tears in her eyes. "You've got lots of friends, honey," she said simply, "and I've left all of mine so far behind me they might as well be dead, as far as ever seeing 'em again is concerned; so it's like finding gold to find a woman friend away out here. I ain't casting no reflections on Jerry, mind," she hastened to warn them, blinking the tears away and leaving the twinkle in full possession; "but good as he is, and satisfying as his company is, he ain't a woman. And, my dear, a woman does get awful hungry sometimes for woman-talk!"

[Illustration: Mrs. Jerry took the señorita's hand and smiled up at her.]

"Santa Maria! that must be true. She shall come and let my mother be her friend also. I will send a carriage, or if she can ride—ask the big señor if he has no horses!"

Jack it was who took up right willingly the burden of translation, for the pure pleasure of repeating the señorita's words and doing her a service; and Dade dropped back beside the don, where he thought he belonged, and stayed there.

"Wall, I ain't got any horses, but I got two of the derndest mules you ever seen, mister. Moll and Poll's good as any mustang in this valley. Mary and me can ride 'em anywheres; that's why I brung 'em along, to ride in case we had to eat the cattle."

"Then they must surely ride Moll and Poll to visit my mother!" the señorita declared with her customary decisiveness. "Padre mio!"

Obediently the don accepted the responsibility laid upon him by his sole-born who ruled him without question, and made official the invitation. It was not what he had expected to do; he was not quite sure that it was what he wanted to do; but he did it, and did it with the courtliness which would have flowered his invitation to the governor to honor his poor household by his presence; he did it because his daughter had glanced at him and said "My father?" in a certain tone which he knew well.

Something else was done, which no one had expected to do when the four galloped up to the trespassers. Jack and Dade dismounted and helped Jerry unload the logs from the wagon, for one thing; while Teresita inspected Mrs. Jerry's ingenious domestic makeshifts and managed somehow, with Mrs. Jerry's help, to make the bond of mutual liking serve very well in the place of intelligible speech. For another, the don fairly committed himself to the promise of a peon or two to help in the further devastation of the trees upon the Picardo mountain slope behind the little, natural meadow, which Jerry Simpson had so calmly appropriated to his own use.

"He is honest," Don Andres asserted more than once on the ride home, perhaps in self-justification for his soft dealing. "He is honest; and when he sees that the land is mine, he will pay; or if he does not pay, he will go—and tilled acres and a cabin will not harm me. Valencia, if he marries the daughter of Carlos (as the señora says will come to pass), will be glad to have a cabin to live in apart from the mother of his wife, who is a shrew and will be disquieting in any man's household. Therefore, Señor Hunter, you may order the peons to assist the big hombre and his beautiful señora, that they may soon have a hut to shelter them from the rains. It is not good to see so gentle a woman endure hardship within my boundary. Many tules, they will need," he added after a minute, "and it is unlikely that the Señor Seem'son understands the making of a thatch. Diego and Juan are skillful; and the tules they lay upon a roof will let no drop of rain fall within the room. Order them to assist."

"I shall tell Margarita to bake many little cakes," cried Teresita, riding up between her father and Dade, that she might assist in the planning. "And madre mia will give me coffee and sugar for the pretty señora. So soft is her voice, like one of my pigeons! And her hair is more beautiful than the golden hair of our Blessed Lady at Dolores. Oh, if the Blessed Virgin would make me as beautiful as she, and as gentle, I should—I should finish the altar cloth immediately, which I began two years ago!"

"Thou art well enough as thou art," comforted her father, trying to hide his pride in her under frowning brows, and to sterilize the praise with a tone of belittlement.

"I love that pretty señora," sighed Teresita, turning in the saddle to glance wistfully back at the meager little camp. "She shall have the black puppy Rosa gave me when last I was at the Mission San José. But I hope," she added plaintively, like the child she was at heart, "she will make that big, ugly beast they called Tige be kind to her; and the milk must be warm to the finger when Chico is fed. To-night, Señor Allen, you shall teach me Americano words that I may say to the señora what is necessary, for the happiness of my black puppy. I must learn to say that her name is Chico, and that the milk must be warm to the finger, and that the big dog must be kind."

Chapter 11

An Ill Wind

A wind rose in the night, blowing straight out of the north; a wind so chill that the señora unpacked extra blankets and distributed them lavishly amongst the beds of her household, and the oldest peon at the hacienda (who was Gustavo and a prophet more infallible than Elijah) stared into the heavens until his neck went lame; and predicted much cold, so that the frost would surely kill the fruit blossoms on the slope behind the house; and after that much rain.

Don Andres, believing him implicitly, repeated the warning to Dade; and Dade, because that was now his business, rode here and there, giving orders to the peons and making sure that all would be snug when the storm broke.

The Señorita Teresa, bethinking her of the "pretty señora" who would have scant shelter in that canvas-topped wagonbox, even though it had been set under the thickest branches of a great live oak, called guardedly to Diego who was passing, and ordered Tejon, her swiftest little mustang, saddled and held ready for her behind the last hut, where it could not be seen from the house.

Tejon, so named by his mistress because he was gray like a badger, hated wind, which the señorita knew well. Also, when the hatred grew into rebellion, it needed a strong hand indeed to control him, if the mood seized him to run. But the señorita was in a perverse mood, and none but Tejon would she ride; even though—or perhaps because—she knew that his temper would be uncertain.

She wanted to beg the pretty Señora Simpson to come and stay with them until the weather cleared and the cabin was finished. But more than that she wanted to punish Señor Jack Allen for laughing when she tried to speak the Americano sentence he had taught her the night before, and got it all backwards. Señor Jack would be frightened, perhaps, when he learned that she had ridden away alone upon Tejon; he would ride after her—perhaps. And she would not talk to him when he found her, but would be absolutely implacable in her displeasure, so that he would be speedily reduced to the most abject humility.

Diego, when she ran stealthily across the patio, her ridinghabit flapping about her feet in the wind, looked at her uneasily as if he would like to remonstrate; but being a mere peon, he bent silently and held his calloused, brown palm for the señorita's foot; reverently straightened the flapping skirt when she was mounted, and sent a hasty prayer to whatever saint might be counted upon to watch most carefully over a foolish little Spanish girl.

"An evil spirit is in the caballo to-day," Diego finally ventured to inform his mistress gravely. "For a week he has not felt the weight of saddle, and he loves not the trees which sway and

sing, or the wind whistling in his ears."

"And for that he pleases me much," retorted the señorita, and touched Tejon with her spurred heel, so that he came near upsetting Diego with the lunge he gave.

When the peon recovered his balance, he stood braced against the wind, and with both hands held his hat upon his head while he watched her flying down the slope and out of sight amongst the trees. No girl in all the valley rode better than the Señorita Teresa Picardo, and Diego knew it well and boasted of it to the peons of other hacendados; but for all that he was ill-at-ease, and when, ten minutes later, he came upon Valencia at the stable, he told him of the madness of the señorita.

"Tejon she would ride, and none other; and to-day he is a devil. Twice he would have bitten my shoulder while I was saddling, and that is the sign that his heart is full of wickedness. Me, I would have put the freno Chilene (Chilian bit) in his mouth—but that would start him bucking; for he hates it because then he cannot run."

Valencia, a little later, met the new majordomo and repeated what Diego had said; and Dade, catching a little of the uneasiness and yet not wanting to frighten the girl's father with the tale, made it his immediate business to find Jack and tell him that Teresita had ridden away alone upon a horse that neither Diego nor Valencia considered safe.

Jack, at first declaring that he wouldn't go where he plainly was not wanted, at the end of an uncomfortable half-hour borrowed Surry, because he was fleet as any mustang in the valley, and rode after her.

In this wise did circumstances and Jack obey the piqued desire of the señorita.

After the first headlong half mile, Tejon became the perfect little saddle-pony which fair weather found him; and Teresita, cheated of her battle of wills and yet too honest to provoke him deliberately, began to think a little less of her own whims and more of the Señora Simpson, housed miserably beneath the canvas covering of the prairie schooner.

She found Mrs. Jerry sitting inside, with a patchwork quilt over her shoulders, her eyes holding a shade more of wistfulness and less twinkle, perhaps, but with her lips quite ready to smile upon her visitor. Teresita sat down upon a box and curiously watched the pretty señora try to make a small, triangular piece of cloth cover a large, irregular hole in the elbow of the big señor's coat sleeve. Sometimes, when she turned it so, the hole was nearly covered—except that there was the frayed rent at the bottom still grinning maliciously up at the mender.

"'Patch beside patch is neighborly, but patch upon patch is beggarly!'" quoted Mrs. Jerry, at the moment forgetting that the girl could not understand.

Whereupon Teresita bethought her of her last night's lesson, and replied slowly and solemnly: "My dear Mrs. Seem'son, how—do—you—*do*?"

"Mrs. Seem'son," realizing the underlying friendliness of the carefully enunciated greeting, flushed with pleasure and for a minute forgot all about the patch problem.

"Why, honey, you've been learnin' English jest so's you can talk to me!" She leaned and kissed the girl where the red blood of youth dyed brightest the Latin duskiness of the cheek. "I wish't you could say some more. Can't you?"

Teresita could; but her further store of American words related chiefly to the diet and general well-being of one very small and very black pup, which was at that moment sleeping luxuriously in the chimney corner at home; and without the pup the words would be no more than parrot-chattering. So the señorita shook her head and smiled, and Mrs. Jerry went back to the problem of the small patch and the large hole.

Hampered thus by having no common language between them, Teresita failed absolutely to accomplish her mission.

Mrs. Jerry, hazily guessing at the invitation without realizing any urgent need of immediate acceptance, shook her head and pointed to her pitifully few household appurtenances, and tried to make it plain that she had duties which kept her there in the little camp which she pathetically called home.

Teresita gathered that the pretty señora did not wish to leave that great, gaunt hombre who was her husband. So, when she could no longer conceal her shiverings, and having no hope that the big señor would understand her any better when he returned with the load of logs he and the peons were after, she rose and prepared to depart. Surely the Señor Jack, if he were going to follow, would by this time be coming, and the hope rather hastened her adieu.

"Adios, amiga mia," she said, her eyes innocently turning from the Señora Simpson to scan stealthily the northern slope.

"Good-by, honey. Come again and see me. Jerry knows a few Spanish words, and I'll make him learn 'em to me so I can talk a little of your kind, next time. And tell your mother I'm obliged for the wine; and them dried peaches tasted fine, after being without so long. Shan't I hold your horse while you git on? Seems to me he's pretty frisky for a girl to be riding; but I guess you're equal to him!"

Teresita smiled vaguely. She had no idea of what the woman was saying, and she was beginning to wish that she had not tried in just this way to punish the Señor Jack; if he were here now, he could make the Señora Simpson understand that the storm would be a very dreadful one—else Gustavo was a liar, and whom should one believe?

Even while she was coaxing Tejon alongside a log and persuading him to stand so until she was in the saddle, she was generously forswearing Señor Jack's punishment that she might serve the pretty señora who had Tejon by the bit and was talking to him softly in words he had never heard before in his life. She resolved that if she met Señor Jack, she would ask him to come back with her and explain to the señora about the cold and the rain, and urge her to accept the hospitality of her neighbors.

For that reason she looked more anxiously than before for some sign of him riding towards her through the fields of flowering mustard that heaved in the wind like the waves on some strange, lemon-colored sea tossing between high, green islands of oak and willow. Surely that fool Diego would never keep the still tongue! He would tell, when some one missed her. If he did not, or if Señor Allen was an obstinate pig of a man and would not come, then she would tell Señor Hunter, who was always so kind, though not so handsome as the other, perhaps.

Señor Hunter's eyes were brown—and she had looked into brown eyes all her life. But the blue! The blue eyes that could so quickly change lighter or darker that they bewildered one; and could smile, or light flames that could wither the soul of one.

Even the best rider among the Spanish girls as far south as Paso Robles should not meditate so deeply upon the color of a señor's eyes that she forgets the horse she is riding, especially when the horse is Tejon, whose heart is full of wickedness.

A coyote, stalking the new-made nest of a quail, leaped out of the mustard and gave Tejon the excuse he wanted, and the dreaming señorita was nearly unseated when he ducked and whirled in his tracks. He ran, and she could not stop him, pull hard as she might. If he had only run towards home! But instead, he ran down the valley, because then he need not face the wind; and he tried to outstrip the wind as he went.

It was when they topped a low knoll and darted under the wide, writhing branches of a live oak, that Jack glimpsed them and gave chase; and his heart forgot to beat until he saw them in the open beyond, and knew that she had not been swept from the saddle by a low branch. He leaned lower over Surry's neck and felt gratefully the instant response of the horse; he had thought that Surry was running his best on such uneven ground; but even a horse may call up an unsuspected reserve of speed or endurance, if his whole heart is given to the service of his master; there was a perceptible quickening and a lengthening of stride, and Jack knew then that Surry could do no more and keep his feet. Indeed, if he held that pace for long without stumbling, he would prove himself a more remarkable horse than even Dade declared him to be.

He hoped to overtake the girl soon, for in the glimpses he got of her now and then, as she flew across an open space, he saw that she was putting her whole weight upon the reins; and that should make a sufficient handicap to the gray to wipe out the three-hundred-yard distance between them. It did not seem possible that Tejon could be running as fast as Surry; and yet, after a half-mile or so of that killing pace, Jack could not see that he was gaining much. Perhaps it was his anxiety to overtake her that made the chase seem interminable; for presently they emerged upon the highway which led south to Santa Clara and so on down the valley, and he saw, on a straight, open stretch, that he was much nearer; so near he could see that her hair was down and blowing about her face in a way that must have blinded her at times.

Tejon showed no disposition to stop, however; and Jack, bethinking him of the trick Dade had played upon the Vigilantes with his riata, threw off the loop that held it. If he could get close enough, he meant to lasso the horse unless she managed by that time to get him under control. Now that they were in the road, Surry's stride was more even, and although his breathing was becoming audible, he held his pace wonderfully well—though for that matter, Tejon also seemed to be running just as fast as at first, in spite of that steady pull; indeed, Tejon knew the trick of curling his chin down close to his chest, so that the girl's strength upon the reins was as nothing.

Jack was almost close enough to make it seem worth while to call encouragement, when a horseman appeared suddenly from behind a willow clump and pulled up in astonishment, as he saw Teresita bearing down upon him like a small whirlwind. Whereupon Tejon, recognizing horse and rider and knowing of old that they meant leisurely riding and much chatter, with little laughs for punctuation, slowed of his own accord and so came up to the man at his usual easy lope, and stopped before him.

So quickly did it happen that a witness might easily have sworn in perfect good faith that the girl was fleeing from Jack Allen and pulled up thankfully when she met José Pacheco. One could not blame José for so interpreting the race, or for the anger that blazed in his eyes for the pursuer, even while his lips parted in a smile at the coming of the girl. He reined in protectingly between her and the approaching Jack, and spoke soothingly because of her apparent need.

"Be not frightened, querida mia. Thou art safe with me—and the accursed gringo will get a lesson he will not soon forget, for daring—"

Teresita, looking back, discovered Jack behind her. He was pulling Surry in, now, and he held his riata in one hand as though he were ready to use it at a moment's notice, and blank astonishment was on his face. That, perhaps, was because of José and José's hostile attitude, standing crosswise of the trail like that, and scowling while he waited, with the fingers of his right hand fumbling inside his sash—for his dagger, perchance! Teresita smiled wickedly, in appreciation of the joke on them both.

"Do not kill him, José," she begged caressingly. "Truly he did not harm me! I but ran from him because—" She sent a smile straight to the leaping heart of José, and fumbled with her tossing banner of hair, and turned eyes of innocent surprise on the Señor Allen, who needed some punishment—and was in fair way to get it.

"What is the pleasure of the señor?" José's voice was as smooth and as keen as the dagger-blade under his sash. "His message must indeed be urgent to warrant such haste! You would do well to ride back as hastily as you came; for truly a blind man could see that the señorita has not the smallest desire for your presence. As for me—" As for him, he smiled a sneer and a threat together.

Jack looked to the girl for a rebuke of the man's insult; but Teresita's head was drooped and tilted sidewise while she made shift to braid her hair, and if she heard she surely did not seem to heed.

"As for you, it wouldn't be a bad idea for you to mind your own business," Jack retorted bluntly. "The señorita doesn't need any interpreter. The señorita is perfectly well-qualified to speak for herself. She knows—"

"The señorita knows whom she can trust—and it is not a low dog of a gringo, who would be rotting now with a neck stretched by the hangman's rope, if he had but received his deserts; murderer of five men in one day, men of his own race at that! Gambler! loafer—"

At the press of silver rowels against his sides, Surry lunged forward. But Teresita's horse sidled suddenly between the two men.

"Señor Jack, we will go now, if this wicked caballo of mine will consent to do his running towards home. Thank you, José, for stopping him for me; truly, I think he was minded to carry me to Santa Clara, whether I wished to go or not! But doubtless Señor Jack would have overtaken him soon. Adios, José. Gracias, amigo mio!" Having put her hair into some sort of confinement, she picked up her reins and smiled at José and then at Jack in a way to tie the tongues of them both; though their brows were black with the hatred which must, if they met again, bear fruit of violence.

Fifty yards away, Teresita looked back and waved a hand at the gay horseman who still stood fair across the highway and stared blankly after them.

"Poor José!" she murmured mischievously. "Very puzzled and unhappy he looks. I wonder if the privilege of tearing you in pieces would not bring the smile to his lips? Señor Jack, if so be you should ever desire death, will you let José do the killing? To serve you thus would give him great pleasure, I am sure."

Jack, usually so headlong in his speech and actions, rode a moody three minutes without replying. He was not a fool, even though he was rather deeply in love; he felt in her that feline instinct to torment which wise men believe they can detect in all women; and angry as he was at José's deliberate insults, he knew quite well in his heart that Teresita had purposely provoked them.

'I've heard," he said at last, looking at her with the hard glint in his eyes that thrilled her pleasurably, "that all women are
either angels or devils. I believe you're both, Señorita!"

Teresita laughed and pouted her lips at him. "Such injustice! Am I then to be blamed because José has a bad temper and speech hotter than the enchilladas of Margarita? I could love him for his rages! When the Blessed Mary sends me a lover—" She looked over her shoulder and sighed romantically, hiding the laughter in her eyes and the telltale twist of her lips as best she could, with lashes downcast and face averted.

Even a kitten the size of your two fists knows how to paw a mouse, even though it lacks the appetite for devouring it after the torture. One cannot logically blame Teresita. She merely used the weapons which nature put into her pink palms.

Chapter 12

Potentiel Moods

So engrossed was the señorita in her truly feminine game of cat-and-mouse that she quite forgot her worry over Mrs. Jerry until she was in her own room and smiling impishly at herself in the mirror, while she brushed the wind-tangles from her hair and planned fresh torment for the Señor Jack. The señorita liked to see his eyes darken and then light with the flames that thrilled her; and it was exceedingly pleasant to know that she could produce that effect almost whenever she chose. Also, her lips would curve of themselves whenever she thought of José's rage and subsequent bafflement when she rode off with Señor Jack; and of Señor Jack's black looks when she praised José afterwards. Truly they hated each other very much—those two caballeros! She was woman enough to know the reason why, and to find a great deal of pleasure in the knowledge.

Still smiling, she lifted a heavy lock of hair to the light and speculated upon the mystery of coloring. Black it was, except when the sun lighted it and brought a sheen that was almost blue; and Señor Jack's was neither red, as was the hair of the big Señor Simpson, nor brown nor gold, but a tantalizing mixture of all; especially where it waved it had many different shades, just as the light gold and the dark of the pretty señora's—It was then that remembrance came to the señorita and made her glance a self-accusing one, when she looked at her reflected face.

"Selfish, thoughtless one that thou art to forget that sweet señora!" she cried. And for punishment she pulled the lock of hair so that it hurt—a little. "I shall ask Señor Hunter if he will not send the carriage for her—and perhaps I shall go with him to bring her; though truly she will never leave the big hombre who speaks so many words over such slight matters. I am glad I did not yet carry Chico to live there in that small camp. Till the house is finished, he shall stay with me. Truly the storm would kill him if he were there. But perhaps the storm will not be so great, after all—not so great as is the storm in the hearts of those two who met and would have fought, had I not so skillfully prevented it! Santa Maria, I truly must have been inspired, to act like the dove with the branch of the olive when I flew between them; and the eyes of José were blazing; and Señor Jack—" There came the smile again, and the dawdling of the brush while she thought of those two. So the pretty señora was forgotten, after all, and left to shiver over her mending in the prairie schooner because Teresita was a spoiled child with more hearts than it is good for a girl to play with.

As a matter of fact, however, the pretty señora was quite accustomed to discomfort in varying degrees, and gave less thought to the weather than did the more tenderly sheltered women of the valley, so that no harm came of the forgetfulness; especially since the storm fell far short of Gustavo's expectations and caused that particular prophet the inconvenience of searching his soul and the heavens for an explanation of the sunshine that reprehensibly bathed the valley next day in its soft glow.

Also, no immediate harm resulted from the rage of the two caballeros, although not even the most partial judge could give the credit to Teresita's "olive branch." Chance herself stepped in, and sent a heavy, dead branch crashing down from a swaying oak upon the head and right shoulder of José, while he was riding into his own patio. Whereupon José, who had been promising himself vengefully that he would send Manuel immediately with a challenge to the gringo who had dared lift eyes to the Señorita Teresa Picardo, instantly forgot both his love and his hate in the oblivion that held him until nightfall.

After that his stiffened muscles and the gash in his scalp gave him time for meditation; and meditation counseled patience. The gringo would doubtless go to the rodeo, and he would meet him there without the spectacular flavor of a formal challenge. For José was a decent sort of a fellow and had no desire to cheapen his passion or cause the señorita the pain of public gossip. It was that same quality of dignity in his love that had restrained him from seeking a deliberate quarrel with Jack before now; and though he fumed inwardly while his outer hurts healed, he resolved to wait. The rodeo would give him his chance.

Because it is not in the nature of the normal human to keep his soul always under the lock and key of utter silence, a little of his hate and a little of his hope seeped into the ears of Manuel, whose poultices of herbs were doing their work upon the bruised muscles of José's shoulder, and whose epithets against the two gringos who were responsible for his exile from the Picardo hacienda had the peculiar flavor of absolute sincerity. Frequently he cursed them while he changed the poultices; and Don José, listening approvingly, added now and then a curse of his own, and a vague prediction of how he meant to teach the blue-eyed one a lesson which he would weep at remembering—if he lived to remember anything.

Manuel did not mean to tattle; he merely let fall a word or two to Valencia, whom he met occasionally in the open and accused bitterly of having a treacherous friendship for the gringos, and particularly for the blue-eyed one.

"Because that mongrel whose hair is neither red nor yellow nor black speaks praise to you of your skill, perchance, and because he makes you laugh with the foolish tales he tells, you would turn against your own kind, Valencia. No honest Spaniard can be a friend of the gringos. Of the patron," he added rather sorrowfully, "I do not speak, for truly he is in his dotage and therefore not to be judged too harshly. But you, Valencia—you should think twice before you choose a gringo for your friend; a gringo who speaks fair to the father that he may cover his love-making to the daughter, who is easily fooled, like all younglings.

"The young Don José will deal with that blue-eyed one, Valencia. Every day he swears it by all the saints. He but waits for the rodeo and until I have healed his shoulder—and then you shall see! There will be no love-making then for the gringo. José will have the señorita yet for his bride, just as the saints have desired since they played together in the patio and I watched them that they did not run into the corrals to be kicked in the head, perchance, by the mustangs we had there. José, I tell you, has loved her too long to stand now with the sombrero in hand while that arrogant hombre steals her away.

When the shoulder is well—and truly, it was near broken—and when they meet at the rodeo, then you shall see what will happen to your new gringo friend."

Valencia did not quarrel with Manuel. He merely listened and smiled his startlingly sunny smile, and afterwards repeated Manuel's words almost verbatim to Jack. Later, he recounted as much as he considered politic to Don Andres himself, just to show how bitter Manuel had become and how unjust. Valencia, it must be admitted, was not in any sense working in the interests of peace. He looked forward with a good deal of eagerness to that meeting of which Manuel prated. He had all the faith of your true hero-worshiper in his new friend, and with the story of that last eventful day which Jack had spent in San Francisco to build his faith upon, he confidently expected to see José learn a much-needed lesson in humility—aye, and

Manuel also.

Since even the best-natured gossip is like a breeze to fan the flames of dissension, Don Andres spent an anxious hour in devising a plan that would preserve the peace he loved better even than prosperity. While he smoked behind the passion vines on the veranda, he thought his way slowly from frowns to a smile of satisfaction, and finally called a peon scurrying across the patio to stand humbly before him while he gave a calm order. His majordomo he would see, as speedily as was convenient to a man as full of ranch business as Dade Hunter found himself.

Dade, tired and hot from a forenoon in the saddle inspecting the horses that were to bear the burden of rodeo work, presently came clanking up to the porch and lifted the sombrero off his sweat-dampened forehead thankfully, when the shade of the vines enveloped him.

The eyes of the don dwelt pleasedly upon the tanned face of his foreman. More and more Don Andres was coming to value the keen common-sense which is so rare, and which distinguished Dade's character almost as much as did the kindliness that made nearly every man his friend.

The don had already fallen into the habit of presenting his orders under the guise of ideas that needed the confirmation of the majordomo, before they became definite plans; and it speaks much for those two that neither of them suspected that it was so. Thus, Don Andres' solution of the problem of preserving peace became the subject for a conference that lasted more than an hour. The don was absolutely candid; so candid that he spoke upon a delicate subject, and one that carried a sting of which he little dreamed.

"One factor I cannot help recognizing," he said slowly. "I am not blind, nor is the señora blind, to the—the—friendship that is growing between Señor Jack and our daughter. We had hoped—but we have long been resolved that in matters of the heart, our daughter shall choose for herself so long as she does not choose one altogether unworthy; which we do not fear, for to that extent we can protect her by admitting to our friendship only those in whose characters we have some confidence. Now that we understand each other so well, amigo, I will say that I have had some correspondence with friends in San Francisco, who have been so good as to make some investigations in my behalf. Their Vigilance Committee," he said, smiling, "was not the only tribunal which weighed evidence for and against your friend, nor was it the only vindication he has received.

"I am assured that in the trouble which brought him to my house he played the part of an honest gentleman fighting to uphold the principles which all honest men espouse; and while he is hot-tempered at times, and perhaps more thoughtless than we could wish, I hear no ill of him save the natural follies of high-stomached youth.

"Therefore I am willing to abide by the choice of my daughter, whose happiness is more dear to her parents than any hope they may have cherished of the welding of two families who have long been friends. I myself," he added reminiscently, "fled to the priest with my sweetheart as if all the fiends of hell pursued us, because her parents had chosen for her a husband whom she could not love. Since we know the pain of choosing between a parent's wishes and the call of the heart, we are resolved that our child shall be left free to choose for herself. Therefore, I think our plan is a wise one; and the result must be as the saints decree."

Dade, because he was engrossed with stifling the ache he had begun to think was dead because it had grown numb, bowed his head without speaking his assent and rose to his feet.

"I'll tell Jack," he said, as he started for the stables. "I guess he'll do it, all right."

Chapter 13

Bill Wilson Goes Visiting

"I Don't know what you've been doing to José Pacheco, lately," was Dade's way of broaching the subject, "but Don Andres asked me to 'persuade' you not to go on rodeo, on account of some trouble between you and José."

"He wants my scalp, is all," Jack explained easily, picking burrs from the fringe of his sash—burrs he had gotten when he ran a race with Teresita from the farther side of the orchard to the spring, a short time before. "Valencia told me—and he got it from Manuel—that José is right on the warpath. If it wasn't for his being laid up—"

"Oh, I know. You'd like to go over and have it out with him. But you can't. The Pachecos and the Picardos are almost like one family. I don't suppose José ever stayed away from here so long since he was a baby, as he has since we came. It's bad enough to keep old friends away, without mixing up a quarrel. Have you seen José lately? Don Andres seemed to think so, but
I told him you'd have said something about it to me if you had."

"I met him in the trail, a week or so ago," Jack admitted with manifest reluctance. "He wasn't overly friendly, but there wasn't any real trouble, if that's what you're afraid of." He looked sidelong at the other, saw the hurt in Dade's eyes at this evidence of the constraint growing intangibly between them, and laughed defiantly.

"Upon my soul!" he exclaimed, "one would think I was simple-minded, the way you act! D'you think a man never scowled my way before? D'you think I'm afraid of José? D'you think I don't know enough to take care of myself? What the devil do you think? Can't go on rodeo—you're afraid I might get hurt! I ain't crazy to go, for that matter; but I don't know as I relish this guardian-angel stunt you're playing. You've got your hands full without that. You needn't worry about me; I've managed to squeak along so far without getting my light put out—"

"By being a tolerably fair shot, yes," Dade assented, his face hardening a little under the injustice. "But since I'm hired to look after Don Andres' interests, you're going to do what I tell you. You'll stay here and boss the peons while I'm gone. A friendship between two families that has lasted as many years as you are old, ain't going to be busted up now, if I can help it. It's strained to the snapping-point right now, just because the don is friendly with us gringos. Of course, we can't help that. He had his ideas on the subject before he ever saw me or you. Just the same, it's up to us not to do the snapping; and I know one gringo that's going to behave himself if I have to take him down and set on him!"

"Whee-ee! Somebody else is hitting the war-post, if I know the signs!" Dade stirred to anger always tickled Jack immensely, perhaps because of its very novelty, and restored him to good humor. "Have it your own way, then, darn you! I don't want to go on rodeo, nohow."

"I know that, all right," snapped Dade, and started off with his hat tilted over his eyes. No one, he reminded himself, would want to spend a month or so riding the range when he could stay and philander with as pretty a Spanish girl as ever played the game of cat-and-mouse with a man. And Jack never had been the kind to go looking for trouble; truth to tell, he had never found it necessary, for trouble usually flew to meet him as a needle flies to the magnet.

But, a wound is not necessarily a deadly one because it sends excruciating pain-signals to a man's heart and brain; and love seldom is fatal, however painful it may be. Dade was slowly recovering, under the rather heroic treatment of watching his successor writhe and exult by turns, as the mood of the maiden might decree. Strong medicine, that, to be swallowed with a wry face, if you will; but it is guaranteed to cure if the sufferer is not a mental and moral weakling.

Dade was quite ready to go out to rodeo work; indeed, he was anxious to go. But, not being a morbid young man, he did not contemplate carrying a broken heart with him. Teresita was sweet and winsome and maddeningly alluring; he knew it, he felt it still. Indeed, he was made to realize it every time the whim seized her to punish Jack by smiling upon Dade. But she was as capricious as beauty usually is, and he knew that also; and after being used several times as a club with which to beat Jack into proper humility (and always seeing very clearly that he was merely the club and nothing more) he had almost reached the point where he could shrug shoulders philosophically at her coquetry; and what is better, do it without bitterness. At least, he could do it when he had not seen her for several hours, which made rodeo time a relief for which he was grateful.

What hurt him most, just now, was the constraint between him and Jack; time was when Jack would have told him immediately of any unpleasant meeting with José. It never occurred to Dade that he himself had fostered the constraint by his moody aloofness when he was fighting the first jealous resentment he had ever felt against the other in the years of their constant companionship. An unexpected slap on the shoulder almost sent him headlong.

"Say, old man, I didn't mean it," Jack began contritely, referring perhaps to his petulant speech, rather than to his mode of making his presence known. "But— come over here in the shade, and let's have it out once for all. I know you aren't

stuck up over being majordomo, but all the same you're not the old Dade, whether you know it or not. You go around as if—well—you know how you've been. What I wanted to say is,
what's the matter? Is it anything I've said or done?"

He sat down on the stone steps of a hut used for a storehouse and reached moodily for his smoking material. "I know I didn't say anything about running up against José—but it wasn't anything beyond a few words; and, Dade, you've been almighty hard to talk to lately. If you've got anything against me—"

"Oh, quit it!" Dade's face glowed darkly with the blood which shame brought there. He opened his lips to say more, took a long breath instead, closed them, and looked at Jack queerly. For one reckless moment he meditated a plunge into that perfect candor which may be either the wisest or the most foolish thing a man may do in all his life.

"I didn't think you noticed it," he said, his voice lowered instinctively because of the temptation to tell the truth, and his glance wandering absently over to the corral opposite, where Surry stood waiting placidly until his master should have need of him. "There has been a regular brick wall between us lately.
I felt it myself and I blamed you for it. I—"

"It wasn't my building," Jack cut in eagerly. "It's you, you old pirate. Why, you'd hardly talk when we happened to be alone, and when I tried to act as if nothing was wrong, you'd look so darned sour I just had to close my sweet lips like the petals of a—"

"Cabbage," supplied Dade dryly, and placed his cigarette between lips that twitched.

Former relations having thus been established after their own fashion, Dade began to wonder how he had ever been fool enough to think of confessing his hurt. It would have built that wall higher and thicker; he saw it now, and with the lighting of his cigarette he swung back to a more normal state of mind than he had been in for a month.

"I'm going up toward Manuel's camp, pretty soon," he observed lazily, eying Jack meditatively through a thin haze of smoke. "Want to take a ride up that way and let the sun shine on your nice new saddle?" Though he called it Manuel's camp from force of habit, that hot-blooded gentleman had not set foot over its unhewn doorsill for three weeks and more.

Jack hesitated, having in mind the possibility of persuading Teresita that she ought to pay a visit to the Simpson cabin that day to display her latest accomplishment by asking in real, understandable English, how the pup was getting along; and to show the pretty señora the proper way to pat tortillas out thin and smooth, as Margarita had been bribed to teach Teresita herself to do.

"Sure, I'll go," he responded, before the hesitation had become pronounced, and managed to inject a good deal of his old heartiness into the words.

"I'm going to have the cattle pushed down this way," Dade explained, "so you can keep an eye on them from here and we won't have to keep up that camp. Since they made Bill Wilson captain of the Vigilantes, there isn't quite so much wholesale stealing as there was, anyway, and enough vaqueros went with Manuel so I'll need every one that's left. I'll leave you Pedro, because he can't do any hard riding, after that fall he got the other day. The two of you can keep the cattle pretty well down this way."

"All right. Say, what was it made you act so glum since we came down here?" Jack, as occasionally happens with a friend, was not content to forget a grievance while the cause of it remained clouded with mystery.

"Are you sore over that trouble I had in town? I know how you feel about—well, about killings; but, Dade, I had to. I hate it myself. You needn't think I like the idea, just because I haven't talked about it. A fellow feels different," he added slowly, "when it's white men. When we fought Injuns, I don't believe it worried either one of us to think we'd killed some. We were generally glad of it. But these others—they were mean enough and ornery enough; but they were humans. I was glad at the time, but that wore off. And I've caught you looking at me kinda queer, lately, as if you hated me, almost. You ought to know—"

"I know you're always going off half-cocked," chuckled Dade, quite himself again. "No, now you mention it, I don't like the idea of shooting first and finding out afterwards what it was all about, the way so many fellows have got in the habit of doing. Guns are all right in their place. And when you get away out where the law doesn't reach, and you have to look out for yourself, they come in mighty handy. But like every other kind of power, most men don't know when and how to use the gun argument; and they make more trouble than they settle, half the time. You had a right to shoot, that day, and shoot to kill. Why, didn't the Committee investigate you, first thing after Bill was elected, and find that you were justified? Didn't they wipe your reputation clean with their official document, that Bill sent you a copy of? No, that never bothered me at all, old man. You want to forget about it. You only saved the Committee the trouble of hanging 'em, according to Bill. Say, Valencia was telling me yesterday—"

"Well, what the dickens did ail you, then?"

Dade threw out both hands helplessly and gave a rueful laugh. "You're harder to dodge than an old cow when you've got her calf on the saddle," he complained.

"The trouble was," he explained gravely, "that these last boots of mine pinched like the devil, and I've been mad for a month because my feet are half a size

bigger than yours. I wanted to stump you for a trade, only I knew yours would cripple me up worse than these did. But I've got 'em broke in now, so I can walk without tying my face into a hard knot. There's nothing on earth," he declared earnestly, "will put me
on the fight as quick as a pair of boots that don't fit."

Jack paid tribute to Dade's mendaciousness by looking at him doubtfully, not quite sure whether to believe him; and Dade chuckled again, well pleased with himself. Even when Jack finally told him quite frankly that he was a liar, he only laughed and went over to where Surry stood rolling the wheel in his bit. He would not answer Jack's chagrined vilifications, except with an occasional amused invitation to go to the devil.

So the wall of constraint crumbled to the nothingness out of which it was built, and the two came close together again in that perfect companionship that may choose whatever medium the mood of man may direct, and still hold taut the bond of their friendship.

While they rode together up the valley, Jack told the details of the encounter with José, and declared that he was doing all that even Dade could demand of him by resisting the desire to ride down to Santa Clara and make José swallow his words.

"I'd have done it anyway, as soon as I brought Teresita home," he added, with a hint of apology for his seeming weakness. "But, darn it, I knew all the time that she made him think she was running away from me. It did look that way, when she stopped as soon as she met him; I can't swear right now whether Tejon was running away, or whether he was just simply running!" He laughed ruefully. "She's an awful little tease—just plumb full of the old Nick, even if she does look as innocent and as meek as their pictures of the Virgin Mary. She had us both guessing, let me tell you! He was pretty blamed insulting, though, and I'd have licked the stuffing out of him right then and there, if she hadn't swung in and played the joker the way she did. Made José look as if he'd been doused with cold water—and him breathing fire and brimstone the minute before.

"It was funny, I reckon—to Teresita; we didn't see the joke. Every time I bring up the subject of that runaway, she laughs; but she won't say whether it was a runaway, no matter how I sneak the question in. So I just let it go, seeing José is laid up now; only, next time I bump into José Pacheco, he's going to act pretty, or there's liable to be a little excitement.

"I wish I had my pistols. I wrote to Bill Wilson about them again, the other day; if he doesn't send them down pretty soon, I'm going after them." He stopped, his attention arrested by the peculiar behavior of a herd of a hundred or more cattle, a little distance from the road.

"Now, what do you suppose is the excitement over there?" he asked; and for answer Dade turned from the trail to investigate.

"Maybe they've run across the carcass of a critter that's been killed," he hazarded, "though this is pretty close home for beef thieves to get in their work. Most of the stock is killed north and east of Manuel's camp."

The cattle, moving restlessly about and jabbing their long, wicked horns at any animal that got in the way, lifted heads to stare at them suspiciously, before they turned tail and scampered off through the mustard. From the live oak under which they had been gathered came a welcoming shout, and the two, riding under the tent-like branches, craned necks in astonishment.

"Hello, Jack," spoke the voice again. "I'm almighty glad to see yuh! Hello, Dade, how are yuh?"

"Bill Wilson, by thunder!" Jack's tone was incredulous.

Bill, roosting a good ten feet from the ground on a great, horizontal limb, flicked the ashes from the cigar he was smoking and grinned down at them unabashed.

"You sure took your time about getting here," he remarked, hitching himself into a more comfortable posture on the rough bark. "I've been praying for you, two hours and more. Say, don't ever talk to me about hungry wolf-packs, boys. I'll take 'em in preference to the meek-eyed cow-bossies, any time."

They besought him for details and got them in Bill's own fashion of telling. Briefly, he had long had in mind a trip down to the Picardo ranch, just to see the boys and the country and have a talk over the stirring events of the past month; and, he added, he wanted to bring Jack his pistols himself, because it was not reasonable to expect any greaser to withstand the temptation of keeping them, once he got them in his hands.

Therefore, having plenty of excuses for venturing so far from his place, and having "tied the dove of peace to the ridge-pole" of town by means of some thorough work on the part of the new Committee, he had boldly set forth that morning, soon after sunrise, upon a horse which somebody had sworn that a lady could ride.

Bill confessed frankly that he wasn't any lady, however; and so, when the horse ducked unexpectedly to one side of the trail, because of something he saw in the long grass, Bill surprised himself very much by getting his next clear impression of the situation from the ground.

"I dunno how I got there, but I was there, all right, and it didn't feel good, either. But I'd been making up my mind to get off and try walking though, so I done it. Say, I don't see nothing so damned attractive about riding horseback, anyway!"

He yelled at the horse to stop, but it appeared that his whoas were so terrifying that the horse ran for its life. So Bill started to walk, beguiling the time, by soliloquizing upon—well, Bill put it this way: "I walked and I cussed, and I cussed and I walked, for about four hours and a half. Say! How do you make out it's only twenty miles?"

"Nearer thirty" corrected Dade, and Bill grunted and went on with the story of his misfortunes. Walking became monotonous, and he wearied of soliloquy before the cattle discovered him.

"Met quite a band, all of a sudden," said Bill. "They throned up their heads and looked at me like I was wild Injuns, and I shooed 'em off—or tried to. They did run a little piece, and then they all turned and looked a minute, and commenced coming again, heads up and tails a-rising. And," he added naïvely, "I commenced going!" He said he thought that he could go faster than they could come; but the faster he departed, the more eager was their arrival. "Till we was all of us on the gallop and tongues a-hanging."

Bill was big, and he was inclined to flesh because of no exercise more strenuous than quelling incipient riots in his place, or weighing the dust that passed into his hands and ownership. He must have run for some distance, since he swore by several forbidden things that the chase lasted for five miles—"And if you don't believe it, you can ride back up the trail till you come
to the dent I made with my toes when I started in."

Other cattle came up and joined in the race, until Bill had quite a following; and when he was gasping for breath and losing hope of seeing another day, he came upon a live oak, whose branches started almost from the roots and inclined upward so gently that even a fat man who has lost his breath need not hesitate over the climbing.

"Thank the good Lord he don't cut all his trees after the same pattern," finished Bill fervently, "and that live oaks ain't built like redwoods. If they was, you'd be wiping off my coat-buttons right now, trying to identify my remains!"

Being polite young men, and having a sincere liking for Bill, they hid certain exchanges of grins and glances under their hat-brims (Bill being above them and the brims being wide) and did not by a single word belittle the escape he had had from man-eating cows. Instead, Dade coaxed him down from the tree and onto Surry, swearing solemnly that the horse was quite as safe as the limb to which Bill showed a disposition to cling. Bill was hard to persuade, but since Dade was a man who inspired faith instinctively, the exchange was finally accomplished, Bill still showing that strange, clinging disposition that made him grip the saddle-horn as a drowning man is said to grasp at a straw.

So they got him to the house, the two riding Jack's peppery palimeno with some difficulty; while Surry stepped softly that he might not dislodge that burden in the saddle, whose body lurched insecurely and made the horse feel at every step the ignorance of the man. They got him and themselves to the house; and his presence there did its part towards strengthening Don Andres' liking for gringos, while Bill himself gained a broader outlook, a keener perception of the rights of the native-born Californians.

Up in San Francisco there was a tendency to make light of those rights. It was commonly accepted that the old land grants were outrageous, and that the dons who prated of their rights were but land pirates who would be justly compelled by the government to disgorge their holdings. Bill had been in the habit of calling all Spaniards "greasers," just as the average Spaniard spoke of all Americans as "gringos," or heathenish foreigners.

But on the porch of Don Andres, his saddle-galled person reclining at ease in a great armchair behind the passion vines, with the fragile stem of a wine-glass twirling between his white, sensitive, gambler-fingers while he listened to the don's courtly utterances as translated faithfully by Dade (Jack being absent on some philandering mission of his own), big Bill Wilson opened his eyes to the other side of the question and frankly owned himself puzzled to choose.

"Seems like the men that came here when there wasn't anything but Injuns and animals, and built up the country outa raw material, ought to have some say now about who's going to reap the harvest," he admitted to Dade. "Don't look so much like gobbling, when you get right down to cases, does it? But at the same time, all these men that leave the east and come out here to make homes—seems like they've got a right to settle down and plow up a garden patch if they want to. They're going to do it, anyway. Looks like these grandees'll have to cash in their chips and quit, but it's a darned shame."

As to the town, Bill told them much that had happened. Politics were still turbulent; but Perkins' gang of hoodlums was fairly wiped out, and the Committee was working systematically and openly for the best interests of the town. There had been a hanging the week before; a public hanging in the square, after a trial as fair as any court properly authorized could give.

"Not much like that farce they pulled off that day with Jack," asserted Bill. "Real lawyers, we had, and real evidence for and against the feller, and tried him for real murder. Things are cooling down fast, up there, and you can walk the streets now without hanging onto your money with one hand and your gun with the other. Jack and you can come back any time. And say, Jack!" Having heard his voice beyond the vines, Bill made bold to call him somewhat peremptorily.

"There's some gold left, you know, that belongs to you. I didn't send it all down; didn't like the looks of that—er—" He checked himself on the point of saying greaser. "And seeing you're located down here for the summer, and don't need it, why don't you put it into lots? You two can pick up a couple of lots that will grow into good money, one of these days. Fact is, I've got a couple in mind. I'd like to see you fellows get some money to workin' for you. This horseback riding is too blamed risky."

"That looks reasonable to me," said Dade. "We've got the mine, of course, but the town ought to go on growing, and lots should be a good place to sink a thousand or two. I've got a little that ain't working." Then seeing the inquiring look in the eyes of Don Andres, he explained to him what Bill had suggested.

Don Andres nodded his white head approvingly. "The Señor Weelson is right," he said. "You would do well, amigos, to heed his advice."

"Just as Jack says," Dade concluded; and Jack amended that statement by saying it was just as Bill said. If Bill knew of a lot or two and thought it would be a good investment, he could buy them in their names. And Bill snorted at their absolute lack of business instinct and let the subject drop into the background with the remark that, for men that had come west with the gold fever, they surely did seem to care very little about the gold they came after.

"The fun of finding it is good enough," declared Jack, unashamed, "so long as we have all we need. And when we need more than we've got, there's the mine; we can always find more. Just now—"

He waved his cigarette towards the darkening hills; and in the little silence that followed they heard the sweet, high tenor of a vaquero somewhere, singing plaintively a Spanish lovesong. When the voice trailed into a mournful, minor "Adios, adios," a robin down in the orchard added a brief, throaty note of his own.

Bill sighed and eased his stiffened muscles in the big chair. "Well, I don't blame either one of you," he drawled somewhat wistfully. "If I was fifteen years limberer and fifty pounds slimmer, I dunno but what I'd set into this ranch game myself. It's sure peaceful."

Foolishly they agreed that it was.

Chapter 14

Rodeo Time

In those days of large leisure and cyclonic bursts of excitement and activity; of midday siestas and moonlight serenades—and a duel, perchance, at sunrise—the spring rodeo was one of the year's events, to be looked forward to all winter by the vaqueros; and when it was over, to be talked of afterwards for months. A mark from which to measure the passing of time, it was; a date for the fixing of incidents in the memory of men.

In the valley of Santa Clara, rodeo time really began when the Picardo vaqueros cinched saddles upon restive mustangs some misty morning, and with shouts and laughter and sombreros waving high over black heads in adieu to those who remained behind, swept down the slope like a charge of gayly caparisoned cavalry, driving the loose saddle horses before them. Past the stone and adobe wall of the home pasture, past the fences where the rails were held to their posts with rawhide thongs, which the coyotes sometimes chewed to pulp and so made extra work for the peons, they raced, exultant with life. Slim young Spaniards they were, clothed picturesquely in velvet and braid and gay sashes; with cumbersome, hairy chaparejos, high-crowned sombreros and big-roweled, silver spurs to mark their calling; caballeros to flutter the heart of a languorous-eyed señorita, and to tingle the pulse of the man who could command and see them ride gallantly to do his bidding.

Fairly in the midst of them, quite as gaudy to look upon and every whit as reckless in their horsemanship, rode Dade and Jack. If their hearts were not as light, their faces gave no sign; and their tongues flung back the good-humored jibes of their fellows in Spanish as fluent as any they heard.

When they left the highway and rode straight down the valley through the mustard that swept the chests of their plunging horses with dainty yellow and green, the two fell behind and slowing their horses to an easy lope, separated themselves from their exuberant fellows.

"I wish you were going along," Dade observed tritely. "If José Pacheco changes his mind and stays at home, I'll send you
word and you can come on, if you want to."

"Thanks." Jack's tone, however, did not sound thankful. "If I wanted to go, do you think I'd hang back because he's going?"

"No, I don't. I think the prospect of a fine, large row would be a temptation; and I must say I'm kinda surprised that you've
been able to resist it. Still, I realize there's compensations."

"Sure, there are. I never denied it, did I?"

"Never. I reckon you've sent by Bill Wilson for a trumpet to proclaim—"

"Oh, shut up. I think," Jack decided suddenly and without any visible cause, "I'll turn off here and ride around by Jerry Simpson's. Adios, old man, and heaps of good luck to you." He swung abruptly off to the right and galloped away, looking back over his shoulder when he had ridden a hundred paces, to wave his sombrero and shout a last word or two of farewell.

"Truly, José will be disappointed when he does not see Señor Jack amongst us," smiled Valencia, reining in beside Dade and looking after the departing horseman with friendly eyes. "Though if he had good sense, he would be thankful. Me, I should not like to have trouble with that friend of yours, Señor. In San Francisco they talk yet of that day when he fired three times from a galloping horse and killed three men. Dios! That was pretty shooting. I would have given much to see it. There will be few men so bold now as to make war with that blueeyed hombre; but José is a fool, when his will is crossed. Me, I fight—yes, and love the heat of fighting in my blood; but I do not bellow threats before, as José has been doing. Carramba! To hear him, one would think he believed that men may die of curses; if they did, the Señor Jack would be lying now with candles burning at his head and his feet! Truly, love takes the sense out of a man quicker than wine."

Dade agreed with him, though his lips did not open to form any words upon the subject.

Their first stopping place was José's ranch down near Santa Clara, and he wondered just how far José's hatred of him would interfere with the traditions of hospitality. It was not likely that José's vaqueros would be ready to start that day; and although he carried his own camp equipment on pack-horses, and, guided by Valencia, ordered the camp set up in its accustomed place beside a little stream half a mile from the house, he sent many a questioning glance that way.

If he feared a hostile reception, he was soon reassured. José and Manuel speedily appeared, galloping side-by-side through the lush yellow and green. José's manner was irreproachable, his speech carefully considered. If his eyes lacked their usual warm glow of friendliness, it was because he could not bring that look at will to beam upon the guest whom his heart failed to welcome. He invited Dade to dinner with him; and Dade, hoping to establish a better understanding between them, accepted.

Dade had not lived half his life amongst the dark-skinned race for nothing. He sipped the home-made wine with José, talked of many things in his soft, easy-natured drawl, and by letting his inner friendliness with the whole world look out of his eyes when they dwelt upon his host, went José one better in courtesy. And José, sauntering afterward across the patio to the porch, met Manuel face to face and paid tribute to Don
Andres' new majordomo in a single sentence.

"If all gringos were like this Señor Hunter, one could tolerate their coming to live amongst us," he said frankly.

"Sí," grudged Manuel. "But then, he is not all gringo. Many years he dwelt with our people in Texas, so that he has the
Spanish ways; but me, I want none of him."

José laughed without much mirth to lighten the sound. "The blue-eyed one—did you find from the vaqueros why he did not come? He need not have been afraid of me—not if his fame was earned honestly." If his tone were patronizing, José perhaps had some excuse, since Fame had not altogether passed him by with face averted.

"Part of the way he came, and turned back. The vaqueros do not know why, except Valencia. And Valencia—he is growing a gringo heart, like the patron. He will speak nothing but boasts of what that blue-eyed one can do. Me, I came near fighting with Valencia; only he would not do anything but smile foolishly, when I told him what I think of traitors like himself."

"Let him smile," advised José, "while he may." Which was not a threat, in spite of its resemblance to one, but rather a vague reference to the specter of trouble that stalks all men as a fox stalks a quail, and might some day wipe that broad smile from the face of Valencia, as it had swept all the gladness from his own.

He went back and smoked a final cigarette in Dade's company; and if he said little, his silences held no hint of antagonism. It was not until Dade rose to return to camp for the night that José put the question that had tickled the tongue of him ever since the arrival on his ranch of the Picardo vaqueros.

"Your friend, the Señor Allen—he is to join you later, perhaps?"

"Jack was left to look after the ranch." Dade's eyes were level in their glance, his voice quiet with the convincing ring of
truth. "He won't be on rodeo at all."

José went paler than he had been two weeks before with his hurt, but a simple word of polite surprise held all his answer. For Jack to stay at home, to be near Teresita every day, to have nothing in the way of his love-making—nothing, since those doting two, her parents, would but smile at whatever she might choose to do—there was acid enough in that thought to eat away all the warmth, all the generosity José possessed. He let Dade go without even the perfunctory phrases of regret, which custom had made almost compulsory; and Manuel, sitting in silent wrath upon the porch, listened to the steady footfalls moving up and down the room behind him until the moon, that had been shining in his smoldering eyes, slipped over the red tiles of the roof and left all but the tree-tops in black shade.

"Dios! There will be one gringo the less when those two meet," he muttered, staring at the tiny glow of his cigarette; and afterward folded his arms tightly over a chest that heaved with the impatience within. When those two met, Manuel meant to be there also to see. "Me, I should like to drag him to death with the six-strand riata he despised!" was the beautiful thought he took to bed with him.

Sunshine was lifting the morning fog high above the treetops when the old, gray mare, whose every movement tinkled the bell hung around her neck, shook her rough coat vigorously to free it from the moisture which the fog had left; and so jangled a peremptory summons to the herd of saddle horses that bore the brand of Don Andres Picardo upon their right thighs. At the camp upon the bank of the Guadalupe, the embaladors were shouting curses, commands, jokes, and civilities to one another while they brought orderly packs out of the chaos of camp-equipment that littered the ground.

The vaqueros were saddling their mounts and fairly bubbling with a purely animal joy in the open; and Dade, his cigarette sending up a tiny ribbon of aromatic smoke as if he were burning incense before the altar of the soul of him that looked steadfastly out of his eyes, walked among them with that intangible air of good-fellowship which is so hard to describe, but which carries more weight among men than any degree of imperious superiority. Valencia looked up and flashed him a smile as he came near; and Pancho, the lean vaquero with the high beak and the tender heart, turned to see what Valencia was smiling at and gave instant glimpse of his own white teeth when he saw Dade behind him.

"To-day will be hot, Señor," he said. "Me, I wish we were already at Tres Pinos."

"No, you don't," grinned Dade, "for then you would not have the Sunal rancho before you, to build hopes upon, but behind you—and hope, they say, is sweeter than memory, Pancho."

Pancho, being ugly to look upon, liked to be rallied upon the one señorita in the valley whose eyes brightened at sight of him. He grinned gratifiedly and said no more.

A faint medley of sounds blended by distance turned heads towards the east; and presently, breasting the mustard field that lay level and yellow to the hills, came José's squad of vaqueros, with José himself leading the group at a pace that was recklessly headlong, his crimson sash floating like a pennant in the breeze he stirred to life as he charged down upon them.

"Only for the silver trimmings, you looked like a band of warlike Injuns coming down on us with the sun at your back," laughed Dade, as José swung down near him. "They're riders—the Indians back there on the plains; and when they pop over a ridge and come down on you like a tidal wave, your backbone squirms a little in spite of you. The way your vaqueros parted and galloped around our camp was a pretty good imitation of their preliminary flourishes."

"Still, I do not come in war," José returned, and looked full at the other. "I hope that we shall have peace, Señor Hunter; though one day I shall meet that friend of yours in war, if the saints permit. And may the day come soon."

"Whatever quarrel you may have with Jack, I hope it will not hinder us from working together without bad feeling between us." Dade threw away his cigarette and took a step nearer, so that the vaqueros could not hear.

"Don José, I know you don't like a gringo major domo to lead Don Andres' vaqueros on rodeo. I don't blame you Californians for being prejudiced against Americans, because you've been treated pretty shabbily by a certain class of them. But you're not so narrow you can't see that we're not all alike. I'd like to be friends, if you will, but I'm not going to apologize for being a gringo, nor for being here in charge of this camp. I didn't choose my nationality, and I didn't ask for my job. I'll give you a square deal, and I want you to know that if there's any grudge between us, it's all on your side."

José's fingers fumbled the little corn-husk wrapping for the cigarette he meant to make. "Señor, I repeat what I said to Manuel last night," he said, after a pause. "If all gringos were like you, we Californians would like the name better. But I thought you would stand by your friend—"

"And so I will, to the last—" Not being of a theatrical temperament, Dade balked at protestations of his loyalty. "Jack and I have worked and fought and played elbow to elbow for a long time, Don José. But I don't mix into his personal quarrels, unless I see him getting a crooked deal. I believe you'll fight fair. The rest lies between you two."

"But is it not your boast that the Señor Allen is the supreme caballero of California?" José was frank, at least, and Dade liked him the better for it. "For three years I have held the medalla oro [gold medal] for riding and for riata throwing; if it is true that you boast—"

Dade, as was the way of him when disgust or chagrin seized him, flung out both hands impatiently. "I did say he couldn't be beat. I said it to Manuel, when Manuel was sneering that Jack didn't know a good riata from a bad one. I won't take it back. I haven't seen your work in the saddle, Don José. I have seen Jack's, and I never saw any better. So, until I do, I can believe he's the best, can't I?"

"Sí." José smiled without effort. "You are honest, Señor Hunter, and that pleases me well. I do not like you less because you are loyal to your friend; but that friend I hope one day to kill." He looked at the other questioningly. "Now I am honest also," his eyes said plainly.

"That's your affair and Jack's, as long as you don't try to get him when he isn't looking."

"I am not an assassin, Señor Hunter," José retorted stiffly.

"Then we understand each other, I guess. Let's get these fellows started. It's going to be hot, they say, and the horses are soft yet—at least, ours are. We took them off pasture yesterday, most of them."

"Mine are the same, Señor. But to-day's marcha will be an easy one. To Sunal Rancho is not far." He turned to remount and give the signal for starting. And with a little of the pride that had impelled Jack to show off his skill that day when the Captain of the Committee commanded him to mount the buckskin, José also vaulted into the saddle without deigning to touch the stirrup.

There was doubt in the señor's mind about his horsemanship being the best in all California? Very good. The señor would have the opportunity to judge for himself. Still, José had put to sleep most of his antagonism towards Dade, and his attitude of friendliness was not so deliberately forced as Manuel, watching eagerly for the first sign of a clash, believed it to be.

Chapter 15

When Camp-Fires Blink

Down the valley they rode, gathering numbers to swell the cavalcade at each ranch they passed. La Laguna Seca, San Vincente, Las Uvas sent their quota of vaqueros, each headed by a majordomo and accompanied by embaladors with the camp equipment and supplies packed upon steady-going little mustangs. The bell-mares of the various herds jangled a chorus of pleasant discords with their little, iron bells. The scent of the mustard rose pungently under the trampling hoofs. At dusk, the camp-fires blinked at one another through the purpling shadows; and the vaqueros, stretched lazily upon their saddle blankets in the glow, stilled the night noises beneath the pleasant murmur of their voices while they talked. From the camp of the San Vincente riders rose a voice beautifully clear and sweet, above the subdued clamor.

Dade was listening to the song and dreaming a little while he listened, with his head lying cradled in his clasped hands and his face to the stars, when the group around the next camp-fire tittered and broke into an occasional laugh. Then a question was called to whoever might be within hearing:

"Who's the best vaquero in California?"

"Jack Allen, the gringo!" shouted a dozen voices, so that every camp must hear. Then came jeering laughter from every camp save one, the camp of the Picardo vaqueros.

Valencia's dark head lifted from the red and green blanket beyond the blaze; and Dade, watching, could see his profile sharply defined in the yellow light of the fire, as he stared toward the offending camp. The lips that smiled so often were drawn tight and thin; the nostrils flared like a frightened horse. While the laughs were still cackling derision, Valencia jumped up and ran; and Dade, even before he sat up to look, knew where he was going.

At the fire where the question was put, a young fellow, whose heavy, black mustache prudently hid lips coarse and sneering, came to his feet like a dummy of a man and glared dazedly at his companions, as if their faces should tell him whose hand it was that gripped the braided collar of his jacket. He was not long in doubt, however. The voice of Valencia grated vitriolic sentences in his ear, and the free hand of Valencia was lifted to deal him a blow fair upon the blank face of him. The circle of faces watched, motionless, above crouched bodies as quiet as the stars overhead.

A hand grasped Valencia's wrist while his arm was lifted to strike, so that the three men stood, taut-muscled and still, like a shadowy, sculptured group that pictured some mythological conflict.

"Let go, Valencia. This is nothing to fight over. Let go."

Valencia's angry eyes questioned the unreadable ones of his majordomo; but he did not let go, and so the three stood for a moment longer.

"But they insult the Señor Allen with their jeers," he protested. "Me, I fight always for my friends who are not present to fight for themselves. Would not the Señor Allen fight this fool who flouts him so?"

"No!" Dade's eyes flicked the circle of faces upon which the firelight danced. "If the Señor Allen were here, there would be no jeering."

"And for that will I fight them all!" Valencia twisted his arm a little, in the hope that Dade would let go his wrist. "Ah, Señor! Shall a man not be true to his friends?"

"Sí, he shall be true, and he shall be sensible. Is the Señor Jack a weakling, that he cannot fight for himself?"

"But he is not here! If he were—" The tone of him gloated over the picture of what would happen in that case.

"There shall be no fighting." If Dade's voice was quiet, it did not carry the impression of weakness, or indecision. "Come to your own fire, Valencia. If it is necessary to fight for the Señor Allen—I am also his friend."

"You are right. There shall be no fighting." Dade started and glanced at José, standing beside him. "If the Señor Allen thinks himself the best, surely it is I, who hold the medalla that calls me el vaquero supremo, who have the right to question his boast; not you, amigos!"

"Who's the best vaquero, the bravest and the best in California?" queried a voice—the voice of the singer, who had come up with others to see what was going on here. And at his elbow another made answer boldly:

"Don José Pacheco!"

José smiled and lifted his shoulders deprecatingly at the tribute, while fifty voices shouted loyally his name. Dade, pressing his hand upon Valencia's shoulder, led him back into the dancing shadows that lay between the fires.

"Let it go," he urged. "Don José holds the medal, and he's entitled to the glory. We must keep peace, Valencia, or else I
must leave the rodeo. Personal quarrels must wait."

"Sí, Señor, personal quarrels must wait," assented José, again coming up unexpectedly behind them. "I but wish to say that I regret the bad manners of those caballeros, whose best excuse is that they are my friends. I hope the señor does not accuse me of spreading the news of the señor's boast. There are others, as the señor well knows, who heard it before even it came to my ears."

"It doesn't matter," Dade repeated. "They'll have their joke, and I don't blame them for putting the joke on a stranger, especially when he's a gringo—and absent."

"The señor is wise as he is loyal," stated José and bowed himself into the shadows. "Buenos noches, Señor."

"Good-night," answered Dade, speaking English to show he was not ashamed of it; and rolled himself in his blankets as a deliberate hint to Valencia that he did not want to discuss the incident, much to that one's disappointment.

It is to be feared that Valencia did not share in Dade's determination to keep the peace; for, before he slept, he promised himself that he would yet tell that pig-faced vaquero from Las Uvas what he thought of him. But outwardly the incident was closed, and closed permanently.

The sun was not risen above the mountains before they were hurriedly drinking their black coffee, and making ready to break camp; the flurry of emotions seemed to have died with the evening fire. If the men of the other camps were cool in their manner towards Dade when they met him, at least they were civil; except Manuel, who passed him by with lowered brows, and of him Dade took no notice. If he were watched curiously, in hope of detecting the awkwardness which would betray unfamiliarity with his work, Dade took no notice of that, either, except to grin now and then when he rode away.

Altogether, he was well pleased with his reception and inclined to laugh at the forebodings he had felt; forebodings born of the knowledge that, unless these natives of California were minded to tolerate the presence of a gringo majordomo, it would be absolutely useless for him to attempt to work with them.

If he had only known it, his own men had done much towards lessening the prejudice of those who joined the main outfit. Valencia was not the only one of the Picardo vaqueros whose friendship might be counted upon. Like Manuel before he became jealous, they forgot that Dade was not of Spanish birth; for his eyes and his hair were dark as many of the native-born Californians, and his speech was as their own; he was good-humored, just in his judgments, reasonable in his demands. He could tell a good story well if he liked, or he could keep silent and listen with that sympathetic attention that never fails to flatter the teller of a tale. To a man they liked him, and they were not slow to show their liking after the manner of their kind.

By the time they reached Tres Pinos, which was the rendezvous of all the vaqueros from the Picardo ranch on the north to San Miguel on the south, Dade had quite lost the constraint that comes of feeling that one is disliked and only tolerated for the moment. He whistled while he rode along the creek bank looking for a comfortable camp site; and when Valencia loped up to him, as he was hesitating over a broad, shaded strip under a clump of willows, he turned and smiled upon his head vaquero.

"See, Señor, how well we Californians work together!" cried Valencia, pointing pridefully. "Here they come, the vaqueros from Agua Amargo, Durasno, Corral de Terre, Salinas—not yet have our embaladors thrown off the ropes from our packs, before they are here, these others whom we came to meet! Not one hour late, even! And the word was given weeks ago that we would meet this day."

From the mouth of the canyon trotted a band of saddle horses, kicking up a dust cloud that filmed the picture made by the gay caballeros who galloped behind. A gallant company were they; and when they met and mingled with those who came down from the north, it was as though a small army was giving itself a holiday in that vivid valley, with the Tres Pinos gurgling at the fun.

Having had experience in these matters, Dade was able to do his part and do it like a veteran, although he tactfully left to the other majordomos all those little details that would make of the various camps one orderly company. Two men he chose from his outfit and sent to the captain, as the Picardo contribution to the detail told off to herd the horses, but beyond that he confined himself chiefly to making himself as unobtrusive as was consistent with dignity.

Six men were sent out after beef; and although Dade had many times in Texas done exactly what they were doing, he watched interestedly these Californians at their work.

Cattle were everywhere except in the immediate vicinity of the camp. Half a mile or so the vaqueros galloped; then two of the leaders singled out a fat, young steer and made after him with their riatas hissing as the rawhide circled over their heads.

A loop dropped neatly over the wide horns, and a moment later the second settled upon the first. The first man turned and headed towards camp with the steer at his heels, ready at the slightest opportunity to make use of those long, sharp-pointed horns which nature had given him for just such need as this. The steer quite forgot the man behind, until he made a vicious lunge and was checked by the rope that had hung slack and unnoticed over his back. Furious, the steer turned and charged resentfully at the caballero who was following him and shouting taunts. But there again he was checked by the first.

So, charging this way and that; galloping wildly in pursuit of the man who seemed to be fleeing for his life, or wheeling to do battle with the rider who kept just so far in his rear, he was decoyed to the very outskirts of the camp.

If he had been qualified to weigh motives, the heart that brindle-roan steer would surely have burst at; the pure effrontery of the thing: not only must he yield his life and give his body for meat, that those yearning stomachs might be filled with his flesh; he must deliver that meat at the most convenient spot, as a butcher brings our chops to the kitchen door. For that purpose alone they were cunningly luring him closer and closer, that they need not carry the meat far when they had slaughtered him.

At least his last moments were lighted with hope. He made one grand, final dash, tripped in a noose that had somehow dropped neatly in the way of his front feet, and went down with a crash and a bellow of dismay. Some one ran lightly in—he did not see that it was the vaquero he had been pursuing all this time—and drove a dagger into the brain just back of the horns. Thus that particular gust of rage was wiped out of existence forever.

Later, when the camp-fires burned low, the pleasant odor of meat broiling upon the forked ends of long, willow branches over the red coals, proved how even a brindle steer may, at the last, in every savory morsel have justified his existence.

Life in those days was painted upon a big canvas, with broad sweep of brushes dipped in vivid colors. Although the branding of the season's calves was a matter of pure business, the manner in which that work was accomplished was a spectacle upon which we of the present generation would give much to look.

When the sun parted the fog and looked down inquisitively, the whole valley was pulsing with life, alight with color. The first real work of the rodeo was beginning, like the ensemble of some vast, spectacular play; and the stage was managed by Nature herself, creator of the harmony of colors. The dark, glossy green of live oak, the tender green of new willow leaves, the pale green of the mustard half buried in the paler yellow of its blossoms, had here and there a splash of orange and blue, where the poppies were refusing to give place to the lupines which April wished to leave for May, when she came smiling to dwell for one sweet month in the valley. The poppies had had their day. March had brought them, and then had gone away and left them for the April showers to pelt and play with; and now, when the redwoods on the mountainsides were singing that May was almost here, a whole slope of poppies lingered rebelliously to nod and peer and preen over the delights of the valley just below. The lupines were shaking their blue heads distressfully at the impertinence; and then here came the vaqueros galloping, and even the lupines and poppies forgot their dispute in the excitement of watching the fun.

As the roundups of our modern cattlemen "ride circle," so did those velvet-jacketed, silver-braided horsemen gallop forth in pairs from a common center that was the chosen rodeo ground. As if they were tracing the invisible spokes of a huge wheel laid flat and filling the valley from mountain range to mountain range, they rode out until they had reached the approximate rim of the circle. Then, turning, they rode more slowly back to the rodeo ground, driving before them the cattle they found there.

Not cattle only; here and there an antelope herd was caught in the circle and ran bewilderedly toward the common center; beautiful creatures with great eyes beseeching the human things to be kind, even while riatas were hissing over their trembling backs. Many a rider rode into camp with an antelope haunch tied to his gorgeous red and black saddle; and the wooden spits held delicious bits of antelope steak that night, broiling over the coals while the vaqueros sang old Spanish love-songs to lighten the time of waiting.

A gallant company, they. A care-free, laughter-loving, brave company, with every man a rider to make his womenfolk prate of his skill to all who would listen; with every man a lover of love and of life and the primitive joys of life. They worked, that company, and they made of their work a game that every man of them loved to play. And Dade, loving the things they loved and living the life they lived, speedily forgot that there was still an undercurrent of antagonism beneath that surface of work and play and jokes and songs and impromptu riding and roping contests (from which José Pacheco was laughingly barred because of his skill and in which Dade himself was, somehow, never invited to join). He forgot

that the antagonism was there—except when he came face to face with Manuel, perhaps, or when he chanced to see on the face of José a brooding look of dissatisfaction, and guessed that he was thinking of
Jack and Teresita.

Chapter 16

"For Weapons I Choose Riatas"

There must have been a good deal of gossip amongst the vaqueros of the various ranches, as they rode on circle or lay upon their saddle blankets around the evening camp-fires. As is ever the case when a man is young, handsome, rich, and holds proudly the gold medal which proclaims him the champion of the whole State—the golden disk which many a young vaquero longed to wrest from him in a fair test of skill—there were those who would rather like to see José humbled. True, they would never choose an alien to do the humbling, and the possibility was discussed with various head-shakings amongst themselves.

But there were the Picardo vaqueros stanchly swearing by all the saints they knew that these two gringos were not as other gringos; that these two were worthy a place amongst true Californians. Could they not see that this Señor Hunter was as themselves? And he was not more Spanish in his speech and his ways than was the Señor Allen, albeit the Señor Allen's eyes were blue as the lupines, and his hair the color of the madrona bark when it grows dark with age—or nearly the color. And he could shoot, that blue-eyed one!

Valencia, having an audience of a dozen or more one night, grew eloquent upon the prowess of the blue-eyed one. And the audience, listening, vowed that they would like to see him matched against José, who thought himself supreme in everything.

"Not in fighting," amended Valencia, his teeth gleaming white in the fire-glow, as he leaned to pull a brand from the blaze that he might relight the cigarette which had gone out while he told the tale of that running fight, when the two Americanos had shamed a whole crowd of gringos—for so did
Valencia make nice distinction of names.

"Not in fighting, amigos, nor yet in love! And because he knows that it is so, the cheeks of Don José hang slack, and he rides with chin upon his breast, when he thinks no one is looking. The medalla oro is his, yes. But he would gladly give it for that which the Señor Allen possesses. Me, I think that the Señor Allen could as easily win also the medalla oro as he has won the other prize." There was a certain fineness in Valencia that would never permit his tongue to fling the name of the Señorita Teresa amongst these vaqueros; but he was sure that they caught his meaning.

"Dios! me, I should like to see him try," cried a tall San Vincente rider, shifting his position to ease a cramp in his long leg; and his tone was neither contemptuous nor even doubtful, but merely eager for the excitement there would be in the spectacle.

Some one in the shadows turned and walked quickly away to another fire-glow with its ring of Rembrandt figures and faces, and none save Valencia knew that it was Manuel gone to tell his master what had been said. Valencia smiled while he smoked.

Presently José was listening unwillingly to Manuel's spitetinged version of the talk at the San Vincente camp. "The vaqueros are making a mock of thy bravery and thy skill!" Manuel declared, with more passion than truth. "They would see thee beaten, in fight as well as in love—"

The stiffening of José's whole figure stopped Manuel short but not dissatisfied, for he saw there was no need that he should speak a single word more upon the subject.

"They shall see him try, unless he is a coward." The voice of José was muffled by the rage that filled him.

So it came to pass that Manuel saddled his best mustang within an hour and rode away to the north. And when Valencia strolled artlessly to the Pacheco fire and asked for him, José hesitated perceptibly before he replied that Manuel had gone home with a message to the foreman there.

Valencia grinned his widest when he heard that, and over two cigarettes he pondered the matter. Being a shrewd young man with an instinct for nosing out mysteries, he flung all uncertainty away with the stub of his second cigarette and sought Dade.

He found him standing alone beside a deep, still pool, staring at the shadows and the moon-painted picture in the middle, and looking as if his thoughts were gone on far journeys. Valencia was too full of his news to heed the air of absolute detachment that surrounded Dade. He went straight to the heart of his subject and as a precaution against eavesdropping he put his meaning into the best English he knew.

"José, she's dam-mad on Señor Jack," he began eagerly. "She's hear talk lak she's no good vaquero. Me, I hear San Vincente vaqueros talk, and Manuel she's hear also and run queeck for tella José. José she's lak for keela Señor Jack.

Manuel, she's ride lak hell for say José, she lak for fight Señor Jack. Me, I theenk Señor Jack keela José pretty dam-queeck!"

Dade had come to know Valencia very well; he turned now and eyed him with some suspicion.

"Are you sure?" he asked, in the tone that demanded a truthful answer. He had seen Manuel ride away in the white light of the moon, and he had wondered a little and then had forgotten all about it in the spell of utter loneliness which the moon brings to those who are cheated by Fate from holding what they most desire.

"Sure, me." Valencia's tone was convincingly positive. "Manuel, she's go lak hell for tella Señor Jack, José, she's lak
for fight duelo. Sure. That's right."

Dade swung back and stared moodily at the moon-painted pool where the trout, deceived by the brightness into thinking it was day, started widening ripple-rings here and there, where they flicked the surface with slaty noses; and the wavering rings were gold-tipped until they slid into the shadows and were lost. Dade watched three rings start in the center and ripple the whole pool.

"How quick could you get to the rancho?" he asked abruptly, just as Valencia's spirits were growing heavy with disappointment. "Could you overtake Manuel, do you think?"

"Me, I could with the caballo which I have in mind—Noches—I could pass Manuel upon the way, though he had two more hours the start of me!" English was too slow now for Valencia's eagerness. "Manuel is fat, and he is not young, and he will not ride too fast for his fat to endure. Also he will stop at the Pacheco hacienda for breakfast, and to rest his bones. Me, I can be at the rancho two hours before Manuel,
Señor."

Valencia was not a deceitful young man, as deceit goes; but he wanted very much to be sent in haste to the ranch, for he was itching with curiosity to know the truth of this matter and if he were indeed right. If Manuel had gone bearing a challenge from José to the Señor Jack, then he wanted to know the answer as soon as possible. Also there was Felice, the daughter of Carlos, whose lips lured him with their sweetness. Truly, Valencia would promise any miracle of speed.

The pool lay calm as the face of a dead child. Dade stooped and tossed a pebble into it as if that stillness troubled him. He took his cigarette from his lips, looked at the glowing tip, and over it at the eager face of Valencia.

"We mustn't let them fight. Take Noches and ride like the devil was at your heels. Get there ahead of Manuel and tell Jack—" He stopped there and bit his lips to hurry his slow thoughts. "Tell Jack he must go to town right away, because—well, tell him Bill Wilson—"

Valencia's face had been lengthening comically, but hope began to live again in his eyes. "If the señor would write what he wishes to say while I am making ready for the start, he will then have more time to think of what is best. The moon will ride clear to-night; and the sun will find me at the rancho, Señor. Me, I have ridden Noches one hundred miles without

rest, before now; these sixty will be play for us both."

"Gracias, Valencia." Dade dropped a hand gratefully upon the shoulder of the other. "I'll write a note, but you must do your part also. You know your people, and I know Jack; if those two fight, the trouble will spread like fire in the grass; for Don José has many friends to take up the quarrel. You've had a long day in the saddle, amigo, and the sixty miles will not be play. I would not ask it if the need were less urgent—but you must beat Manuel. If you don't, Jack will accept the challenge; and once he does that—" he flung out both hands in his characteristic gesture of impatience or helplessness.

"Sí, Señor. If the saints permit, Manuel shall not see him first." It was like Valencia to shift the responsibility from his own conscience to the shoulders of the saints, for now he could ride with a lighter heart. Perhaps he was even sincere when he made the promise; but there were sixty miles of moonlight in which his desire could ride with him and tempt him; and of a truth, Valencia did greatly desire to see those two come together in combat!

The saints were kind to Valencia, but they were also grimly just. Because he so greatly desired an excuse for delay, they tricked Noches with a broken willow branch that in the deceptive moonlight appeared to be but the shadow of the branch above it. It caught him just under an outflung knee as he galloped and flipped him neatly, heels to the stars. He did not struggle to his feet even when Valencia himself, a bit dazed by the fall, pulled upon the reins and called to him to rise. The horse lay inert, a steaming, black mass in the road. The moon was sliding down behind the Santa Cruz Mountains, and the chill breeze whispered that dawn was coming fast upon the trail of the moonbeams.

Valencia, when he saw that Noches would never gallop again, because he had managed to break his sweat-lathered neck in the fall, sat down beside the trail and rolled a cornhusk cigarette. His mood swung from regret over the passing of as fleet and true a horse as ever he bestrode, to gratitude to the saints for their timely hindrance of his prompt delivery of the note. Truly it was now no fault of his that he could never reach the hacienda before Manuel! He would have to walk and carry his saddle, heavy with silver and wide skirts of stamped leather; and he was a long way from the end of his journey, when he must cover the distance with his own feet. Eight or ten miles, he estimated it roughly; for he had passed José's hacienda some time before, and had resisted the temptation to turn aside and find out if Manuel were there or had gone on. He had not passed Manuel in the trail as he had boasted that he would do, and not once had he glimpsed him anywhere, though there had been places where the road lay straight, and he could see it clear in the moonlight for a mile or more.

When he had finished the cigarette and his thanks to Fate—or whatever power had delayed him—he removed his saddle and bridle from the horse and went on; and it was then that he began to understand that he must do a penance for desiring war rather than peace amongst his fellows. Valencia, after the first hour of tramping with his saddle on his shoulders, had lost a good deal of his enthusiasm for the duel he felt sure was already a certainty.

When he left the road for a straight cut to the hacienda, the wild range cattle hindered him with their curiosity, so that, using all the methods known to a seasoned vaquero for driving them back, his progress had been slow. But he finally came out into the road again and was plodding along the stone wall within half a mile of the house, his face very disconsolate because of his protesting feet and the emptiness in his stomach, when Manuel himself confronted him suddenly coming from the house.

Manuel was looking well pleased with himself, in spite of his night ride. He pulled up and stared wide-eyed at Valencia, who had no smile with which to greet him but swore instead a pensive oath.

"Dios! Is it for a wager that you travel thus?" grinned Manuel, abominably comfortable upon a great, sorrel horse that pranced all round Valencia in its anxiety to be upon its way home. "Look you, Valencia! Since you are travelling, you had best go and tell the padres to make ready the sacrament for your gringo friend, that blue-eyed one; for truly his time on earth is short!"

Valencia, at that, looked up into Manuel's face and smiled in spite of the pain in his feet and the emptiness in his stomach.

"Does it please you, then, Valencia? All night I rode to bear a message to that blue-eyed one who thinks himself supremo in all things; a challenge from Don José, to fight a duelo if he is not a coward; so did José write. 'Unless you are afraid to meet me'—and the vanity of that blue-eyed one is great, Valencia. Of a truth, the man is loco. What think you, Valencia? He had the right to choose the weapons—and José believed that he would choose those pistols of which you make so much talk. Madre de Dios! What says the blue-eyed one, then?—and laughed in my face while he spoke the words! 'Go tell Don José I will fight him whenever and wherever he likes; and for weapons I choose riatas.' Heard you anything—"

"Riatas!" Valencia's jaw dropped an inch before he remembered that Manuel's eyes were sharp and eager to read the thoughts of a man in the twitching muscles of his face.

"Sí, riatas!" Manuel's whole fat body shook with laughter. "Even you, who are wholly bewitched by those gringos, even you are dismayed! Tell me, Valencia, have you seen him lasso anything?"

But Valencia, having pulled himself together, merely lifted his shoulders and smiled wisely, so that even Manuel was almost deceived into believing that Valencia's faith was great because it was built upon a secret knowledge of what the blueeyed one could do.

"Me, I heard you boasting to those San Vincente vaqueros," Manuel accused, shifting the talk to generalities. "And the Señor Hunter boasts also that the blue-eyed one is supremo with the riata, as he is with everything else!" The tone of Manuel was exceeding bitter. "Well, he will have the chance to prove what he can do. No gringo can come among us Californians and flap the wings and crow upon the tule thatch for naught. There has been overmuch crowing, Valencia. Me, I am glad that boaster must do something more than crow upon the thatch, Valencia!"

"Sí, there has been overmuch crowing," Valencia retorted, giving to his smile the lift that made it a sneer, "but the thatch has not been of Picardo tules. Me, I think they grew within hearing of the mission bells of Santa Clara! And the gallo [rooster] which crows is old and fat, and feeds too much upon the grapes that are sour! Adios! I must haste to give congratulations to the Señor Jack, that he will have opportunity to wring the necks of those loud-crowing gallos of the Pacheco thatches."

Whereupon he picked up his saddle and walked on, very straight in the back and patently unashamed of the injustice of his charge; for it was the crowing of Valencia himself beside the San Vincente camp-fire that had brought Manuel with the message, and Valencia knew that perfectly well.

The family of Don Andres had been breakfasting upon the wide veranda when Manuel strode grimly across the patio and confronted them. They were still seated there when Valencia, having deposited his riding gear at the saddle-hut, limped to the steps and stood with his sunny smile upon his face and his sombrero brim trailing the dust. It seemed to Valencia that the don was displeased; he read it in the set of his head, in the hardness that was in his glance, in a certain inflexible quality of his voice.

"Ah, Valencia," he said, rising as if the interruption was to put an end to his lingering there, "you also seem to have ridden in haste from the rodeo. Truly, I think that same rodeo has been but the breeding-ground of gossip and ill-feeling, and is like to bear bitter fruit. Well, you have a message, I'll warrant. What is it?"

Valencia's mien was respectful almost to the point of humility. "The majordomo sent me with a letter, which I was to deliver into the hands of the Señor Allen," he said simply. "My hope was that I might arrive before Manuel"—he caught a flicker of wrath in the eyes of the don at the name and smiled inwardly—"but the moonlight played tricks upon the trail, and my caballo tripped upon a willow-branch and fell upon his head so that his neck was twisted. I was forced to walk and carry the saddle, and there were times when the cattle interrupted with their foolish curiosity, and I must stop and set the riata hissing to frighten them back, else they would perchance have trampled me. So I fear that I arrive too late, Don Andres. But truly I did my best; a full hour behind Manuel I started, and

have walked ten miles of the sixty. The saints know well—"

Don Andres checked his apologies with a wave of the hand, and sat down somewhat heavily in his favorite chair, as if he were tired, though the day was but fairly begun.

"We do not doubt your zeal," he observed dryly. "Give the letter to the señor and begone to your breakfast. And," he added impressively, "wait you and rest well until the answer is ready; for perchance there will be further need to test the kindness of the saints—and the speed of a horse."

Valencia fumbled within his sash and brought forth the small, folded square of paper, went up two steps and placed it in Jack's upturned palm, gave Jack also a glance more kindly and loyal than ever he had received from that minx, Teresita, and went away to the vaqueros' quarters. Valencia had learned nothing from the meeting, except that the don was in one of his rare fits of ill-temper.

"Yet I know that there will be a duelo," he comforted himself with thinking, as he limped wearily across the patio. "The face of the patron is black because of it, and a little devil-flame burns in the eyes of the señorita because for love of her men would fight—(Such is the way of women, to joy in those things which should give them, fear!)—and the señora's face is sagged with worry, and Señor Jack—ah, there is the fighting look in those eyes! Never have I seen them so dark: like the bay when a storm is riding upon the wind. And it will be riatas—for so Manuel told me. Me, I will wager my saddle upon the Señor Jack, even though riatas be the weapons. For he is wily, that blue-eyed one; never would he choose the rawhide unless he knew its hiss as he knows his own heartbeats. Let it be riatas, then, if so the señor chooses!"

Chapter 17

A Fiesta We Shall Have

Jack, unfolding the crumpled paper, read twice the note from Dade, and at each reading gave a little snort. He folded the paper, unfolded it and read again:

"Dear Jack,

"If José wants to fight, take a fool's advice and don't. Better quit the ranch and go back to town for a while—Valencia will get there ahead of Manuel, he says, and you can pull out before Manuel shows up. A licking might do José good, but it would stir up a lot of trouble and raise hell all around, so crawl into any hole you come to. I'll quit as soon as rodeo is over, and meet you in town. Now don't be bull-headed. Let your own feelings go into the discard for once, and do what's best for the whole valley. Everything's going smooth here. Noah's dove ain't got any the best of me and José, and the boys are working fine.

"Dade."

"At least your majordomo agrees with you, Don Andres," he said, twisting the note unthinkingly in his fingers. "Dade wants me to sneak off to town and hide in Bill Wilson's cellar." There was more resentment in his tone than the note itself had put there; for the argument which Valencia had unwittingly interrupted had been threatening to become acrimonious.

"My majordomo," replied Don Andres, his habitual courtesy just saving the words from becoming a retort, "continues to show that rare good sense which first attracted me to him."

The señora moved uneasily in her chair and smiled deprecatingly at Jack, then imploringly at her husband. This was washing day, and those shiftless ones within would overlook half the linen unless she was on the spot to watch and direct. But these two had come to their first clash of wills, and her husband had little liking for such firm defiance of his wishes. Well she knew the little weather-signs in his face. When his eyebrows took just that tilt, and when the nostrils were drawn in and quivered with his breathing, then was it wise that she should remain by his side. The señora knew well that words are never so harsh between the male of our species when their women are beside them. So, suffering mental torment because of the careless peonas, she, nevertheless, sent Teresita after the fine, linen apron from which she meant to remove a whole two inches of woof for the new pattern of drawnwork which the Donna Lucia had sent her. She would remain as a buffer between these two whose eyes were too hard when they looked at each other.

"It seems a pity that young men nowadays cannot contain themselves without quarreling," sighed the señora, acting upon the theory that anger is most dangerous when it is silent, and so giving the conversational ball a push.

"Is there no way, Señor, in which you might avert this trouble? Truly it saddens me to think of it, for José has been as my own son. His mother and I were as twin sisters, Señor, and his mother prayed me to watch over him when she had gone. 'Sí, madre mia' would he tell me, when I gave him the good counsel. And now he comes no more, and he wants to fight the
duelo! Is there no way, Señor?"

The hardness left Jack's lips but not his eyes, while he looked from her to the don, smoking imperturbably his cigar beside her.

"There is no way, Señora, except for a coward. I have done what I could; I know that José's skill is great with riatas, and the choice was mine. I might have said pistols," he reminded her gently, but with meaning.

The plump hands of the señora went betrayingly into the air and her earrings tinkled with the horror that shook her cushiony person. "Not pistols! No, no—for then José would surely be killed! Gracias, Señor! With riatas my José can surely give good account of himself. Three times has he won the medalla oro in fair contest. He is a wizard with the rawhide. Myself, I have wept with pride to see him throw it at the fiestas—"

"Mother mine, Margarita would have you come at once," the señorita interrupted her. "Little Francisco has burned his legs with hot water, and Margarita thinks that your poultice—"

With twittering exclamations of dismay over the, accident the two women hurried away to minister to the burned legs of Francisco, and Jack rose and flung away his cigarette. His mouth had again the stubborn look which Dade knew so well, and dreaded also.

"I am sorry for this unpleasantness," he said perfunctorily, stopping before Don Andres. "But as I told the señora, I have done all that I can do. I have named riatas. I don't think even you, Don Andres, could ask more of me. Surely you wouldn't
want to know that your roof had sheltered a coward?"

Don Andres waved away the challenge which the question carried. "Still, it seems a pity that my family must be made the subject of gossip because of the foolishness of two young men," he said doggedly, returning to his argument. "They will say that it is because of my daughter that you fight; and the friendship of years must be set aside while two hot-heads vent their silly spite—"

"It need not." Jack's head went up an inch. "I can leave your employ, Don Andres, at any moment. There is no need for you to be caught between the duties of hospitality and those of friendship. I can do anything—I am willing to do anything—except crawl into a hole, as Dade wrote for me to do." A fine, spirited picture he made, standing there with the flames of wrath in his eyes and with neck stiff and his jaws set hard together.

Don Andres looked up at him with secret approval. He did not love a coward, and truly, this young fellow was brave. And José had deliberately sought the quarrel from the first; justice compelled him to remember that.

"If it might be arranged—" The don was studying the situation and the man together. "Almost have I grasped the thread that will unravel the whole. No, no! I do not mean your going, Señor. That would but limber the tongue of scandal; and besides, I do not mean that I withdraw my friendship from you. A man must be narrow, indeed, if he cannot carry more than one friendship in his soul.

"Sit you down, Señor, while I think a moment," he urged. "Surely it can be arranged without hurt to the fair name of—of any. Riatas—ah, now I have it, Señor! Dullard, not to have thought of it at once! Truly must I be in my dotage!" He did not mean that, of course, and he was quite openly pleased when Jack smiled and shook his head.

"Listen, Señor, and tell me if the plan is not a good one! Tomorrow Valencia shall ride back to the rodeo, with a message to all from me, Don Andres Picardo. I shall proclaim a fiesta, Señor—such a fiesta as even Monterey never rivaled in the good old days when we were subject to his Majesty, the King. A fiesta we shall have, as soon as may be after the rodeo is over. There will be sports such as you Americanos know nothing of, Señor. And there openly, before all the people, you shall contest with José for a prize which I shall give, and for the medalla oro if you will; for you shall have the privilege of challenging José, the champion, to contest for the medalla. And there will be a prize—and I doubt not—" He was thinking that there would probably be two prizes, though only one which he could proclaim publicly.

"Myself, I shall write to José and beg him to consider the honor of his father's name and of the name of his father's friend, and consent that the duelo shall take place under the guise of sport. It must not be to the death, Señor. Myself, I shall insist that it shall not be to the death. Before all the people, and women, and niños—and besides, I do not wish that José should—" There again he checked himself, and Jack's lips twitched at the meaning he read into the break.

"But if there should be an accident?" Jack's eyes probed for the soul of the old man; the real soul of the Spanish grandee under the broad-minded, easy-natured, Californian gentleman. He probed, and he thought he found what he was seeking; he thought it showed for just an instant in his eyes and in the upward lift of his white mustache.

"An accident would be deplorable, Señor," he said. "We will hope that there will be no accident. Still, José is a very devil when the riata is hissing over his head, and he rides recklessly. Señor, permit me to warn you that José is a demon in the
saddle. Not for nothing does he hold the medalla oro."

"Gracias, Don Andres. I shall remember," said Jack, and walked away to the stables.

He felt that the heart of Don Andres Picardo was warring with his intelligence. That although his wide outlook and his tolerance would make friends of the gringos and of the new government—and quite sincerely—still, the heart of him was true Spanish; and the fortunes of his own blood-kin would send it beating fast or slow in sympathy, while his brain weighed nicely the ethics of the struggle. Jack was not much given to analyzing the inner workings of a man's mind and heart, but he carried with him a conviction that it was so.

He hunted up Diego, and found him putting a deal of gratuitous labor upon the silver trimmings of the new saddle. Diego being the peon in whose behalf Jack had last winter interfered with Perkins, his gratitude took the form of secret polishings upon the splendid riding-gear, the cleaning of Jack's boots and such voluntary services. Now the silver crescents which Teresita ridiculed were winking up at him to show they could grow no brighter, and he was attacking vigorously the "milky way" that rode behind the high cantle. Diego grinned bashfully when Jack's shadow flung itself across the saddle and so announced his coming, and stood up and waited humbly before the white señor who had fought for him, a mere peon, born to kicks and cursings rather than to kindness, and so had won the very soul of him.

"Bueno," praised Jack patronizingly. "Now I have some real work for you, Diego, and it must be done quickly and well."

"Gracias, Señor," murmured Diego, abashed by such favor, and bowed low before his god.

"The riata must be dressed now, Diego, and dressed until it is soft as a silken cord, sinuous as the green snakes that live in the streams, and not one strand must be frayed and weakened. Sabe? Too long have I neglected to have it done, and now it must be done in haste—and done well. Can you dress it so that it will be the most perfect riata in California, Diego?" A twinkle was in Jack's eyes, but Diego was too dazzled by the graciousness of his god to see it there. He made obeisance more humble than before.

"Sí, Señor," he promised breathlessly. "Never has riata been dressed as this riata shall be. By the Holy Mother I swear it."

"Bueno. For listen! Much may hang upon the strength and the softness of it." He fixed his eyes sternly upon the abject one. "It may mean my life or my death, Diego. For in a contest with Don José Pacheco will I use it."

"Sí, Señor," gasped Diego, awed into trembling. "By my soul I swear—"

"You needn't. Save some of your energy for the rawhide. You'll want all you've got before you're through." Jack, having made an impression deep enough to satisfy the most exacting of masters, dropped to his natural tone and speech. "Get some one to help, and come with me to the orchard."

From the saddle-house he brought the six-strand, rawhide riata which Manuel had bought for him and which his carelessness had left still stiff and unwieldy, and walked slowly into the orchard, examining critically each braided strand as he went. Manuel, he decided, was right; the riata was perfect.

Diego, trailing two horsehair ropes and carrying a stout, smooth stick of oak that had evidently been used before for the work, came running after Jack as if he were going to put out a fire. Behind him trotted a big, muscular peon who saw not half the reason for haste that blazoned itself across the soul of Diego.

Thus the three reached the orchard, where Jack selected two pear trees that happened to stand a few feet more than the riata length apart; and Diego, slipping a hair rope through the hondo of the riata, made fast the rope to a pear tree. The other end he tied to the second hair rope, drew the riata taut and tied the rope securely to the second tree. He picked up the oaken stick, examined it critically for the last time, although he knew well that it was polished smooth as glass from its work on other riatas, twisted the riata once around it and signed to the other peon.

Each grasping an end of the stick and throwing all their weight against it, they pushed it before them along the stretched riata. As they strained toward the distant pear tree the rawhide smoked with the friction of the stick in the twist. It was killing work, that first trip from tree to tree, but Diego joyed in thus serving his blue-eyed god. As for the other, Roberto, he strained stolidly along the line, using the strength that belonged to his master the patron just as matter-of-factly as he had used it since he was old enough to be called a man.

Jack, leaning against a convenient tree in the next row, smoked a cigarette and watched their slow, toilsome progress. Killing work it was, but the next trip would be easier after that rendering of the stiff tissue. When the stick touched the hondo, the two stopped and panted for a minute; then Diego grasped his end of the stick and signaled the return trip. Again it took practically every ounce of strength they had in their muscular bodies, but they could move steadily now, instead of in straining, spasmodic jerks. The rawhide sizzled where it curled around the stick. They reached the end and stopped, and Jack commanded them to sit down and have a smoke before they did more.

"It is nothing, Señor. We can continue, since the señor has need of haste," panted Diego, brushing from his eyes the sweat that dripped from his eyebrows.

"Not such haste that you need to kill yourselves at it," grinned Jack, and went to examine the riata. Those two trips had accomplished much towards making it a pliable, live thing in the hands of one skilled to direct its snaky dartings here and there, wherever one willed it to go. Many trips it would require before the riata was perfect, and then—

"The señor is early at his prayers," observed a soft, mocking voice behind him.

Jack dropped the riata and turned, his whole face smiling a welcome. But Teresita was in one of her perverse moods and the mockery was not all in her voice; her eyes were maddeningly full of it as she looked from him to the stretched riata.

"The señor is wise to tell the twists in his riata as I tell my beads—a prayer for each," she cooed. "For truly he will need the prayers, and a riata that will perform miracles of its own accord, if he would fight José with rawhide." There was the little twist of her lips afterward which Jack had come to know well and to recognize as a bull recognizes the red serape of the matador.

"Señor," she added impressively, holding back her hair from blowing across her face and gazing at him wide-eyed, with a wicked assumption of guileless innocence, "at the Mission San José there is a very old and very wise woman. She lives in a tule hut behind the very walls of the Mission, and the Indians go to her by night when dreams have warned them that death threatens. She is a terribly wise old woman, Señor, for she can look into the past and part the curtain which hides the future. For gold will she part it. And for gold will she put the curse or the blessing where curse or blessing is needed most. Go you to the old woman and have her put a blessing upon the riata when it is dressed and you have prayed your prayers upon it, Señor! For five pesos will she bless it and command it to fly straight wherever the señor desires that it shall fly. Then can you meet José and not tremble so that the spur-bells tinkle."

Jack went hot inside of him, but he made his lips smile at the jest; for so do brave men try to make light of torment, whether it be fire or flood or the tongue of the woman they love.

"All right," he said. "And I think I'll have the judges rule that the fight shall be at fifty paces, as I would if we were to fight with pistols." He tried to keep his irritation out of his voice, but there must have been enough to betray him.

For Teresita smiled pleasedly and sent another barb. "It would be wise. For truly, José's equal has never been seen, and caballeros I have known who would swear that José's riata can
stretch to fifty paces and more to find its mark."

"Is it anxiety for me that makes you so solicitous?" demanded Jack, speaking low so that the peons could not overhear.

"Perhaps—and perhaps it is pride; for I know well the skill and the bravery of my José." Again the twist of her pretty, pouting lips, blood-red and tempting.

Her José! For just a minute the face of Teresita showed vague to him before his wrathful eyes.

"When you tell your beads again, Señorita," he advised her crisply, "say a prayer or two for your José also. For I promise you now that I will shame him before your face, and if he lives afterward to seek your sympathy, it will be by grace of my mercy!"

"Santa Maria, what a fierce señor!" Her laughter mocked him. "Till the fiesta I shall pray—for you!" Then she turned and ran, looking over her shoulder now and again to laugh at him.

Always before, when she had teased and flouted and fled laughing, Jack had pursued her with long strides, and in the first sequestered nook had made her lips pay a penalty. But this time he stood still and let her go—which must have puzzled the señorita very much, and perhaps piqued her pride as well. For the girl who flouts and then flees laughing surely invites pursuit and an inexorable exaction of the penalty. And if she is left to flee in safety, then must the flouted one pay for his stupidity, and pay high in the coin of love.

Chapter 18

What Is Love Worth

Valencia swung down from his belathered horse as lightly as though he had not spent seven hours in the saddle and during those seven hours had covered more miles than he would have years to live. His smile was wide and went as deep as his emotions had thus far plumbed his nature, and his voice had the exultant note of a child who has wonderful news to tell. He gave Dade a letter, and his very gesture was triumphant; and the eyes were eager that watched his majordomo read. He bubbled with words that he would like to say, but he waited.

"So you didn't get there in time, after all," Dade observed, looking up from Jack's characteristic signature, in which the tail of the "k" curled around the whole like a mouse lying asleep. "Manuel came back this morning, and the whole camp
is talking nothing but duelo. I thought you said—"

"Señor, the saints would not permit that I should arrive first," Valencia explained virtuously. "A stick tripped Noches and he fell, and broke his neck in the fall. The señor knows well the saints had a hand in that, for hundreds of horses fall every day thus without hurt. Never before in my life have I seen a horse die thus, Señor! I was compelled to walk and carry the saddle, yet such haste I made that Manuel met me by the stone wall as
he was leaving. And at least twelve miles I walked—"

"Oh, all right," Dade waved away further apology. "I reckon you did your best; it can't be helped now. They're going to fight with riatas, Manuel says. Is that right?"

"But not the duelo, Señor—no, but in the contest. For sport, that all may witness, and choose who is champion, after the bull-fighting, and the—"

"What are you talking about, man?" Dade's hand fell heavily upon the shoulder of Valencia, swaying his whole body with the
impact. "Are you loco, to talk of bull-fightings?"

"It is the fiesta, Señor! The patron himself has proclaimed the grand fiesta, such as they have in Monterey, only this will be greater; and then those two will fight their duelo with riatas, yes; but not to the death, Señor. The patron himself has declared it. For the medalla oro and also for a prize will they fight; and the prize—what think you, Señor?"

Valencia, a-quiver with eagerness, laid a slim hand upon the braided front of Dade's close-fitting buckskin jacket.

"The prize will be Solano! That beautiful caballo—beautiful even as thy Surry—which the patron has not permitted rawhide to touch, except for the branding. Like the sunshine he is, with his hair of gold; and the tail that waves to his heels is like the ripples on the bay at sunrise. Who wins the duelo shall have Solano for his own, and shall ride him before all the people; for such is the patron's word. From his own lips I heard it! Me, I think that will be the greatest sport of all, for he is wild as the deer on the mountain slopes—that yellow caballo, and strong as the bull which the patron will choose to fight the grizzly he will bring from the mountains.

"Listen, Señor! The mother of Solano was a she-devil under the saddle, and killed two men by throwing herself upon them; and the sire was Satanas, of whom stories are told around the camp-fires as far south as San Luis Obispo.

"Ah, he is wise, the patron! 'Then let them also prove their courage in other ways. Let the victor pray to the saints and ride Solano, who is five years old and has never felt the riata since he left his mother's side—who was a devil.' Me, I heard the soul of the patron speak thus, while the lips of the patron said to me:

"'Go back to the rodeo, Valencia, and proclaim to all that I will give the grand fiesta with sports to please all. Tell them that already two have agreed to contest with riatas for a prize—' Look you, Señor, how wily is the patron!—'And for the prize I name the gelding, Solano, who has never known weight of saddle. Tell them, Valencia, that the victor shall ride his prize for all the crowd to see. And if he is thrown, then Solano will be forfeit to the other, who must ride him also. There will be other sports and other prizes, Valencia, and others may contest in riding, in the lassoing and tying of wild steers, in running. But say that Don José Pacheco and the Señor Jack Allen will contest with riatas for the possession of Solano.' Ah, Señor—"

"Ah, Valencia, why not scatter some of your enthusiasm over the other camp-fires?" Dade broke in quizzically. "Go and proclaim it, then. Tell the San Vincente men, and the Las Uvas, and all the other vaqueros."

Valencia, grinned and departed, leaving behind him in the loose sand tracks more than three feet apart to show how eager was his obedience; and Dade sat down upon a dead log that had been dragged to the Picardo camp-fire, to consider how this new phase of the affair would affect the temper of the people who owned such warm hearts and such hot heads.

A fiesta, with the duelo fought openly under the guise of a contest for the medal and a prize which was well worth any man's best efforts—surely, Don Andres was wily, as Valencia said. But with all the people of the valley there to see, their partisanship inflamed by the wine of festivity and the excitement of the sports themselves—what then?

Dade thoughtfully rolled a corn-husk cigarette, and tried to peer into the future. As it looked to him, he and Jack were rather between the devil and the deep sea. If Jack were beaten, they would be scorned and crowed over and humiliated beyond endurance. Neither was made of the stuff to stand much of that, and they would probably wind up with both hands and their hats full of trouble. And to himself he admitted that there was a fair chance of that very result. He had not been blind, and José had not shrunk into the background when there was riata-work and riding to be done on the rodeo ground. Dade had watched him as jealously as it was in his nature to do, and the eyes of jealousy are keen indeed; and he had seen José make many throws, and never a miss. Which, if you know anything of rope-work, was a remarkable record for any man. So there was a good chance of José winning that fight. In his heart
Dade knew it, even if his lips never would admit it.

Well, supposing José was beaten; suppose Jack won! What then? Dade blew a mouthful of smoke towards the camp-fire, deserted except for himself, while his vaqueros disported themselves with their neighbors, and shook his head. He had a little imagination; perhaps he had more than most men of his type. He could see a glorious row, if José were beaten. It would, on the whole, be more disastrous than if he won.

"And she's just fickle-minded enough to turn up her nose at Jack if he got beat," Dade grumbled, thinking of a certain señorita. "And if he don't, the whole bunch will pile onto us. Looks to me like a worse combination than that Vigilance row, for Jack. If he wins, he gets knifed; if he don't, he gets hell. And me the only one to back him up! I'll wish I was about forty men seven foot high and armed with—"

"Pardon, Señor. The señor has of course heard the news?" José came out of the shadows and stood with the firelight dancing on his face and picking out the glittery places on his jacket, where was the braid. "I have a letter from Don Andres. Would the señor care to read it? No? The señor is welcome to read. I have no wish to keep anything hidden which concerns this matter. I have brought the letter, and I want to say that the wishes of my friend, Don Andres, shall be granted. Except," he added, coming closer, "that I shall fight to the death. I wish the Señor Allen to understand this, though it must he held a secret between us three. An accident it must appear to those who watch, because the duelo will be

proclaimed a sport; but to the death I will fight, and I trust that the Señor Allen will
fight as I fight. Does the señor understand?"

"Yes, but I can't promise anything for Jack." Dade studied José quietly through the smoke of his cigarette. "Jack will fight to please himself, and nobody can tell how that will be, except that it won't be tricky. He may want to kill you, and he may not. I don't know. If he does, he'll try his damnedest, you can bank on that."

"But you, Señor—do you not see that to fight for a prize merely is to belittle—" José waved a hand eloquently.

"I see you're taking life pretty serious," Dade retorted, moving farther along the log. "Sit down, José, and be sociable. Nothing like seeing the point of a joke, if there is one. Do you reckon anything's worth all the heart-burnings you're indulging in? Some things are tough; I've waded kinda deep, myself, so I know. But there's nothing you can't get over, with time and lots of common sense, except being a sneak—and being dead. To me, one's as bad as the other, with maybe first choice on death. You aren't a sneak, and I don't see why you hanker to be
dead. What do you want to fight to the death for?"

[Illustration: "An accident it must appear to those who watch"]

José did not sit down beside Dade, but he came a little closer, "Why do I want to fight to the death? I will tell you, Señor; I am not ashamed. Since I was a child I have loved that señorita whom I will not name to you. Only last Christmas time the señora, her mother, said I must wait but a year longer till she was a little older. They would keep their child a little longer, and truly her heart is the heart of a child. But she knew; and I think she waited also and was happy. But look you, Señor!
Then comes a stranger and steals—

"Ah, you ask me why must I fight to the death? Señor, you are a man; perchance you have loved—for of a truth I see sometimes the sadness in your eyes. You know that I must fight thus. You know that to kill that blue-eyed one is all there is left to do. Me, I could have put him out of the way before now, for there are many knives ready to do me the service. Kill him I shall, Señor; but it shall be in fight; and if the señorita sees—good. She shall know then that at least it is not a coward or a weakling who loves her. Do you ask why—"

Dade's hands went out, dismissing the question. "No, I don't ask another blamed thing. Go ahead and fight. Fight to kill, if that's the only thing that will satisfy you. You two aren't the first to lock horns over a woman. Jack seems just as keen for it as you are, so I don't reckon there's any stopping either one of you. But it does seem a pity!"

"Why does it seem a pity?" José's tone was insistent.

"It seems a pity," Dade explained doggedly, "to see two fine fellows like you and Jack trying to kill each other for a
girl—that isn't worth the life of either one of you!"

In two steps José confronted him, his hand lifted to strike. Dade, looking up at him, flicked the ashes from his cigarette with his forefinger, but that was the only move he made. José's hand trembled and came down harmlessly by his side.

"I was mistaken," he said, smiling queerly. "You have never loved any woman, Señor; and I think the sadness I have seen in your eyes is for yourself, that life has cheated you so. If you had known love, you could never have said that. Love, Señor, is worth everything a man has to give—even his life. You would know that, if you had ever loved." He waited a moment, closed his teeth upon further words, turned abruptly on his heel and went away into the fog-darkened night.

Dade, with a slight curl to his lips that did not look quite like a smile, stared into the fire, where the embers were growing charred for half their length, and the flames were waving wearily and shrinking back to the coals, and the coals themselves were filmed with gray. The cigarette went cold and clammy in his fingers, and in his eyes was that sadness of which José had spoken; and something else besides.

They would fight, those two, and fight to kill. Since the world was first peopled, men had fought as they would fight—for love; for the possession of a pretty thing—warm, capricious, endearing, with possibly a heart and a soul beneath; possibly. And love—what was love, after all? What is love worth? He had loved her, too; at least, he had felt all the emotions that either of them had felt for her. He was not sure that he did not still feel them, or would if he let himself go. He did not believe, however, that those emotions were worth more than everything else in the world; more than his life, or honor, or friendship. He had choked love, strangled it, starved it for sake of friendship; and, sitting there staring abstractedly into the filming coals, he wondered if he had done wrong; if those two were right, and love was worth fighting for.

The man who fought the hardest, he felt, would in this case win that for which he fought. For he felt in his heart, that Teresita was only a pretty little animal, the primitive woman who would surrender to strength; and that he would win in the end who simply refused to yield before her coquetries.

With a quick, impatient gesture he threw his cigarette into the coals, kicked viciously a lazily smoking brand which sent up a little blaze and a spurt of sparks that died almost immediately to dull coals again.

"Love's like that," he muttered pessimistically, standing up and stretching his arms mechanically. "And the winner loses in the end; maybe not always, but he will in this case. Poor old Jack! After all, she ain't worth it. If she was—" His chin went down for a minute or two, while he stared again at the fire. "If she was, I'd—But she ain't. Love's worth—what is love worth, anyway?"

He did not answer the question with any degree of positiveness, and he went to bed wishing that he had never seen the valley of Santa Clara.

Chapter 19

Anticipation

To give a clear picture of the preparations for that fiesta, one should be able to draw with strokes as swift as the horses that galloped up and down the valley at the behest of riders whose minds titillated with whatever phase of the fiesta appealed to them most; and paint with colors as vivid as were the dreams of the women, from the peonas in the huts to the señoritas and señoras murmuring behind the shelter of their vines.

One would need tell of those who went boldly into the mountains to find a grizzly bear and bring it alive and unhurt to the pen, which the peons, with feverish zeal and much chattering amongst themselves, were building close beside the smallest corral.

A great story it would make—the tale of that hunt! A man came back from it with a forearm torn sickeningly, to show how brave he had been. And the bear came also—a great, gaunt she-bear with two cubs whimpering beside her in the cage, and in her eyes a sullen hunger for the giant redwoods that stood so straight and strong together upon the steep slopes while they sang crooningly the songs she knew of old, and a glowing hatred for her captors.

A story that would make! A story in which Jerry Simpson and Tige played valiant part and bore more than their share of the danger, and became heroes to those who went with them.

One would need to picture somehow the bubbling excitement of Teresita, while she planned and replanned her festal garments, and tell how often she found it necessary to ride with Jack across the valley to talk the matter over with the "pretty Señora" Simpson, or to the Mission San José to see what Rosa had at last decided to wear.

Then, there would be the solemn conferences in the kitchen, between Margarita and the señora herself; conferences that had to do with cakes and preserves and the like, with the niños getting in every one's way, while they listened and smacked lips over the very naming of so many good things to eat.

One would need see the adobe corral that was to be transformed into an amphitheater where were hammering and clatter from sunrise till dark, without even a pause for midday siesta amongst those lazy peons who would sleep over their cigarettes, though the padres stood over them predicting the end of the world the next moment.

Well in the foreground of the picture would be Jack, to be sure; Jack riding far afield upon Surry, whom he had found the best horse for his purpose upon the whole ranch; lassoing cattle to get his hand in, practising certain little twists of his own invention, and teaching Surry to know without fail just what certain signals meant, and obey instantly and implicitly when they were given.

Sometimes, when the señorita was not in a perverse mood, she would ride with him and applaud his dexterity; at other times she would boast of José's marvelous skill, and pity Jack in advance for the defeat which she pretended was inevitable. Whether she pitied or praised, she seemed always sincere for the moment, so that Jack gave up any lingering hope of knowing how she really felt about it, and contented himself with the determination to deflect all the pity towards José when the time came, and keep the praise for himself.

There would be other contests; and scarce a day passed wherein no horse loped heavily up the slope and stopped with heaving flanks in the patio, while its rider dismounted and bowed low before Don Andres, giving news of some vaquero who wished his name to be listed as a contestant in the riding, or the lassoing and tying of steers, or in the bull-fight, perchance.

But there was no third name offered in the riata contest for which Solano was announced as a prize. All up and down the valley; at the ranches, on the trails when men met and stopped to talk awhile, and around the camp-fires of the rodeo they talked of it; and many bets would have been laid upon the outcome, had not all men been of one mind. When José was not present, or Dade, or the more outspoken of the Picardo vaqueros, always they spoke of it as the duelo riata, and took it for granted that it would be fought to the death. Thus are secrets kept from men who can read from their own natures the truth! The men of Santa Clara lowered lids and smiled whenever they spoke of it as a contest, for as a duel had the word first gone forth from the exultant lips of Manuel; as a duel would it still remain among themselves, spite of the fiesta and the prize that was offered, and the reiteration that it was but sport.

One should picture the whole valley for the background; a sunken paradise of greenery, splotched with color, made alive with bird-songs and racing cloud-shadows on the grass; with the wooded slopes of the Santa Cruz mountains closing in upon the west and sheltering it from the sweeping winds from off the ocean, and the grassy hills rising high and rugged on the east, giving rich pasturage to the cattle and all the wild things that fed there.

When it was complete—that picture—then might one weep to be there in the midst of it all! For there would be much laughter, and the love-making would make young pulses beat fast to think upon. There would be dancing, and the tinkle of guitars and mandolins, and a harp or two to beat a harmonious surf-song beneath the waves of melody. There would be feasting, with whole beeves roasted over pits which the peons were already digging in their dreams; with casks of wine from the don's own vineyard to wash down the juicy morsels. There would be all that throughout one long, moonlit night, with the day of sports to think back upon. And through the night they would talk of the duelo riata between two men who loved one little señorita who laughed much and cared little, said certain wise señoras, and nodded their heads while they said it.

What if some hearts were bitter over the prospect? From Santa Barbara, even, were they coming to the fiesta! (Gustavo had the news from a peon who came straight through from
Paso Robles on an errand for his master.)

What if Dade, thinking and thinking until his brain was dizzy, lay long hours awake in his blankets and stared up at the starsprinkle in the purple night-sky, trying to find a path that would lead to peace? The señorita lay awake also, thinking smilingly that she had nearly finished the embroidery upon the bodice she meant to wear, and that the pretty señora had promised to do her black hair in a new and wonderful way that should smart with envy the eyes of all the other señoritas when they saw; and that the señora her mother had reluctantly promised that she should wear the gold chain with the rubies glowing along every little thumb-length of it; thinking also, perhaps, of how she had made the Señor Jack's eyes grow dark and then flash anger-lights, when she taunted him again about going to the wise old woman at the Mission San José for a charm to make the riata fly true!

What if the old don, seeing also that trouble hung like a vulture over the feast, paced uneasily up and down the vine-hidden veranda, while he meditated upon the follies of youth? The young steers that had been driven in for the roasting-pits were trampling uneasily about the little corral where they had been put to fatten; and Gustavo walked with his head thrown back upon his shoulders that he might read that open page which was the sky, and to any anxious ones who asked, he had but one answer and that a comforting one:

"The day will be a day of sunshine, with linnets singing in the trees and the smallest breeze to cool the cheek." The anxious ones, hearing so good an augury, would pass on, their thoughts upon the day-of-days and on their lips a little smile.

Chapter 20

Lost ! Two Hasty Tempers

"One more throw, and then no more until the contest," Jack announced placatingly, when he spied a lone bull standing just before a thicket of chaparral and staring at them with stupid resentment that his siesta had been disturbed. "A kiss for luck, little one!"

Riata coiled in his hand, Jack rode closer and leaned to the girl, his eyes and his voice caressing, his lips quivering for the kiss he craved. It had come to kisses long before then, and to half promises, when her mood was tender, that she would marry her blue-eyed one—sometime.

Just now her mood was not tender. Jack was not to blame, nor was the pretty Señora Simpson, although Mrs. Jerry was quite innocently and unconsciously the cause. Mrs. Jerry had a headache, that day, and a fit of the blues; and from the first moment when Teresita had entered the cabin she had felt a lack of warmth in the pretty señora's manner that had piqued her, who had lived upon adoration all her life. Mrs. Jerry had even shown a disposition to shirk keeping her promise anent the new way of doing Teresita's hair.

She said that she didn't think she'd go to the fiesta, after all—which was like calmly telling a priest that one does not, after all, feel as if heaven is worth striving for.

Teresita failed to see how the wistfulness was quite submerging the twinkle in Mrs. Jerry's eyes, and if she had seen, she would never have guessed what put it there; nor would she have understood why Mrs. Jerry might shrink from attending that magnificent festival, perhaps the only gringo woman in all the crowd, and a pitifully shabby gringo woman at that. To her mind, Mrs. Jerry was beautiful and perfect, even in her shapeless brown dress that was always clean. Teresita herself would never have worn that dress at all, yet it did not occur to her that Mrs. Jerry might have some very feminine quality of pride crowded down into some corner of her sweet nature. So Teresita was mightily offended at what she considered a slight from the only gringo woman she had ever known; and she was also bitterly disappointed over the abandonment of the new coiffure.

"Why don't you wear it just the way it is, honey?" Mrs. Jerry had suggested— and very sensibly, too. "I wouldn't go and twist it all up and stick pins through it, if I was you. It's prettier just that way."

Teresita had understood enough of that, thanks to the teachings of her blue-eyed one, to know that the pretty señora did not mean to keep her promise. She had gone almost immediately to the cabin door to tell Jack that she was ready to go home. And Jack, deep in one of those interminable conversations with Jerry himself, over on the pile of logs that would one day be a stable if Jerry's hopes reached fruition, had merely waved his hand carelessly when he saw her, and had given all his attention to Jerry again.

Of course, Teresita could not know that they were discussing a brief but rancorous encounter which Jerry had had with Manuel that morning, when the two happened to meet farther down the valley while Manuel was riding his share of the rodeo circle. Two of José's men had been with Manuel, and their attitude had been "purty derned upstropolus," according to Jerry. (Jack decided after a puzzled minute that the strange word which Jerry spoke with such relish must be Simpsonese for obstreperous.) They had, in fact, attempted to drive off three of Jerry's oxen to the rodeo ground, and only the characteristic "firmness" of Jerry had prevented them from doing it. Jemina, he said, had helped some when pointed at Manuel's scowling face; but Jerry opined that he would hereafter take the twins along too when he rode out anywhere, and that he guessed he'd cut another loophole or two in his cabin walls.

All of these various influences had created an atmosphere which Teresita felt and resented without attempting to understand. The big señor had not given her the smiles and the funny attempts at conversation which she had come to accept as a matter of course. The pretty señora had not been as enthusiastic as she should have been, when Teresita showed her the ruby chain which, like a child, she had brought over for the pretty señora to admire.

Therefore, Jack's lips found reason to tighten and cease their eager quivering for a kiss. For Teresita twitched her shoulders pettishly and her reins dexterously, and so removed herself some distance from the kissing zone.

"No? Well, I'll have to depend on my good riata, then. I'll take that gentleman at twenty-five feet, and if I can get him to run
right, I'll heel him. Don't ride any closer, Teresita."

He had not called her dulce corazon (sweetheart) as she had expected him to call her; he had not even insisted upon the kiss, but had given up altogether too tamely; and for that she rode closer to the bull in spite. She even had some notion of getting in Jack's way, and of making him miss if she could. She was seventeen, you see, and she was terribly spoiled.

Jack had never made any attempt to study the psychological twists of a woman's nature. He contented himself with loving, and with being straightforward and selfish and a bit arrogant in his love, after the manner of the normal man. It would never occur to him that Teresita was piqued because he had not called her sweetheart, and he straightway sinned more grievously still.

"Go back, the other way! He's liable to start in your direction," he cried, intent upon her safety and his own whim to rope the beast.

Teresita deliberately kicked her horse and loped forward.

It would not be nice to say that bulls are like some humans, but it is a fact that they are extremely illogical animals, full of impulses and whims that have absolutely no relation to cause or effect. This bull had not moved except to roll his eyes from one to the other of the riders. If he meditated war he should, by all the bovine traditions of warfare, have bellowed a warning and sent up a whiff or two of dirt over his back, as one has a right to expect a pessimistic bull to do. Instead of which he flung down his head and made an unexpected rush at Teresita—and Jack had left his pistols at home.

Jack's riata was coiled in his hand and his head was turned towards the girl, his brain busy with his thoughts of her and her wilfulness. From the tail of his eye he caught the first lunge of the bull, and that automatic mental adjustment to unexpected situations, which we call presence of mind, sent a knee-signal to Surry which that intelligent animal obeyed implicitly.

Surry rushed straight at the bull, but the triangle was a short one, and there was much to do in that quarter of a minute. Teresita was stubborn and would not turn and run; but she happened to be riding Tejon, who knew something about bulls and was capable of acting upon his knowledge. He whirled with hind feet for a pivot and ducked away from the horns coming at him, and it was not one second too soon. The bull swept by, so close that a slaver of foam was flung against Teresita's skirt as he passed.

He whirled to come back at the girl—and that time he seemed sure to give that vicious, ripping jab he had so narrowly missed giving before; even the girl saw that he would, and turned a little pale, and Tejon's eyes glazed with terror.

But Jack had gained the second he needed—the second that divided adventure from tragedy. The riata loop shot from his upflung hand and sped whimperingly on its errand, even as Tejon tried to swing away, tripped, and tumbled to his knees. The riata caught the lifted forefeet of the bull just as he stiffened his neck for the lunge. Surry braced himself automatically when Jack drew tight the loop, and the bull went down with a thud and lay with his forefeet held high in air, so close to his quarry that the tip of one horn struck Tejon upon the knee and flicked a raw, red spot there.

Then Jack, in the revulsion from deadly fear to relief, was possessed by one of those gusts of nervous rage that seized him sometimes; such a brief fit of rage as made him kill lustfully three men in the space of three heart-beats, almost, and feel regret because he could not keep on killing.

He did not run to Teresita and comfort her for her fright, as a lover ought to have done. Instead he gave her one look as he went by, and that a look of indignation for her foolishness. He ran to the bull, drew his knife from his sash and tried to stab it in the brain; but his hand shook so that he missed and only gave it a glancing gash that let much blood flow. He swore and struck again, snapping the dagger blade short off against the horns. Whereupon he threw the dagger violently from him and gave an angry kick at the animal, as if he would kill it that way.

"Savage!" cried Teresita, hysterically shrill. "Brute! Leave the poor thing alone! It has done nothing, that you should beat it while it cannot fight back."

Jack, lifting his spurred foot for another kick, set it down and turned to her dazedly.

In her way as shaken by her narrow escape as he was himself, she straightway called him brute and savage again, and sentimentally pitied the bull because he lay upon his back with his front feet in the air, and because the gash on his head was bleeding.

Jack's rage passed as quickly as it came; but it left him stubborn under her recriminations.

"You are very soft-hearted, all of a sudden, señorita," he said, with a fairly well-defined sneer, when he could bear no more. "You won't enjoy the bull-fighting, then, to-morrow—for all you have been looking forward to it so anxiously, and have robbed yourself of ribbons to decorate the darts. It's not half so brutal to kill a bull that tries to kill you, as it is to fill it with flagtrimmed arrows for fun, and only put it out of its misery when you're tired of seeing it suffer! This bull came near killing you!
That's why I'm going to kill it."

"You are not! Santa Maria, what a savage beast you are! Let
him go instantly! Let him go, I say!"

If she had been on the ground, she would have stamped her foot. As it was, she shook an adorably tiny fist at Jack, and blinked her long lashes upon the tears of real, sincere anger that stood in her black eyes, and gritted her teeth at him; for the señorita had a temper quite as hot as Jack's, when it was roused, and all her life she had been given her own way in everything.

"Let him go this moment, or I shall never speak to you again!" she threatened rashly.

For answer, Jack walked deliberately past her to where Surry stood with his feet braced still against the pull of the riata and his neck arched knowingly, while he rolled the little wheel in the bit with his tongue. Jack made himself a cigarette, lay down in the shade of his horse, and smoked just as calmly as though his heart was not thumping so that he could hear it quite plainly. She had gone the wrong way about making him yield; threats had always acted like a goad upon Jack's anger, just as they do upon most of us.

Teresita looked at him in silence for a minute. And Jack, his head upon his arm in a position that would give him a fair view of her from the brim of his sombrero while he seemed to be taking no notice of her, wondered how soon she would change her mood to coaxing, and so melt that lump of obstinacy in his throat that would not let him so much as answer her vixenish upbraidings. A very little coaxing would have freed the bull then, and he would have kissed the red mouth that had reviled him, and would have called her "dulce corazon," as she loved to have him do. Such a very little coaxing would have been enough!

"Dios! How I hate a gringo!" she cried passionately, just when Jack believed she was going to cry "Señor Jack?" in that pretty, cooing tone she had that could make the words as tender as a kiss. "José is right. Gringos are savages and worse than savages. Stay and torture your bull, then! I hate you! Never have I known hate, till now! I shall be glad when José drags you from your horse to-morrow. I shall laugh and clap my hands, and cry, 'Bravo, bravo, querido mio!' [my beloved] when you are flung into the dirt where you belong. And when he kills you, I shall kiss him for his reward, before all the people, and I shall laugh when they fling you to the coyotes!" Yes, she said that; for she had a temper—had the Señorita Teresita—and she had a tongue that could speak words that burned like vitriol.

She said more than has been quoted; epithets she hurled upon the recumbent form that seemed a man asleep save for the little drift of smoke from his cigarette; epithets which she had heard the vaqueros use at the corrals upon certain occasions when they did not know that she was near; epithets of which she did not know the meaning at all.

"Bravo!" applauded some one, and she turned to see that Manuel and Carlos, José's head vaquero, had ridden up to the group very quietly, and had been listening for no one knew how long.

The señorita was so angry that she was not in the least abashed by the eavesdropping. She smiled wickedly, drew off a glove and tossed it to Manuel, who caught it dexterously without waiting to see why she wanted him to have it.

"Take that to José, for a token," she cried recklessly. "Tell him I have put a wish upon it; and if he wears it next his heart in the duelo to-morrow he will win without fail. Tell José I shall ask the Blessed Virgin to-night to let no accident befall him, and that I shall save the first two dances for him and none other!"

She was not a finished actress, because of her youth. She betrayed by a glance his way that she spoke for Jack's benefit. And Jack, in the hardening of his stubborn anger, blew a mouthful of smoke upward into a ring which the breeze broke almost immediately, and laughed aloud.

Teresita heard, bit her lips cruelly at failing to bring that stubborn gringo to his feet—and to hers!—and wheeled Tejon close to Manuel and Carlos. She rode away between the two towards home, and she did not once look behind her until she had gone so far she feared she could not see what her blueeyed one was doing. Then she turned, and her teeth went together with a click. For Jack was lying just as she had left him, with his head upon his arm as if he might be asleep.

Chapter 21

Fiesta Day

Dade, rolling over in bed and at the same moment opening his eyes reluctantly upon the new day, that he hated, beheld Jack half-dressed and shaving his left jaw, and looking as if he were committing murder upon an enemy. Dade watched him idly; he could afford the luxury of idleness that morning; for rodeo was over, and he was lying between linen sheets on a real bed, under a roof other than the branches of a tree; and if his mind had rested as easily as his body, he would have been almost happy.

But this was the day of the fiesta; and with the remembrance of that vital fact came a realization that on this day the Picardo ranch would be the Mecca toward which all California was making pilgrimage; and, he feared, the battle-ground of the warring interests and prejudices of the pilgrims themselves.

Dade listened to the voices shouting orders and greetings without as the vaqueros hurried here and there in excited preparations for the event. He judged that not another man in the valley was in bed at that moment, unless sickness held him there; and for that very reason he pulled a blanket snugger about his ears and tried to make himself believe that he was enjoying to the full his laziness. He had earned it; and last night had been the first one of deep, unbroken sleep that he had had since that moonlit night when Manuel and Valencia rode in haste to meet this surly-browed fellow before him.

Jack did not wipe off the scowl with the lather, and Dade began to observe him more critically; which he had not before had an opportunity to do, for the reason that Jack had not returned to the ranch the night before until Dade was in bed and asleep.

"Say, you don't want to let the fellows outside see you looking like that," he remarked, when Jack had yanked a horn comb through his red-brown mop of hair as if he were hoeing corn.

"Why?" Jack turned on him truculently.

"Well, you look a whole lot like a man that expects a licking. And I don't see any excuse for that; you're sure to win, old man. I'd bet my last shirt on that." Which was Dade's method of wiping off the scowl.

"Say, Dade," Jack began irrelevantly, "I'm going to use Surry. You don't mind, do you? He's the best horse I ever threw a rope off from, without any exceptions. I've been training him up a little, and I tell you what, Surry's going to have a lot to do with that duel."

Dade sat up in bed as if he had been pulled up. "Jack, are you going to make it a sure-enough duel?" he asked anxiously.

"Why?" Jack's eyes hardened perceptibly. "That's what José wants."

"Do you want it?" Dade scowled absent-mindedly at the wall, felt the prick of an unpleasant thought, and glanced sharply at Jack.

"Say, I feel sorry for José," he began straightforwardly. "As a man, I'd like him fine, if he'd let me. And, Jack, you've got everything coming your way, and—well, seems like you might go easy on this fight, no matter what José wants. He's crazy jealous, of course—but you want to recollect that he has plenty of cause. You've stepped in between him and a girl he's known
all his life. They were practically engaged, before—"

"I don't know as José's love affairs interest me," put in Jack harshly. "Do you care if I use Surry? I kinda took it for granted it would be all right, so I went ahead and trained him so I can bank on him in a pinch."

"Of course you can use him." That Dade's hesitation did not cover more than a few seconds was proof of his absolute loyalty to Jack. Not another man living could have used Surry in a struggle such as that would be; a struggle where the danger was not all for the rider, but must be shared equally by the horse. Indeed, Dade himself would not have ridden him in such a contest, because his anxiety lest Surry should be hurt would have crippled his own dexterity. But Jack wanted to ride Surry, and Dade's lips smiled consent to the sacrifice.

"All right, then. That horse is sure a wonder, Dade. Sensible? You never saw anything like it! I never saw a horse so sensitive to—well, I suppose it's muscular reactions that I'm unconscious of. I've tried him out without a bridle on him; and, Dade, I can sit perfectly still in the saddle, and he'll turn wherever I make up my mind to go! Fact. You try it yourself, next time you ride him. So I've cultivated that faculty of his, this last month.

"And besides, I've got him trained to dodge a rope every time. Had Diego go out with me and try to lasso me, you know. I had one devil of a time with the Injun, too, to make him disrespectful enough to throw a rope at me. But Surry took to it like a she-bear to honey, and he's got so he can gauge distances to a hair, now, and dodge it every pass. I'm going to ride him to-day with a hackamore; and you watch him perform, old man! I can turn him on a tin plate, just with pressing my knees. That horse will—"

"Say, you're stealing my thunder," drawled Dade, grinning. "That's my privilege, to sing Surry's praises. Haven't I told you, right along, that he's a wonder?"

"Well, you told the truth for once in your life, anyway. Get up, you lazy devil, and come out and take a look at him. I'm going to have Diego give him a bath, soon as the sun gets hot enough. I've got a color scheme that will make these natives bug their eyes out! And Surry's got to be considerably whiter than snow—"

"Huh!" Dade was watching him closely while he listened. For all Jack's exuberance of speech, there was the hard look in his eyes still; and there was a line between his eyebrows which Dade had never noticed there before, except as a temporary symptom of anger. He had, Dade remembered, failed to make any statement of his intentions toward José; which was not like Jack, who was prone to speak impulsively and bluntly his mind. Also, it occurred to Dade that he had not once mentioned Teresita, although, before the rodeo his talk had been colored with references to the girl.

"Oh, how's the señorita, by the way?" Dade asked deliberately.

"All right," returned Jack promptly, with a rising inflection,
"Are you going to get up, or shall I haul you out by the heels?" Dade, observing an evasion of that subject also, did some hard thinking while he obediently pulled on his clothes. But he said not a word more about the duel, or José's love-tragedy, or
Teresita.

Since the first flush of dawn the dismal squeal of woodenwheeled ox-carts had hushed the bird songs all up and down El Camino Real, and the popping of the drivers' lashes, which punctuated their objurgations to the shambling oxen, told eloquently of haste. Within canopies formed of gay, patchwork quilts and gayer serapes, heavy-jowled, swarthy señoras lurched resignedly with the jolting of the carts, and between whiles counseled restive señoritas upon the subject of deportment or gossiped idly of those whom they expected to meet at the fiesta.

The Picardo hacienda was fairly wiped clean of its, comfortable home-atmosphere, so immaculate was it and so plainly held ready for ceremonious festivities. The señora herself went about with a linen dust-cloth in her hand, and scolded because the smoke from the fires which the peons had tended all night in the barbecue pits was borne straight toward the house by the tricksy west wind, and left cinders and grime upon windows closed against it. The patio was swept clean of dust and footprints, and the peons scarce dared to cross it in their scurrying errands hither and thither.

In the orchard many caballeros fresh from the rodeo were camped, their waiting-time spent chiefly in talking of the thing they meant to do or hoped to see, while they polished spurshanks and bridle trimmings.

Horses were being groomed painstakingly at the corrals, and there was always a group around the bear-pen where the two cubs whimpered, and the gaunt mother rolled wicked, little, bloodshot eyes at those who watched and dropped pebbles upon her outraged nose and like cowards remained always beyond her reach.

In the small corral near by, the bulls bellowed hoarsely at the scent of their grizzly neighbor and tossed dirt menacingly over their backs; while above them the rude tiers of seats waited emptily for the yelling humans who would crowd them later. Beyond, under a great, wide-spreading live oak near the roasting pits, three fat young steers swung by their heels from a horizontal limb, ready for the huge gridirons that stood leaning against the trunk behind them. Indeed, the heads of those same steers were even then roasting in their hide in the smaller pit of their own, where the ashes were still warm, though the fire had been drawn over-night.

The sun was not more than two hours high when Don Andres himself appeared in his gala dress upon the veranda, to greet in flowery Spanish the first arrivals among his guests. The señora, he explained courteously, was still occupied, and the señorita, he averred fondly, was sleeping still, because there would be no further opportunity to sleep for many hours; but his house and all that he had was half theirs, and they would honor him most by entering into their possessions.

Whereupon the señoras and the señoritas settled themselves in comfortable chairs and waited, and inspected the house of this lord of the valley, whose luxury was something to envy. Some of those señoras walked upon bare, earthen floors when they were at home, and their black eyes rested hungrily upon the polished, dark wood beneath their feet, and upon the rugs that had come from Spain along with the paintings upon the walls. They looked, and craned, and murmured comments until the señora appeared, a little breathless and warm from her last conference with Margarita in the kitchen, and turned their tongues upon the festival.

Dade was just finishing the rite of shaving, and thinking the while that he would give all that he possessed, including Surry, if he could whisk Jack and himself to the cool, pine slope in the Sierras where was their mine. Every day of waiting and gossiping over the duel had but fostered the feeling of antagonism among the men of the valley, and whatever might be the outcome of that encounter, Dade could see no hope of avoiding an open clash between the partisans of the two combatants. Valencia and Pancho and two or three others of the Picardo vaqueros, who hated Manuel—and therefore had no love for José—would be more than likely to side with him and Jack, though he honestly wished that they would not; for the more friends they had when the test was made, the greater would be the disturbance, especially since there would be wine for all; and wine never yet served to cool a temper or lull excitement.

Without in the least realizing it, Dade's face while he shaved wore a scowl quite as pronounced as the one that had called his attention to Jack's mood. And, more significant, he had no sooner finished than he looked into his little box of pistol caps to see how many he had left, and inspected the pistol as well; for the law of self-preservation strikes deeper than most emotions, and his life had mostly been lived where men must frequently fight for the right to live; and in such surroundings the fighting instinct wakes at the first hint of antagonism.

"My riata's gone!" announced Jack breathlessly, bursting into the room at that moment as if he expected to find the thief
there. "I left it on my saddle last night, and now—"

"And that was a fool thing to do, I must say!" commented Dade, startled into harshness. He slid the pistol into its holster and buckled the belt around his muscular body with fingers that moved briskly. "Well, my riata's no slouch—you can use it. You've used it before."

"I don't want yours. I've got used to my own. I know to an inch just where it will land—oh, damn the luck—It was some of those fellows camped by the orchard, and when I find out which—"

"Keep your head on, anyway," advised Dade more equably. "Your nerves must be pretty well frazzled. If you let a little thing like this upset you, how do you expect—"

"It ain't a little thing!" gritted Jack, loading his pistols hurriedly. "That six-strand riata has got a different feel, a different weight—oh, you know it's going to make all the difference in the world when I get out there with José. Whoever took it knew what it meant, all right! Some one—"

"Where's Surry?" A sudden fear sent Dade hurrying to the door. "By the Lord Harry, if they've hurt Surry—" He jerked the door open and went out, Jack hard upon his heels.

"I didn't think of that," Jack confessed on the way to the stable, and got a look of intense disgust from Dade, which he mitigated somewhat by his next remark. "Diego was to sleep in the stall last night."

"Oh." Dade slackened his pace a bit. "Why didn't you say so?"

"I think," retorted Jack, grinning a little, "somebody else's nerves are kinda frazzled, too. I don't want you to begin worrying over my affairs, Dade. I'm not," he asserted with unconvincing emphasis. "But all the same, I'd like to get my fingers on the fellow that took my riata!"

Since he formulated that wish after he reached the doorway of the roomy box-stall where Surry was housed, he faced a badly scared peon as the door swung open.

"Señor—I—pardon, Señor! But I feared that harm might come to the riata in the night. There are many guests, Señor, who speak ill of gringos, and I heard a whisper—"

Jack, gripping Diego by the shoulders, halted his nervous explanations. "What about the riata?" he cried. "Do you know where it is?"

"Sí, Señor. Me, I took it from the señor's saddle, for I feared harm would be done if it were left there to tempt those who would laugh to see the señor dragged to the death to-day. Señor, that is José's purpose; from a San Vincente vaquero I heard—and he had it from the lips of Manuel. José will lasso the señor, and the horse will run away with José, and the señor will be killed. Ah, Señor!—José's skill is great; and Manuel swears that now he will truly fight like a demon, because the prayers of the señorita go with José. Her glove she sent him for a token—Manuel swears that it is so, and a message that he is to kill thee, Señor!"

"But my riata?" To Diego's amazement, his blue-eyed god seemed not in the least disturbed, either by plot or gossip.

"Ah, the riata! Last night I greased it well, Señor, so that today it would be soft. And this morning at daybreak I stretched it here in the stall and rubbed it until it shone. Now it is here, Señor, where no knife-point can steal into it and cunningly cut the strands that are hidden, so that the señor would not observe and would place faith upon it and be betrayed." Diego lifted his loose, linen shirt and disclosed the riata coiled about his middle.

The eyes of his god, when they rested upon the brown body wrapped round and round with the rawhide on which his life would later hang, were softer than they had been since he had craved the kiss that had been denied him, many hours before. It was only the blind worship and the loyalty of a peon whose feet were bare, whose hands were calloused with labor, whose face was seamed with the harshness of his serfdom. Only a peon's loyalty; but something hard and bitter and reckless, something that might have proved a more serious handicap than a strange riata, dropped away from Jack's mood and left him very nearly his normal self. It was as if the warmth of the rawhide struck through the chill which Teresita's unreasoning spite had brought to the heart of him, and left there a little glow.

"Gracias, Diego," he said, and smiled in the way that made one love him. "Let it stay until I have need of it. It will surely fly true, to-day, since it has been warmed thus by thy friendship."

From an impulse of careless kindness he said it, even though he had been touched by the peon's anxiety for his welfare. But Diego's heart was near to bursting with gratitude and pride; those last two words—he would not have exchanged the memory of them for the gold medal itself. That his blue-eyed god should address him, a mere peon, as "thy," the endearing, intimate pronoun kept for one's friends! The tears stood in Diego's black eyes when he heard; and Diego was no weakling, but a straight-backed stoic of an Indian, who stood almost as tall as the Señor Jack himself and who could throw a full-grown steer to the ground by twisting its head. He bowed low and turned to fumble the sweet, dried grasses in Surry's manger; and beneath his coarse shirt the feel of the rawhide was sweeter than the embrace of a loved woman.

"You want to take mighty good care of this little nag of mine," Dade observed irrelevantly, his fingers combing wistfully the crinkly mane. "There'll never be another like him in
this world. And if there was, it wouldn't be him."

"I reckon it's asking a good deal of you, to think of using him at all." For the first time Jack became conscious of his selfish-
ness. "I won't, Dade, if you'd rather I didn't."

"Don't be a blamed idiot. You know I want you to go ahead
and use him; only—I'd hate to see him hurt."

To Dade the words seemed to be wrenched from the very fibers of his friendship. He loved that horse more than he had ever believed he could love an animal; and he was mentally sacrificing him to Jack's need.

Jack went up and rubbed Surry's nose playfully; and it cost Dade a jealous twinge to see how the horse responded to the touch.

"He won't get hurt. I've taught him how to take care of himself; haven't I, Diego?" And he put the statement into Spanish, so that the peon could understand.

"Sí, he will never let the riata touch him, Señor. Truly, it is well that he will come at the call, for otherwise he would never again he caught!" Diego grinned, checked himself on the verge of venturing another comment, and tilted his head sidewise instead, his ears perked toward the medley of fiesta sounds outside.

"Listen, Señors! That is not the squeal of carts alone, which I hear. It is the carriage that has wheels made of little sticks, that chatters much when it moves. Americanos are coming,
Señors."

"Americanos!" Dade glanced quickly at Jack, mutely questioning. "I wonder if—" He gave Surry a hasty, farewell slap on the shoulder and went out into the sunshine and the clamor of voices and laughter, with the creaking of carts threaded through it all. The faint, unmistakable rattle of a wagon driven rapidly, came towards them. While they stood listening, came also a confused jumble of voices emitting sounds which the two guessed were intended for a song. A little later, above the highpitched rattle of the wagon wheels, they heard the raucous, long-drawn "Yank-ee doo-oo-dle da-a-andy!" which confirmed their suspicions and identified the comers as gringos beyond a doubt.

"Must be a crowd from San Francisco," said Jack needlessly. "I wrote and told Bill about the fiesta, when I sent up after some clothes. I told him to come down and take it in—and I guess he's coming."

Bill was; and he was coming largely, emphatically, and vaingloriously. He had a wagon well loaded with his more intimate friends, including Jim. He had a following of half his Committee of Vigilance and all the men of like caliber who could find a horse or a mule to straddle. Even the Roman-nosed buckskin of sinister history was in the van of the procession that came charging up the slope with all the speed it could muster after the journey from the town on the tip of the peninsula.

In the wagon were a drum, two fifes, a cornet, and much confusion of voices. Bill, enthroned upon the front seat beside the driver of the four-horse team, waved both arms exuberantly and started the song all over again, so that they had to sing very fast indeed in order to finish by the time they swung up to the patio and stopped.

Bill scrambled awkwardly down over the wheel and gripped the hands of those two whose faces welcomed him without words. "Well, we got here," he announced, including the whole cavalcade with one sweeping gesture. "Started before daylight, too, so we wouldn't miss none of the doings." He tilted his head toward Dade's ear and jerked his thumb towards the wagon. "Say! I brought the boys along, in case—" His left eyelid lowered lazily and flew up again into its normal position as Don Andres, his sombrero in his hand, came towards them across the patio, smiling a dignified welcome.

Dade spoke not a word in reply, but his eyes brightened wonderfully. There was still the element of danger, and on a larger scale than ever. But it was heartening to have Bill Wilson's capable self to stand beside him. Bill could handle turbulent crowds better than any man Dade had ever seen.

They lingered, greeting acquaintances here and there among the arrivals, until Bill was at liberty again.

"Got any greaser here that can talk white man's talk, and you can trust?" was Bill's mild way of indicating his need of an interpreter, when the fiesta crowd had grown to the proportions of a multitude that buzzed like giant bees in a tree of ripe figs.

"Why? What do you want of one? Valencia will help you out, I guess." Dade's hesitation was born of inattention rather than reluctance. He was watching the gesticulating groups of Californians as a gambler watches the faces of his opponents, and the little weather-signs did not reassure him.

"Well, there's good money to be picked out of this crowd," said Bill, pushing his hands deep into his pockets. "I can't understand their lingo, but faces talk one language; and I don't care what's the color of the skin. I've been reading what's wrote in their eyes and around their mouths. I can get big odds on Jack, here, if I can find somebody to talk for me. How about it, Jack? I've heard some say there's more than the gold medal and a horse up on this lariat game. I've heard some say you two have put your necks in the jack-pot. On the quiet, what do you reckon you're going to do to the greaser?"

Jack shifted his glance to Dade's face, tense with anxiety while he waited. He looked out over the slope dotted thickly with people, laughed briefly and mirthlessly, and then looked full at Bill.

"I reckon I'm going to kill him," he said very quietly.

Big Bill stared. "Say! I'm glad I ain't the greaser," he said dryly, answering a certain something in Jack's eyes and around his lips. Bill had heard men threaten death, before now; but he did not think of this as a threat. To him it seemed a sentence of death.

"Jack, you'll be sorry for it," warned Dade under his breath. "Don't go and—"

"I don't want to hear any remarks on the subject." Never in all the years of their friendship had Jack spoken to him in so harsh a tone. "God Almighty couldn't talk me out of it. I'm going to kill him. Let it go at that." He turned abruptly and walked away to the stable, and the two stood perfectly still and watched him out of sight.

"He'll do it, too," said Dade distressfully. "There's something in this I don't understand—but he'll do it."

Chapter 22

The Battle of Beasts

Sweating, impatient humans wedged tight upon the seats around the rim of the great adobe corral, waited for the bulls to dash in through the gate and be goaded into the frenzy that would thrill the spectators pleasurably. Meantime, those spectators munched sweets and gossiped, smoked cigarettes and gossiped; sweltered under the glare of the sun and gossiped; and always they talked of the gringos, who had come one hundred strong and never a woman among them; one hundred strong, and every man of them dangling pistols at his hips—pistols that could shoot six times before they must be reloaded, and shoot with marvelous exactness of aim at that; one hundred strong, and every one of the hundred making bets that the gringo with the red-brown hair would win the medalla oro from Don José, who three times had fought and kept it flashing on his breast, so that now no vaquero dared lift eyes to it!

Truly, those gringos were a mad people, said the gossips. They would see the blue-eyed one flung dead upon the ground, and then—would the gringos want to fight? Knives were instinctively loosened under sashes when the owners talked of the possibility. Knives are swift and keen, but those guns that could shoot six times with one loading—Gossip preferred to dwell greedily upon the details of the quarrel between the young Don José and his gringo rival.

There were whispers also of a quarrel between the señorita and her gringo lover, and it was said that the young señorita prayed last night that José would win. But there were other whispers than that: One, that the maid of the señorita had been seen to give a rose and a written message into the hands of the Señor Allen, not an hour ago; and had gone singing to her mistress again, and smiling while she sang. Truly, that did not look as if the señorita had prayed for José! The Señor Allen had kept the rose. Look you! It was a token, and he would doubtless wear it upon his breast in the fight, where he hoped later to wear the medalla oro—but where the hands would be folded instead while the padres said mass for him; if indeed mass could be said over a dead gringo! There was laughter to follow that conceit. And so they talked, and made the tedious time of waiting seem shorter than it was.

Late comers looked for seats, found none, and were forced to content themselves with such perches as neighboring trees and the roofs of the outbuildings might afford. Peons who had early scrambled to the insecure vantage-point of the nearest stable roof, were hustled off to make room for a group of Salinas caballeros who arrived late. This was merely the bull-fighting coming now; but bull-fighting never palls, even though bigger things are yet in store. For there is always the chance that a horse may be gored to death—even that a man may die horribly. Such things have been and may be again; so the tardy ones climbed and scurried and attained breathlessness and a final resting-place together.

Came a season of frenzied yelling, breathless moments of suspense, and stamping that threatened disaster to the seats. Two bulls in succession had been let into the corral, bellowed under the shower of be-ribboned barbs and went down, fighting valiantly to the last.

Blood-lusting, the great crowd screamed importunities for more. "Bring out the bear!" was their demand. "Let us see that she-bear fight the big bull which has been reserved for the combat!"

Now, this was ticklish work for the Picardo vaqueros who were stage-managing the sport. From the top of the corral above the bear-cage they made shift to slide the oaken gate built across an opening into the adobe corral. Through the barred ceiling of the pen they prodded the bear from her sulking and sent her, malevolent and sullen, into the arena. (Señoras tucked vivid skirts closer about stocky ankles and sent murmurous appeals to their patron saints, and señoritas squealed in trepidation that was at least half sincere. It was a very big bear, and she truly looked very fierce and as if she would think nothing of climbing the adobe wall and devouring a whole front seat full of fluttering femininity! Rosa screamed and was immediately reassured, when Teresita reminded her that those

fierce gringos across the corral had many guns.)

The bear did not give more than one look of hatred at the flutter above. Loose-skinned and loose-jointed she shambled across the corral; lifted her pointed nose to sniff disgustedly the air tainted with the odor of enemies whom she could not reach with her huge paws, and went on. Clear around the corral she walked, her great, hand-like feet falling as silently as the leaf shadows that splashed one whole corner and danced all over her back when she passed that way; back to the pen where her two cubs whimpered against the bars, and watched her wishfully with pert little tiltings of their heads. (Teresita was confiding to Rosa, beside her, that they would each have a cub for a pet when the mother bear was killed).

Valencia and Pancho and one other were straining to shift the gate of another pen. It was awkward, since they must work from the top; for the adobe corral was as the jaws of a lion while the bear circled watchfully there, and the pen they were striving to open was no safer, with the big, black bull rolling bloodshot eyes at them from below. He had been teased with clods of dirt and small stones flung at him. He had shaken the very posts in their sockets with the impact of his huge body while he tried to reach his tormentors, until they desisted in the fear that he would break his horns off in his rage and so would cheat them of the sight of the good, red blood of the shebear. Now he was in a fine, fighting mood, and he had both horns with which to fight. From his muzzle dribbled the froth of his anger, as he stiffened his great neck and rumbled a challenge to all the world. Twice, when the gate moved an inch or two and creaked with straining, he came at it so viciously that it jammed again; indeed, it was the batterings of the bull that had made it so hard to open.

Valencia, catching a timbered crosspiece, gave it a lift and a heave. The gate came suddenly free and slid back as they strained at the crosspiece. The bull, from the far side of the pen where he had backed for another rush, shot clear through the opening and half-way across the adobe corral before he realized that he was free.

The bear, at pause in her circlings while she snuffed at the bars that now separated her from her cubs, whirled and lifted herself awkwardly upon her haunches, her narrow head thrust forward sinisterly as she faced this fresh annoyance. Midway, the bull stopped with two or three stiff-legged jumps and glared at her, a little chagrined, perhaps, at the sudden transformation from human foe to this grizzled hill-giant whom instinct had taught him to fear. In his calf-hood he had fled many times before the menace of grizzly, and perhaps he remembered. At any rate he stiffened his forelegs, stopped short, and glared.

Up above, the breaths that had been held came in a shout together. Everyone who saw the pause yelled to the bull to go on and prove his courage. And the bull, when the first shock of surprise and distaste had passed, backed ominously, head lowered, tail switching in spasmodic jerks from side to side. The bear stood a little straighter in her defiance; her head went forward an inch; beyond that she did not move, for her tactics were not to rush but to wait, and to put every ounce of her terrible strength into the meeting.

The neck of the bull swelled and curved, his eyeballs showed glassy. His back humped; like a bowlder hurled down a mountain slope he made his rush, and nothing could swerve him.

The bear might have dodged, and sent him crashing against the wall. Men hoped that she would, and so prolong the excitement. But she did not. She stood there and waited, her forepaws outspread as if for an embrace.

Like a bullet sent true to the target, the head of the bull met the gaunt, ungainly, gray shape; met and went down, the tip of one sharp horn showing in the rough hair of her back, her body collapsing limply across the neck she had broken with one tremendous side-blow as he struck. A moment she struggled and clawed futilely to free herself, then lay as quiet as the bull himself. And so that spectacle ended swiftly and suddenly.

In the reaction which followed that ten-seconds' suspense, men grumbled because it had ended so soon. But, upon second thoughts, its very brevity brought the duel just that much closer, and so they heaved great sighs of relaxation and began craning and looking for the two to enter who would fight to the death with riatas.

Instead, entered the gringo whom Don Andres had foolishly chosen for majordomo, and stood in the middle of the corral, quietly waiting while the vaqueros with their horses and riatas dragged away the carcasses of the bull and the bear.

When the main gate slammed shut behind them Dade lifted his eyes to that side of the corral where the Californians were massed clannishly together, and raised his hands for silence; got it by degrees, as a clamoring breaker subsides and dwindles to little, whispering ripple sounds; and straightway began in the sonorous melody of the Castilian tongue which had been brought, pure and undefiled, from Spain and had not yet been greatly corrupted into the dialect spoken to-day among the descendants and called Spanish.

"Señors, and Señoras" (so he began), "the hour is now midday, and there are many who have come far and are wearied. In the orchard you will find refreshment for all; and your host, Don Andres Picardo, desires me to say for him that he will be greatly honored if you will consider that all things are yours to be used for your comfort and pleasure.

"In two hours, further sports will take place, in the open beyond this corral, so that the seats which you now occupy will serve also to give a fair view of the field. There will be riding contests, free for all caballeros to enter who so desire, and the prize will be a beautiful silver-trimmed bridle that may be seen at the saddle house. After the riding, there will be a contest in the lassoing and tying down of wild steers, for which a prize of a silver hatband and spurs will be given by Don Andres Picardo, your host. Also there will be the riding of bulls; and the prize for the most skillful rider will be a silver-mounted quirto of beautiful design.

"Immediately after these various contests"—Dade could see the tensing of interest among his listeners then—"there will be a contest with riatas between Don José Pacheco and Señor Jack Allen, an Americano vaquero from Texas. As the prize for this contest, Don Andres offers Solano, a gelding, four years of age and unbroken. But Don Andres makes this condition: that the winner shall lasso his prize in this corral, and ride him before you all. If he should chance to be thrown, then the prize shall be forfeited to the other contestant, who will also be required to ride the horse before you all. If he also shall fail to ride the caballo, then will the horse revert to Don Andres, who will keep him for his own saddle horse!" He waited while the applause at this sly bit of humor gradually diminished into the occasional pistol-popping of enthusiastic palms, and gestured for silence that he might speak again.

"I am also instructed to inform you that not alone for the prize which Don Andres offers will the contest be fought. I am requested to announce that the Texas vaquero, Señor Jack Allen, hereby publicly challenges Don José Pacheco to contest for the gold medal which now rests in the possession of Don José. Señors and Señoras, I thank you for attending so graciously to my words, and I wish to ask for continued attention while I announce the sports to these Americanos who do not understand the Spanish, and who are also the guests of Don Andres Picardo, your host."

He bowed low before them, turned and told Bill Wilson's solemnly attentive crowd what was to take place after the feast. Not so elaborate; terse, that he might not try the politeness of that other crowd too far. And when he was done he stopped himself on the verge of saying more, reconsidered and, trusting to the fact that scarce a Spaniard there spoke English, added a warning.

"I hope you all realize," he said, "that we're anxious to have everything go off peaceably. We look to you men to see that, whatever may happen, there shall be no disturbance. Such things are easier started than stopped; and, just as a hint of what will do the most to keep the peace, I want to announce that the water on this rancho can't be beat, and can safely be used for drinking purposes!"

"Water goes, m' son, or I'll know the reason why," called Bill Wilson, and the palms of his crowd clapped vigorous assent.

"That thar's the sensiblest thing you've said, so fur," approved Jerry Simpson, beside Bill. "Me an' the twins'll stand guard, if necessary, and see't that thar hint is took." Whereat Bill Wilson clapped him on the shoulder approvingly.

There was the hum of confusion while the hungry sought the barbecue pits. Dade, his face settled into gloomy foreboding in spite of certain heartening circumstances, went slowly away to his room; where Jack, refusing to take any interest in the sports, lay sprawled upon the bed with a cigarette gone cold between his lips and his eyes fixed hardly upon the ceiling.

Dade gave him a look to measure the degree of his unapproachable mood, sighed wearily and flung his silver-spangled sombrero petulantly into a corner.

"Damn!" he said viciously, as if his vocabulary was so inadequate to voice his emotions that the one expletive would do as well as any to cover his meaning; and sat down heavily in a cushioned chair.

Two minutes, perhaps, of silence, while from sheer force of habit he rolled a cigarette he did not want.

Then Jack moved his head on the pillow so that he could look at Dade.

"I wish you wouldn't take my affairs so to heart," he said, apathy fighting his understanding and his appreciation of a friend like this. "I'd be a whole lot easier in my mind if I didn't know you were worried half to death. And it's no good worrying, Dade. Some' things just come at a fellow, head down; and they have to be met, if we expect to look anybody in the face again." He shifted his head impatiently and stared again at the ceiling. "I'd rather be dead than a coward," he said, speaking low.

"Oh, I know. But—men are just beasts with clothes on their backs. Did you hear them yelling, awhile ago? That was when beasts just as human as they are under the skin, fought and killed each other, so those yelling maniacs could get a thrill or two." He searched his pockets for a match, found one and drew it glumly along the sole of his high-heeled, calfskin boot with its embroidered top of yellow silk on red morocco.

"That's what makes me sick to the stomach," he went on. "They'll sit and watch you two, and they'll gloat over the spectacle—"

A brisk tattoo of knuckles on the oaken door stopped him.

Bill came in, grinning with satisfaction over something.

"Say, I've been getting bets laid down five and six to one, on the greaser," he exulted. "You go in and clean him up, Jack, and we'll skin this outfit down to their shirts! All the boys have been taking every bet that was offered; and the old don, I guess, is about the only greaser on the place that ain't bet all he's got. Three-to-one that José gets you the third pass, m' son!

Now, I don't know a damned thing about this here lasso business, but I took 'em on that, and so did a lot of the boys; and from that up to six-to-one that he'll get you! Want to lay a few bets yourself, you and Dade? That's what I come to find out."

Dade threw out both hands in disgust with the idea; revolted unexpectedly at the thought of being accused of failing to back his friendship with money as well as with every fiber of his loyal being, and turned sourly to Bill. "I've got something like six or eight hundred, in dust," he said. "Lend me enough to make it a thousand, and put 'er up. Take any odds they offer, damn 'em. It'll be blood money, win or lose, but—put 'er up. They can't yowl around that I'm afraid to back him down to my boots."

"That's the kinda talk!" approved Bill. "Make 'em take water all around, the swine! And the boys'll see they cough up afterwards, too. I guess—" He checked himself and went out, still grinning.

Chapter 23

The Duel of Riatas

"They're riding the last bull," announced Dade, coming into the room again where Jack was dressing for the supreme test of the day. "I've got your plan for the ground explained to Valencia and Pancho, and Diego's shining Surry up till you can see your face in him. You ought to be thankful there's somebody on the lookout as faithful as that Injun. I just discovered he hasn't had a bite to eat since last night, because he wouldn't leave
Surry long enough to get anything. I hope you're grateful."

"I am," said Jack shortly. "But I've no business to be. Right now I don't believe much in the sloppy whine of gratitude or the limber-backed prayer for mercy. Thankful or not, we get what we get. Fate hands it out to us; and we may as well take
it and keep our mouths shut."

"That's the result of cooping yourself in here all day, just thinking and smoking cigarettes," grumbled Dade, himself worried to the point of nervous petulance. If he could have taken his own riata and fought also, he would have been much nearer his usual calm, humorous self.

"Say, I told José the rules you suggested, and he agreed to every one like a gentleman. He just came, and Manuel with him leading the horse José means to use; a big, black brute with a chest on him like a lion. His crowd stood on their hind legs and yelled themselves purple when they saw him come riding up."

"Well, that's what they've come for—to yell over José." Jack held three new neckties to the light, trying to choose the one he would wear.

"Say—" Dade hesitated, looking doubtfully at the other.

"Well? Say it." Jack chose a deep crimson and flung the loop over his head as if he were arraying himself for a ball.

"It may be some advantage to know ... I've watched José
lasso cattle; he always uses—"

"Step right there!" Jack swung to face him. "I don't want to know how José works with his riata. He don't know any of my little kinks, don't you see? I never," he added, after a little silence, "started out with the deliberate intention of killing a man, before. I can't take any advantage, Dade; you know that, just as well as I do." He tried to smile, to soften the rebuff—and he failed.

Dade went up and laid a contrite hand upon his shoulder. "You're a better man than I am, Jack," he asserted humbly. "But it's hell for me to stand back and let you go into this thing alone. I've got piles of confidence in you, old boy—but José never got that medal by saying 'pretty, please' and holding out his hand. The best lassoer in California means something. And he means to kill you—"

"If I'll let him," put in Jack, stretching his lips in what passed for a grin.

"I know—but you've been off the range for two years, just about; and you've had a little over three weeks to make up for that lost practice." His eyes caught their two reflections in the glass, and something in Jack's made him smile ruefully. "Kick me good," he advised. "I need it. I've got nerves worse than any old woman. I know you'll come out on top. You always do.
But—what'n hell made you say riatas?"

"What'n hell made you brag about me to Manuel?" Jack came back instantly, and was sorry for it when he saw how Dade winced. "Honest, I'm not a bit scared. I know what I can do, and I'm not worrying."

"You are. I never saw you so queer as you have been since I
came back. You're no more like yourself than—"

"Well—but it ain't the duel altogether." Jack hesitated. "Say, Dade! Did—er—did Teresita take in all the sports? Bull fight and all?"

"Yes. She and that friend of hers from the Mission were in the front row having the time of their lives. Is that talk true about—" Dade eyed him sharply.

"You go on and get things ready. In five minutes I'll expect to make my little bow to Fate."

Outside in the sunshine, men waited and clamored greedily for more excitement. All day they had waited for the duel, at most merely appeased by the other sports; and now, with José actually among them, and with the wine they had drunk to heat their blood and the mob-psychology working its will of them, they were scarce human, but rather a tremendous battle beast personified by dark, eager faces and tongues that wagged continually and with prejudice.

A group of spur-jingling vaqueros, chosen because of their well-broken mounts, rode out in front of the adobe corral and the expectant audience, halted and dispersed to their various stations as directed by Dade, clear-voiced, steady of glance, unemotional, as if he were in charge of a bit of work from habit gone stale.

He might confess to "nerves" in private; in public, there were men who marveled at his calm.

Riatas uncoiled and with each end fastened to a saddle horn, the vaqueros filed out from the corral in two straight lines, with Dade and Valencia to lead the way. When they were placed to Dade's liking, the riatas fenced in a rectangle two hundred yards long, and one-third that distance across. At each riata length, all down the line, a vaquero sat quiet upon his horse, a living fence-post holding the riata fence tight and straight. Down the middle of the arena thus formed easily with definite boundaries, peons were stretching, upon forked stakes, a rope spliced to reach the whole six hundred feet—save that a space of fifty feet was left open at each end so that the combatants might, upon occasion, change sides easily.

Twice Dade paced the width of the area to make sure that the dividing line marked the exact center. When the last stake was driven deep and the rope was knotted securely in place, he rode straight to the corral and pulled up before the judges' stand for his final announcement.

It was a quiet crowd now that he faced. A mass of men and women, tense, silent, ears and eyes strained to miss no smallest detail. He had no need to lift his hand for their attention; he had it—had it to the extent that every man there was unconscious of his neighbor. That roped area was something new, something they had not been expecting. Also the thing Dade told them sounded strange to these hot-blooded ones, who had looked forward to a whirlwind battle, with dust and swirling riatas and no law except the law of chance and superior skill and cunning.

"The two who will fight with riatas for the medalla oro and for the prize which Don Andres offers to the victor," he began, "have agreed upon certain rules which each has promised to observe faithfully, that skill rather than luck may be the chief factor in the fight. These are the rules of the contest:

"None but those two, Don José Pacheco and Señor Allen, will be permitted within the square we have marked off for them after the first signal shot is fired. They will toss a coin for first position and will start from opposite ends of the ground. At the signal, which will be a pistol shot, they will mount and ride with the center rope between them. Upon meeting"—he stopped long enough for a quick smile—"they will try what they can do. If both miss, they will coil their riatas and hang them from the horn, and ride on to the end; there they will dismount and wait for the second signal for starting.

"They will repeat these maneuvers until the contest is decided, one way or the other, but at no time will they start before the signal is given.

"Remember, no one else will be permitted inside the line, at any time; also, neither of the contestants may pass the dividing line unless he has the other at his mercy—when—he may cross if he chooses." It cost Dade something, that last sentence, but he said it firmly; repeated the rules more briefly in English and rode out of the square, a vaquero slackening the first riata of the line to leave a space for him to pass. And as he went, there was nothing in his manner to show how ticklish he felt the situation to be.

Only, when he came upon Jack, just riding out from the stable upon Surry, his lips drew tight and thin. But he merely waved his hand and went on to tell José that he wanted Manuel to give the signals, for then all would be sure that there would be no unfairness.

He was gone perhaps two minutes; yet when he returned with Manuel glowering beside him, that fenced area was lined four deep with horsemen all around; and so had they segregated themselves instinctively, friend with friend, that the northern side was a mass of bright colors to show that there stood the Spanish caballeros; and opposite them, a more motley showing and yet a more sinister one, stood the Americanos, with Bill Wilson pressed against the rope half-way down the line, and beside him big Jerry Simpson, lounging upon Moll, his black mule.

Instinctively, Dade rode around to them, beckoning Manuel to follow; and placed him between Jerry and Bill; explained that Manuel was to fire the starting signals, and smiled his thanks when Jerry promptly produced one of his "twins" and placed it in Manuel's hands.

"P'int her nose in the air, mister, when you turn her loose," he advised solemnly. "She's loaded fur b'ar!"

"Keep your eyes open," Dade warned Bill Wilson when he turned to ride back; and Bill nodded understandingly. Bill, for that matter, usually did keep his eyes open, and to such purpose that nothing escaped them.

Back at the corral, Dade saw Jack waiting upon Surry in the shade of the adobe wall until the moment came for entering the arena. Near to him, José calmed his big, black horse and waited also, cold hauteur the keynote of his whole attitude. Dade waved his hand to them, and they followed him into the empty rectangle. From the crowd came a rustle as of a gust of wind through tree-tops; then they were still again, watching and waiting and listening.

Those for whom they had watched all day at last stood side by side before them; and the picture they made must have pleased the most exacting eye that looked down upon them.

For José was all black and silver, from the tasseled, silver cord upon his embroidered sombrero to the great silver rowels of his spurs. Black velvet jacket, black velvet breeches with silver braid glistening in heavy, intricate pattern; black hair, black eyes—and a black frown, withal, and for good reason, perhaps. For, thinking to win a smile from her who had sent the glove and the message, José looked towards the nearest and most comfortable seat, where Teresita sat, smiling and resplendent, between her mother and Rosa. He had looked, had José, and had seen her smile; but he saw that it was not at him she smiled, but at Jack. It is true, the smile may have been merely scornful; but José was in no mood for nice analysis, and the hurt was keen enough because she smiled at all, and it made his mood a savage one.

Jack was all white and red save for the saddle, which was black with silver trimmings; and Surry, milk white from ears to heel, served to complete the picture satisfyingly. Diego must have put an extra crimp in mane and tail, for the waves were beautiful to behold; he had surely polished the hoofs so that they shone; and nature had done the rest, when she made Surry the proud, gentle, high-stepping animal he was. Jack wore breeches and jacket of soft, white leather—and none but Bill Wilson knew what they had cost in time, trouble, and money. A red, silk sash was knotted about his middle; the flaming, crimson tie fluttered under his chin; and he was bareheaded, so that his coppery hair lifted from his untanned forehead in the breeze, and made many a señorita's pulse quicken admiringly. For Jack, think what you will of him otherwise, was extremely good to look upon.

"Heads for Don José!" A Mexican dollar, spun high in air from Dade's fingers, glittered and fell straight. Three heads bent to see which side came uppermost, and thousands of necks craned futilely.

"Don José will choose his starting-point," Dade called out. "But first the two will lead their horses over the ground, so that they may make sure that there are no holes or stones to trip them."

Even in that preliminary, they showed how differently two persons will go about doing the same thing. José, trailing immense, silver spur-rowels, walked with the bridle reins looped over his arm, his eyes examining critically every foot of the ground as he passed.

Jack, loosening his riata as he dismounted, caught the loop over the high horn and let the rope drop to the ground. He wore no spurs; and as for Surry, he had no bridle and bit, but a hackamore instead.

Jack threw the reins over the neck of the horse. "Come, old fellow," he said, quite as if he were speaking to a person, and started off. And Surry, his neck arched, his ears perked knowingly, stepped out after him with that peculiar, springy gait that speaks eloquently of perfect muscles and a body fairly vibrating with energy; the riata trailed after him, every little tendency towards a kink taken out of it.

"Dios! What a caballo is that white one!" Dade heard a Salinas man exclaim, and flushed at the praise.

Back they came, Jack and Surry, with Jack ten feet in advance of the horse; for José had chosen to remain at the southern end, with the sun at his left shoulder.

Jack, for all his eagerness to begin, found time to shake hands with Bill and say a word to some others as he passed—and those eyes up there that watched did not miss one single movement.

"Look, you! The gringo is telling his friends adios while he may!" some one shouted loudly from across the arena; and a great laugh roared from the throats that were dark, and handclapping at the witticism made the speaker a self-conscious caballero indeed.

At the corral, which was his starting-point, Jack took up the dragging riata, and with his handkerchief wiped off the dust while he coiled it again; hung it over the saddle horn and waited for the signal.

He was scowling now at certain remarks that came to his ears from the seats, with titters and chuckles to point their wit. But he sent a cheering eye-signal to Dade, whose face was strained and noticeably white under the tan.

Half-way down the line, among the Americans, there was a little stir, and then a pistol barked with that loud crash which black powder makes. Jack, on the instant when the smoke curled up in a little, balloon-like puff, turned and leaped into the saddle. The duel of riatas was begun.

Chapter 24

For Love and a Medal

Down the roped lane thundered José, whirling his riata over his head till the loop had taken full twenty of the sixty feet of rawhide.

Galloping to meet him, Jack gave his rope a forward, downward fling and formed a little loop—a loop not one-third the size of José's—and held it dangling beside Surry's shoulder. So, at the very start, they showed themselves different in method, even though they might be the same in skill.

They met, with fifteen feet between them as they flashed past. José flung out his lifted hand. The loop hissed and shot straight for Jack's head.

Jack flung out his little loop, struck the big one fairly, and threw it aside. Even so, the end might have caught him, but for the lengthening lunge which Surry made in mid-air. The loop flecked Surry's crinkled tail and he fled on to the far end and stopped in two short, stiff-legged jumps.

As Jack coiled his riata and slid off he heard the caballeros yelling praise of José. But he did not mind that in the least. In that one throw he had learned José's method; the big loop, the overhead swirl—direct, bullet-swift, deadly in its aim. He knew now what Dade had wanted to tell him—what it was vital that he should know. And—he hugged the thought—José did not know his method; not yet.

A shot, and he was off again with his little loop. José, like a great, black bird, flew towards him with the big loop. As they neared he saw José's teeth show in the smile of hate. He waited, his little loop ready for the fling should his chance come.

José was over-eager. The great, rawhide hoop whistled and shot down aslant like the swoop of a nighthawk. Surry's eye was upon it unwinkingly. He saw where the next leap would bring him within its terrible grip, and he made that leap to one side instead, so that the rawhide thudded into the dust alongside his nose. He swerved again lest José in jerking it up should catch his feet, and went on with an exultant toss of his white head. It was the game he knew—the game Diego had played with him many times, to the discomfiture of the peon.

"He is a devil—that white caballo!" cried a chagrined voice from among the vaqueros crowding the ropes so that they bulged inward.

"Hah! devil or no, they will go down, those two white ones! Saw you the look of José as he passed? He has been playing with them for the sport of the people. Look you! I have gold on that third throw. The next time—it is as José chooses—"

The bark of the pistol cut short the boastings of that vaquero. This was the third pass, and much Spanish gold would be lost upon that throw if José missed.

"Three to one, m' son," bawled Bill Wilson remindingly, as Jack loped past with his little loop hanging beside him, ready but scarcely seeming so. José was coming swiftly, the big horse lunging against the Spanish bit, his knees flung high with every jump he made, like a deer leaping through brush. And there was the great, rawhide loop singing its battle-song over his head, with the soft *who-oo-oo* before he released it for the flight.

He aimed true—but Surry had also a nice eye for distance. He did not swerve; he simply stiffened every muscle and stopped short. Even as he did so the black horse plunged past; and Jack, lifting his hand, whirled his loop swiftly once to open it, and gave it a backward fling.

Straight past his shoulder it shot, whimpering, following, reaching—the force of the fling carrying it far, far ... José heard it whining behind him, glanced quickly, thought to beat it to the end of its leash. He leaned far over—farther, so that his cheek touched the flying black mane of his horse. He dug deep with his spurs—but he dug too late.

The little loop narrowed—it had reached as far as sixty feet of rawhide could reach and have any loop at all. It sank, and caught the outflung head of the black horse; slid back swiftly and caught José as the horse lunged and swung short around; tightened and pressed José's cheek hard against the black mane as the rawhide drew tight across the back of his neck.

The black horse plunged and tried to back away; the white one stiffened against the pull of the rope. Between the two of them, they came near finishing José once for all. And from the side where stood the white men came the vicious sound of a pistol shot.

"Slack, Surry!" Jack, on the ground, glimpsed the purpling
face of his foe. "Slack, you devil!"

Near sixty feet he had to run—and José was strangling before his eyes; strangling, because Surry's instant obedience was offset by José's horse, who, facing the other at the first jerk of the riata, backed involuntarily with the pull of the pinioned reins. The Spanish bit was cutting his mouth cruelly, and José's frenzied clawing could not ease the cruel strain upon either of them.

A few terrible seconds, and then Jack overtook them, eaught the horse by the bridle, and stopped him; and the blood which the cruel bit had brought when the spade cut deep, stained
Jack's white clothes red where it fell.

"Slack, Surry! Come on!" he cried, his voice harsh with the stress of that moment. And when the rawhide hung loose between the two horses he freed José of the deadly noose, and saw where it had burnt raw the skin of his neck on the side where it touched. A snaky, six-strand riata can be a rather terrible weapon, he decided, while he loosed it and flung it from him.

José, for the first time getting breath enough to gasp, tried to straighten himself in the saddle; lurched, and would have gone off on his head if Jack had not put up a hand to steady him. So he led him, a shaken, gasping, disarmed antagonist, across the little space that separated them from where Don Andres and four other Spanish gentlemen sat before the middle gate of the corral.

"Bravo!" cried a sweet, girl voice; and a rose, blood-red and heavy with perfume, fell at Jack's feet. He gave it one cold glance and let it lie. In another moment the black horse crushed it heedlessly beneath his hoof, as Jack turned to the judges.

"Señors, I bring you Don José Pacheco."

So suddenly had the contest ended that those riders who helped to form the riata fence stood still in their places, as if another round had yet to be fought. Beyond the pistol shot and the girl voice crying well done, the audience was quiet, waiting.

Then José, sitting spent upon his horse, lifted a hand that shook weakly. His fingers fumbled at his breast, and he held out the shining medal of gold—the medal with diamonds prisoning the sunlight so that the trinket flashed in his hand.

"Señor," he said huskily, "the medalla—it is yours."

Jack looked at him; looked at the bent faces of the frowning judges; looked up at Teresita, watching the two with red lips parted and breath coming quickly; looked again queerly at José, gasping still, and holding out to him the medalla oro. Jack did a good deal of thinking in a very short space of time.

"I don't want your medal," he said. "Let some Californian fight you for it, if he likes. That is not for a gringo."

Perhaps there was a shade of the theatrical element in his speech and his manner, but he was perfectly innocent of any such intention; and the people before him were nothing if not dramatic. He got his response in the bravos and the applause that followed the silence of sheer amazement. "Gracias!" they cried, in their impulsive appreciation of his generosity.

"The horse which you offered for a prize, Don Andres, I will claim," Jack went on, when he could be heard—and he did not wait long, for short-lived indeed is the applause given to an alien. "And I will ride him as soon as you desire."

"Yes! Let us see him ride that caballo!" cried the fickle mass of humanity. "By a trick of chance he won the duelo, and the medalla he refused because he knows it was not won fairly. Where is that yellow caballo which no man has ridden? Let him show us what he can do with that yellow one!"

Dade, pushing his way exultantly toward him, saw the blaze of anger at their fickleness leap into Jack's eyes.

"Sí, I will show you!" he called out. "It is well that you should see some horsemanship! Bring the yellow caballo, then. Truly, I will show you what I can do."

"Come, Surry," called Dade, and the white horse walked up to him and nibbled playfully his bearskin chaparejos. "Solano's
in the little corral, off this big one. I'll bring your saddle—"

"I don't want any saddle. I'm going to ride him bareback, with a rope over his nose. Let me have your spurs, will you? Did you hear them say I won the duel with luck? I'll show these greasers what a gringo can do!" He spoke in Spanish, to show his contempt of their opinion of him, and he curled his lip at the jibes they began to fling down at him; the jibes and the taunts—and vague threats as well, when those who had wagered much upon the duelo began to reckon mentally their losings.

In the adobe corral he stood with his riata coiled in his hand and Dade's spurs upon his heels, and waited until Solano, with a fling of heels into the air, rushed in from the pen where the big bull had waited until he was let out to fight the grizzly.

"Bareback he says he will ride that son of Satanas!" jeered a wine-roughened voice. "Boaster that he is, look you how he stands! He is afraid even to lasso that yellow one!"

Jack was indeed deliberate in his movements. He stood still while the horse circled him twice with head and tail held high. When Solano brought up with a flourish on the far side of the corral, Jack turned to Dade and Valencia standing guard at the main gate, their horses barring the opening.

"See that it's kept clear out in front," he told them. "I'll come out a-flying when I do come, most likely."

Whereat those who heard him laughed derisively. "Never to the gate will you ride him, gringo—even so you touch his back! Not twice will the devil give you luck," they yelled, while they scrambled for the choicest positions.

Jack, standing in the center quietly, smiled at them, and gave the flip downward and forward that formed the little loop to which he seemed so partial. He tossed that loop upward, straight over his head; a careless little toss, it looked to those who watched. His hand began to rotate upon his supple wrist joint— and like a live corkscrew the rawhide loop went up, and up, and up, and grew larger while it climbed.

Solano snorted; and the noise was like a gun in the dead silence while those thousands watched this miracle of a rawhide riata that apparently climbed of its own accord into the air.

The loop, a good ten feet in diameter, swirled horizontally over his head. The coil in his hand was paid out until there was barely enough to give him power over the rest. His hand gave a quick motion sidewise, and the loop dropped true, and settled over the head of Solano.

Jack flung a foot backward and braced himself for the pull, the riata drawn across one thigh in the "hip-hold" which cowboys use to-day when they rope from the ground. Solano gave one frightened lunge and brought up trembling with surprise.

That he knew nothing of the feel of a rope worked now to Jack's advantage, for sheer astonishment held the horse quiet. A flip, and the riata curled in a half-hitch over Solano's nose; and Jack was edging slowly towards him, his hands moving along the taut riata like a sailor climbing a rope.

Solano backed, shook his head futilely, snorted, and rolled his eyes—mere frills of resentment that formed no real opposition to Jack's purpose. Five minutes of maneuvering to get close, and Jack had twisted his fingers in the taffy-colored mane; he went up, and landed fairly in the middle of Solano's rounded back and began swiftly coiling the trailing riata.

"Get outa the way, there!" he yelled, and raked the big spurs backward when Solano's forefeet struck the ground after going high in air. Like a bullet they went out of that corral and across the open space where the duel had been fought, with Dade and
Valencia spurring desperately after.

It took a long ten minutes to bring Solano back, chafing, but owning Jack's mastery—for the time being, at least. He returned to a sullen audience, save where the Americans cheered him from their side of the corral.

"He is a devil—that blue-eyed one!" the natives were saying grudgingly to one another; but they were stubborn and would not cheer. "Saw you ever a riata thrown as he threw it? Not José Pacheco himself ever did so impossible a thing; truly the devil is in that gringo." So they muttered amongst themselves when he came back to the corral and slipped, laughing, from Solano's sweat-roughened back.

"You can have your Surry!" he cried boastfully to Dade, who was the first to reach him. "Give me a month to school him, and this yellow horse will be mighty near as good as your white
one. I'd rather have him than forty gold medals!"

"Señor,"—it was José, his neck wrapped in a white handkerchief, coming forward from where he had sat with Don Andres—"Señor, I am sorry that I did not kill you; but yet I admire your skill, and I wish to thank you for your generosity; the medalla is not mine, even though you refuse it. Since I have found one better than I, Don Andres shall keep the medalla until I or some other caballero has won it fairly. For my life,
which you also refused to take, I—cannot thank you."

Jack looked at him intently. "You will thank me," he said grimly, "later on."

José's face went white. "Señor, you do not mean—"

"I do mean—just that."

"But, Señor—" There are times when pride drops away from the proudest man and leaves him weak to the very core of him; weak and humbled beyond words.

Big Jerry Simpson saved that situation from becoming intolerable. With Moll's great ears flopping solemnly to herald his approach, Jerry rode up, perfectly aware that he brought a murmur of curiosity from those who saw his coming.

For Jerry was leading Manuel by the ear; Manuel with his hands tied behind him with Jerry's red bandanna; Manuel with his lips drawn away from his teeth in the desire to kill, and his eyes sullen with the impotence of that desire.

"Sa-ay," drawled Jerry, when he came up to the little group, "what d'ye want done with this here greaser that fired on Jack? Some of the fellers over there wanted to take him out and hang him, but I kinda hated to draw attention away from Jack's p'formance—which was right interesting. Bill Wilson, he reckoned I better fetch him over here and ask you fellers about it; Bill says this mob of greasers might make a fuss if the agony's piled on too thick, but whatever you say will be did." With his unoccupied hand he helped himself to a generous chew of tobacco, and spat gravely into the dust.

"Fer as I'm concerned," he drawled lazily, "I'm willin' to help string him up. He done as dirty a trick as ever I seen, and he done it deliberate. I had m' eye peeled fer him all the time, and I seen he wasn't goin' to stand back and let Jack git the best of that greaser if he could help it. He was cunnin'—but shucks! I see all along why he kept that gun p'inted out front—"

"Turn him loose," said Dade suddenly, interrupting him. "We don't want to start any trouble, Jerry. He may need hanging, but we can't afford to give him what he deserves. It's a ticklish crowd, right now; they've lost a lot on the duel, and they've drunk enough wine to swim a mule. Turn him loose. I mean it," he added, when he caught the incipient rebellion in Jerry's weather-beaten face. "I'm bossing things here to-day. He didn't hit anybody, and I'm beginning to think we can get through the

day without any real trouble, if we go easy."

"Wa-al—" Jerry scratched his stubbly jaw reflectively with his free hand, and looked down at his captive. "I'll give him a derned good wallopin', then, just to learn him manners. I've been wantin' to lick him since yesterday mornin' when he tried to drive off Bawley and Lay-fayette and William Penn. I lost two hours off'n my work, argyin' with him. I'll take that outa his hide, right now."

He induced Moll to turn around, and led Manuel away from the presence of the women lest they should be shocked at his deed; and on the cool side of the farthest shed he did indeed give Manuel a "derned good walloping." After which he took a fresh chew of tobacco, lounged over to where Moll waited and switched desultorily at the flies, mounted, and went placidly home to his Mary.

Bill Wilson, having collected their winnings and his own, sought Dade and Jack, where they were lying under the shade of a sycamore just beyond the rim of the crowd chattering shrilly of the later events. With a grunt of relief to be rid of the buzzing, Bill flung himself down beside them and plucked a cigar from an inner pocket.

"Say," he began, after he had bitten off the end of the cigar and had moistened the whole with his tongue. "Them greasers sure do hate to come forward with their losings! Some bets I never will be able to collect; but I got a lot—enough to pay for the trouble of coming down." He rolled over upon his back and lay smoking and looking up into the mottled branches of the tree; thought of something, and lifted himself to an elbow so that he faced Jack.

"Sa-ay, I thought you said you was going to kill that greaser," he challenged quizzically.

Jack shrugged his shoulders, took two long draws on his cigarette, and blew one of his pet smoke-rings. "I did." He moistened his lips and blew another ring. "At least, I killed the
biggest part of him—and that's his pride."

Bill grunted, lay down again, and stared up at the widepronged sycamore leaves. "Darn my oldest sister's cat's eyes if I ever seen anything like it!" he exploded suddenly, and closed his eyes in a vast content.

From the barbecue pits there came an appetizing odor of roasting beef; high-keyed voices flung good-humored taunts, and once they heard a great shout of laughter surge through the crowd gathered there. From the great platform built under a group of live oaks near the patio they heard the resonant plunk-plunk-plunk of a harp making ready for the dance, and the shrill laughter of slim señoritas hovering there. Down the slope before the three the shadows stretched longer and longer. A violin twanged in the tuning, the harp-strings crooning the key.

"You fellows are going to dance, ain't yuh?" Bill inquired lazily, when his cigar was half gone to ashes and smoke. "Jack, here, can get pardners enough to keep him going fer a week—judging by the eyes them Spanish girls have been making at him since the duel and the horse-breaking.

"Say! How about that sassy-eyed Picardo girl? I ain't seen you and her in speaking distance all day; and the way you was buzzing around her when I was down here before—"

"Say, Jack," Dade interrupted, diplomacy winning against politeness, "I never dreamed you'd have the nerve to try that fancy corkscrew throw of yours before all that crowd. Why, after two years to get out of practice, you took an awful chance of making a fool of yourself! Y'see, Bill," he explained with a deliberate garrulity, "that throw he made when he caught the horse was the finest bit of rope-work that's been done to-day. I don't believe there's another man in the crowd that could do it; and the chances are they never saw it done before, even! I know I never saw but one man beside Jack that could do it. Jack was always at it, when we happened to be laying around with nothing to do, and I know he had to keep his hand in, or he'd make a fizzle of it. Of course," he conceded, "you didn't miss—but if you had—Wow!" He shook his head at the bare possibility.

Jack grinned at him. "I'm not saying how much moonlight I used up, practicing out in the orchard when everybody else was asleep. I reckon I've made that corkscrew five thousand
times in the last three weeks!"

"Where you belong," bantered Dade, "is on the stage. You do
love to create a sensation, better than any one I ever—"

"Señors—" Diego came hurriedly out of the shadows behind them. "The patron begs that you will honor his table by dining with him to-night. In one little half-hour will he hope to see you; and Don José Pacheco will also be happy to meet the señors, if it is the pleasure of the señors to meet him and dine in his company. The patron," added Diego, with the faintest suspicion of a twinkle in his pensive black eyes, "desires also that I shall extend to you the deep regret of the señora and the
señorita because it will be impossible for them to be present."

The three looked at one another, and in Bill's eyes dawned slowly the light of understanding.

"Tell the patron we are honored by the invitation, and that it gives us much pleasure to accept," Dade replied for the three of them, after a moment spent in swift, mental measuring of the situation. "Jack, you've got to get them bloody clothes off, and some decent ones on. Come on, Bill; half an hour ain't any
too much time to get ready in."

Half-way to the house they walked without saying a word. Then Dade, walking between the two, suddenly clapped a hand down upon the shoulder of each.

"Say, I could holler my head off!" he exulted. "I'm going to quit worrying about anything, after this; the nights I've laid awake and worried myself purple over this darned fiesta—or the duel, rather! And things are turning out smooth as a man could ask.

"Jack, I'm proud to death of you, and that's a fact. With that temper of yours, I kinda looked for you to get this whole outfit down on you; but the way you acted, I don't believe there's a man here, except Manuel, that's got any real grudge against you, even if they did lose a lot of money on the fight. And it's all the way you behaved, old boy—like a prince! Just—like a—blamed prince!"

"Oh, I don't know—José acted pretty white, himself. You've got to admit that it's José that took the fight out of the crowd. I'm glad—" He did not finish the sentence, and they were considerate enough not to insist that he should.

Warm sunlight, and bonfires fallen to cheerless, charred embers and ashes gone gray; warm sunlight, and eyes grown heavy with the weariness of surfeited pleasure. Bullock carts creaked again, their squealing growing gradually fainter as the fat-jowled señoras lurched home to the monotony of life, while the señoritas drowsed and dreamed, and smiled in their dreaming.

At the corrals, red-lidded caballeros cursed irritably the horses they saddled. In the patio Don Andres gave dignified adieu to the guests that still lingered. The harp was shrouded and dumb upon the platform, the oaken floor polished and dark with the night-long slide of slippered feet. The fiesta was slipping out of the present into the past, where it would live still under the rose-lights of memory.

There was a scurry of little feet in the rose-garden. A door slammed somewhere and hushed the sound of sobbing. A señorita—a young and lovely señorita who had all her life been given her way—fled to her room in a great rage, because for once her smiles had not thawed the ice which her anger had frozen.

The señorita flung something upon the floor and trampled it with her little slipper-heels; a rose, blood-red and withered, yet heavy with perfume still; a rose, twin to the one upon which the black horse of José had set his foot in the arena. A note she tore in little bits, with fingers that tingled still from the slap she had given to Diego, who had brought it. She flung the fragments from her, and the writing was fine and feminine in every curve—her own, if you wish to know; the note she had sent, twenty-four hours before, to her blue-eyed one whom she had decided to forgive.

"Santa Maria!" she gasped, and gritted her teeth afterwards. "This, then, is what he meant—that insolent one! 'After the fiesta will I send the answer'—so he told that simpering maid who took my letter and the rose. And the answer, then, is my rose and my letter returned, and no word else. Madre de Dios! That he should flout me thus! Now will I tell José to kill him—and kill him quickly. For that blue-eyed gringo I hate!" Then she flung herself across her bed and wept.

Let the tender-hearted be reassured. The señorita slid from sobbing into slumber, and her dreams were pleasant, so that she woke smiling. That night she sang a love-song to José, behind the passion vines; and her eyes were soft; and when young Don José pulled her fingers from the guitar strings and kissed them many times, her only rebuke was such a pursing of lips that they were kissed also for their mutiny.

After awhile the señorita sang again, while José, his neck held a little to one side because of his hurt, watched her worshipfully, and forgot how much he had suffered because of her. She was seventeen, you see, and she was lovely to look upon; and as for a heart—perhaps she would develop one later.

Chapter 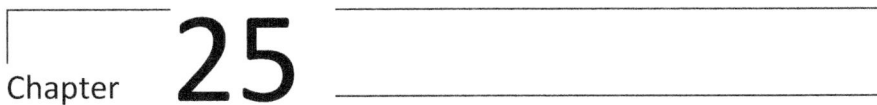 25

Adios

The sun was sliding past the zenith when Jack yawned himself awake. He lay frowning at the ceiling as if he were trying to remember something, sat up when recollection came, and discovered that Dade was already up and getting into his jacket.

"Dade, let's go back to the mine," he suggested abruptly, reaching for his boots. "You aren't crazy about this job here,
are you? I know you didn't want to take it, at first."

"And I know you bullied me into it," Dade retorted, with some acrimony. He had danced until his feet burned with fatigue, and there was the reaction from a month of worry to roughen his mood. Also, he had yet to digest the amazing fact that the sight of Teresita had not hurt him so very much—not one quarter as much as he had expected it would do. Now, here was Jack proposing to leave, just when staying would be rather agreeable!

"Well—but times have changed, since then. I'm ready to go." Jack pulled on a boot and stamped his foot snugly into it.
"What's more, I'm going!"

"You'll eat, first, won't you?"

Jack passed over the sarcasm. "No, sir, I won't. I'm not going to swallow another mouthful on this ranch. I held myself down till that damned fiesta was over, because I didn't want folks to say I was scared off. But now—I'm going, just as quick as the
Lord'll let me get a saddle on that yellow mustang."

"Why, you—"

"Why, nothing! I'm going. If you want to go along, you can; but I won't drag you off by the heels. You can suit yourself." He stamped himself into the other boot, went over and splashed cold water into his eyes and upon his head, shook off the drops that clung to his hair, made a few violent passes with towel and brush, and reached for his sombrero.

"It's a long ways to ride on an empty stomach," Dade reminded him dryly.

"We can stop at Jerry Simpson's and eat. That won't be more than a mile or so out of the way." Jack's hand was on the latch.

"And that yellow horse ain't what you can call trail-broke."

"He will be, by the time I get to the mine!"

Dade threw out both hands in surrender. "Oh, well—you darned donkey, give me time to tell Don Andres good-by, anyway."

Jack's eyes lighted with the smile Dade knew and loved to see. "Dade, they don't make 'em any better than you," he cried, and left the door to try and break a shoulder-blade with the flat of his hand, just to show his appreciation of such friendship. "Bill Wilson has got enough gold that he pulled out of the crowd for us yesterday to grub-stake us for a good long while, and—I can't get out of this valley a minute too soon to suit me," he confessed. "You go on and hunt up Don Andres, while I tackle Solano. I'll wait for you—but don't ask me to stay till after dinner, because I won't do it.

"We don't want to go off without saying good-by to Jerry and his wife, anyway; and we'll beg a meal from the old Turk, and listen to some more yarns about Tige, just to show we're friendly. I'll have Surry saddled, so all you've got to do is make your talk to the don and pack your socks."

Dade grinned and followed him outside. "Good thing I'm used to you," he commented grimly, "or my head would be whirling, right now." Not a word, you will observe, as to whether his own interests would be furthered by this sudden departure; but that was Dade's way. Not a word about the sudden change from last evening, when Jack had eaten at Don Andres' table and had talked amiably with José—amiably in spite of the fact that every one of them understood perfectly that the amiability was but the flowers of courtesy strewn over a formal—and perhaps a temporary—truce. But José was not a fixture upon the ranch, and the don's friendship for the two seemed unchanged.

Dade did not argue nor did he question. Barring details, he thought he understood why it was that Jack wanted to go—why it was impossible for him to stay. A girl may be only seventeen and as irresponsible as a kitten, but for all that she may play an important part in the making and the marring of a man's most practical plans.

When he returned from the house, Don Andres walked beside him. The two of them reached the corral just as Jack released Solano's foot from the rawhide loop that had held it high while Jack cinched the saddle in place. When Jack saw them he came forward, wiping from his face the beads of perspiration which the tussle had brought there.

"Señor Hunter tells me that you are going away," Don Andres began almost at once. "That you are acting wisely I am truly convinced, Señor Allen, though it irks me to say that it is so. For a little time would all be well, perchance; for as long as your generosity fills the heart of José with gratitude, so that no ill will finds room there. But his temper is hot and hasty, as is yours; and with other considerations which one must face—"

He held out his hand for farewell.

"Adios, Señor. I am indeed sorry that you must leave us," he said simply. "Under other circumstance I should urge you to remain; but my lips are sealed, as you well know. Adios, amigo mio. I have liked thee well." He gripped Jack's hand warmly, and turned away. Dade he gave a final handclasp, and walked slowly back to the house, his proud old head bowed upon his chest.

Valencia, yawning prodigiously, came forth from the vaqueros' hut and glimpsed them just as Jack was bringing Solano to something like decent behavior before they started down the slope.

"Dios!" cried Valencia, and ran to see what was taking place. For while the taming of a mustang is something which a man may undertake whenever the mood of him impels, the somewhat bulky packages tied behind the high cantles could mean nothing save a journey.

When they told him, he expostulated with tears in his eyes. He had been nursing since yesterday a secret hope that the blue-eyed one would teach him that wonderful trick of making a riata climb upward of its own accord as if it were a live thing. Beyond that he was genuinely distressed to see them go, and even threatened to go with them before he yielded finally to the inevitable—remembering Felice, perhaps, and the emptiness of life without her.

"Señor, should you chance to see that great hombre who whipped Manuel so completely, you would do well to give the warning. Me, I heard from Ronaldo last night that Manuel spoke many threats against that gringo who had beaten him. Carlos also—and I think they mean ill towards the Señor Seem'son. Me, I thought to ride that way to-morrow and give the word of warning."

"We're going there now," said Jack, with some difficulty holding the yellow horse quiet, while he shook hands with Valencia. "Adios, Valencia. If you ever come near our mine, remember
that what we have will be yours also."

"Gracias, gracias—adios—" He stood staring regretfully after them when they started erratically down the slope; erratically, because Solano preferred going backward or sidewise, or straight up and down, to going forward. They were not two hundred yards away from the stable when Valencia overtook them, having saddled in haste that he might ride with them for a way.

"That caballo, he needs two to show him the way, Señors," grinned Valencia, to explain his coming. "Me, I shall help to get him started, and we will say adios farther up the valley, unless the señors desire to ride to Señor Seem'son's cabin."

"That's where we're headed for, believe it or not!" laughed Jack, who at that moment was going round and round in a circle. "When he gets so dizzy he can't tell up from down,
maybe he'll do as I say about going straight ahead."

Eventually Solano did decide to move forward; and he did so at such a pace that speedily they reached Jerry's claim and galloped furiously up the slope to the cabin.

"Must be asleep," Dade remarked carelessly, when they faced a quiet, straight-hanging bullock hide.

But when a loud hallo brought no sign, even from Tige, he jumped off and went to investigate the silence.

"There ain't a single soul here," he announced, "and that's funny, too. They always leave Tige to watch the place, you
know—or they did before I went on rodeo."

"They do yet," said Jack. "Only Mrs. Jerry never goes anywhere. She stays at home to watch their garden. That's it, over
there; her 'truck patch,' she calls it."

"Things are all upset here. Get off, Jack, and let's see what's up. I don't like the looks of things, myself." Dade's face was growing sober.

Valencia, on the ground, was helping Jack with Solano. But he turned suddenly and cast an uneasy glance towards the quiet log hut.

"Señors, for these two who live here I am afraid! It is as I told you; that Manuel was speaking threats against the big señor, last night; and he had drunk much wine, so that he walked not steady. And with Carlos and perhaps one or two others—of that I am not sure—he rode away soon after dark. Dolt, that I did not tell thee at the time! But I was dancing much," he confessed, "and the fiesta dance makes drunken the feet, that they must dance—"

"Well, tie up that mustang and never mind." Dade was walking aimlessly about, looking for something—what, he did not know. "There's tracks all around, and—" he disappeared behind the cabin.

In a minute he was calling them, and his tone brought them on the run. "Now, what do you make of that?" he wanted to know, and pointed.

Two fresh mounds of earth, narrow, long—graves, if size and shape meant anything at all. The form of a "T" they made there in the grass; for one was short and extended across, near one end of the larger one.

"What do you make of that?" Dade repeated, much lower than before.

"Señors, evil has been done here. Me, I think—"

"Don't think! Bring that shovel, over there—see it, by the tree?—and dig. There's one way to find out what it means."

Valencia did not want to dig into those mounds, but the voice was that of his majordomo, whom he had for a month obeyed implicitly. He got the shovel and he dug. And since it seemed too bad to make him do all the work, Jack and Dade each took their turn in opening the grave.

And in that grave they found Mrs. Jerry, wrapped in her faded patchwork quilt, her hands folded at peace, her wistful brown eyes closed softly—There was no need to speculate long upon the cause of her death. Her shapeless brown dress was stained dark from throat to waist. Dade, shuddering a little, very gently lifted the hands that were folded; beneath was the hole where the bullet had struck.

"Dios!" said Valencia, in a whisper.

They were three white-faced young men who stood there, abashed before the tragedy they had uncovered. After a little, they filled the grave again and stood back, trying to think the thing out and to think it out calmly. They drew away from the spot, Dade leading.

"We don't need to open the other one," he said. "That holds Tige, of course. I wonder—"

"Let's look around out there in the bushes," Jack suggested. "I can see how the thing must have happened; somebody came and started shooting—and that rifle he called Jemina, and the two pistols—don't you reckon they did some good for themselves?"

"Probably—if Jerry was here."

"Man, he must have been here! Who else—" he tilted his head towards the graves. Surely, no one but Jerry would have buried them so, with Tige lying at the feet of his mistress. And, as Jack presently pointed out, if the shooting had taken place in Jerry's absence, he would certainly have notified them at the ranch. And Jack had a swift mental picture of Jerry galloping furiously up to the patio on one of his mules, brandishing his rifle, while he shouted to all around him the news of this terrible, unbelievable thing that had befallen him.

They did not search long before they found plenty of evidence that Jerry had been there at the time of the trouble. They found Manuel lying on his back, with his beard clotted and stained red, and his black eyes staring dully at the sky. Farther along they came upon Carlos, lying upon his face, with a bloodstained trail behind him in the grass to show how far he had crawled before death overtook him. But they did not find Jerry, look where they would.

In the cabin, where they finally went to search systematically for clews, they found places where the logs had been splintered near the loopholes with bullets from without. A siege it had been, then.

Jack, more familiar with the interior than either of the others because of his frequent visits there with Teresita, missed certain articles; the frying pan, an iron pot, a few dishes, and the bedding, to be exact.

So, finally, they decided that Jerry, having had the worst befall him, had buried his dead, packed a few necessary things upon one of the mules, mounted the other, and had gone—where? There was no telling where, in that big land. Somewhere into the wilderness, they guessed, where he could be alone with the deadly hurt Fate and his enemies had given him.

The oxen, when they went outside, came shambling up the slope to the oak tree where they were wont to spend the night near the prairie schooner that had been their homing place for many a month. But without a doubt the mules were gone; otherwise, Jack insisted, they would be near the oxen, as was their gregarious habit.

"Jerry's gone—pulled out," Jack asserted for the third or fourth time. "And the mules, and—the pup. Where's Chico? I
haven't seen or heard anything of him; have you?"

They had not; and they immediately began calling and looking for Chico, who was at that stage of puppyhood that insists upon getting in front of one and then falling down and lying, paws in the air, waiting to be picked up and petted. But Chico did not come lumbering up like an animated black muff, and they could not find his little, dead body.

It occurred to Dade that he might be buried with Tige; and, once the idea was presented to Jack, he could not content himself to leave the place until he knew to a certainty. He would never have admitted it, but there were certain sweet memories which made that particular pup not at all like other black pups. He got the shovel, and he dug in the little grave until he was certain that Tige lay there, and that he was alone.

"Well, he's taken the pup along, then; and that proves to me that Jerry wasn't crazy, or anything like that. He's just pulled out, because he couldn't stand it around here any longer—and I don't blame him. But I wish I knew where; we'd take him up to the mine with us; huh?"

"Yes—but we're about fourteen hours too late to find out where he went. If I'm any judge, these bodies have been dead that long. And if we found him, the chances are he wouldn't go. If I'm any good at guessing poor Jerry's state of mind, right now, he don't want to see or speak to any human being on earth."

"I guess you're right," Jack assented, after a meditative pause. "He just worshiped that poor little woman."

Beyond that, neither of them attempted to put into speech the tragedy; it was beyond the poor words we have thus far coined for our needs, like many another thing that happens in these lives we live. They waited a little while longer, wondering what they could or should do.

Mrs. Jerry lay easily where she had been placed by the man who loved her. The killers had been killed by the same hand that laid her deep, in her faded, patchwork quilt. There seemed nothing further to be done.

But Valencia, when he had ridden a thoughtful half-mile, did think of something.

"Me, I shall give ten pesos of the gold I won yesterday upon the duelo," he said, glancing back at the grim little cabin, "that mass may be said for the repose of the Señora Seem'son's soul. For thus will sleep come easier to me, Señors. And you?"

"I think, Valencia, if I were going to say any prayers, they'd be said for Jerry," Dade told him. "He needs 'em worse than she does."

"Oh, come on, Dade; let's be getting out of this valley!" Jack urged irritably. "And I hope," he added, "I'll never see the place again!"

"But, Señor!" Valencia rode alongside to protest almost tearfully, "The valley, it is not to be blame. Saw you ever a sweeter land than this?" He flung his arm outward to include the whole beautiful expanse of it. "The valley, it is glorious! Am I not right? Blame not the beautiful land, Señor, for the trouble that has come; for trouble will find a man out, though he climb the loneliest mountain peak and hide himself among the rocks there! And the valley—Señors, the valley will hold friends that are true to thee."

Jack flushed at the reproach; flushed and owned himself wrong. "I'll remember the friends," he said. "And I'll forget the things that hurt; I'm a selfish brute— whee-ee! I should say!" He pulled up as short as Solano would let him, and stared from
Dade to Valencia with guilty eyes.

"Diego—I forgot that Injun, Dade; and next to you, I believe he's the best friend I've got on earth! I was so wrapped up in my own bruises that I clean overlooked something that I ought to be mighty grateful for. Dade, do you think he'd like to go along to the mine? You know his wife died a few months ago,
and he's kind of alone; do you think he'd go?"

"I think the chance to go would look like a ticket to glory," Dade assured him sententiously.

Whereupon Jack dismounted, that he might write a few lines as he had written the note to Bill Wilson, a couple of months before: with a leaf from his memorandum book and a bullet for pencil.

"Give that to Don Andres, will you, Valencia? It's to ask how much is Diego's debt, and to say that I'll pay it if the peon wants to come with me. We'll wait in

town until we hear; perhaps Don Andres will let you come up with Diego—that is, if
Diego wants to come. You ask him, Valencia."

"He will come, Señor; nothing would give him greater joy. And," he added wishfully, "but for my sweetheart, Señors, I would ask that I might come with you also!"

"You stick to your sweetheart, Valencia—if she's true," Jack advised him somberly. "Now, Dade, I guess we're ready for the long ride to supper. Why don't you kick me for being such a selfish cuss?"

"Maybe because I'm used to you," Dade's lips quirked humorously after the retort. "You're just Jack—and you couldn't be any different, I reckon, if you tried. Well, come along, then. Adios, Valencia."

Once more they shook hands solemnly with the vaquero, who had no smile for the parting.

"Adios, adios," Valencia called lingeringly after them, and held his horse quiet that he might gaze after them until a willow bend hid them finally from his view.

Printed in Great Britain
by Amazon